GUTTER MAGE

J. S. Kelley

SAGA  PRESS

LONDON SYDNEY **NEW YORK** TORONTO NEW DELHI

SAGA PRESS
AN IMPRINT OF SIMON & SCHUSTER, INC.

1230 AVENUE OF THE AMERICAS, NEW YORK, NEW YORK 10020

First Saga Press hardcover edition September 2021

SAGA PRESS and colophon are trademarks of Simon & Schuster, Inc.

For information about special discounts for bulk purchases, please contact Simon & Schuster Special Sales at 1-866-506-1949 or business@simonandschuster.com

The Simon & Schuster Speakers Bureau can bring authors to your live event. For more information or to book an event, contact the Simon & Schuster Speakers Bureau at 1-866-248-3049 or visit our website at www.simonspeakers.com.

Interior design by Erika R. Genova

Manufactured in the United States of America

1 3 5 7 9 10 8 6 4 2

Library of Congress Cataloging-in-Publication Data is available.

ISBN 978-1-9821-3400-6
ISBN 978-1-9821-3402-0 (ebook)

For Stana. She knows why.

"O! for a muse of fire, that would ascend the brightest heaven of invention."

—*William Shakespeare*

"What fire does not destroy, it hardens."

—*Oscar Wilde*

GUTTER
MAGE

PART ONE

NOTHING IN THIS TOWN BUT BAD LUCK AND MAGIC

ONE

The Skinned Cat was a tavern down in Quartz Harbor with an unsavory reputation. Not coincidentally, it was also one of the few places I was still welcome. I sat at a scarred wooden table, sipping whiskey while I waited for Lysander to show up. He said we were meeting a new client he'd found, and I was curious to know who'd be willing to meet us in such a notorious dump.

There were three guys at the next table getting drunk on the horse urine that passed for ale around here. They looked like the sort who maybe did some honest labor unloading cargo down at the docks when they had to, but would take something less legal and better paying whenever they could find it. Not that I blamed them. Honest labor was for chumps. The trio was already impressively drunk for noon, and their voices had been rising in volume with each round.

Other than the knuckleheads, the tavern was pretty quiet. Two men in neat, dark clothes sat in the back corner and whispered suspiciously over their tankards. Hired assassins, if I had to guess. The barmaid, Julia, looked haggard for so early in the day. Maybe she'd gotten back together with that blacksmith from Henslow and spent the previous night making up for all the sex she'd been missing out on the last few weeks. Apparently, it was the one thing he was good for.

Chester, the owner, was behind the bar, serving drinks to the usual line of sad, silent old men who grimly downed pint after pint to quiet the losses and regrets they'd accrued over their long lives. Or maybe just to escape the harping of their equally sad old wives at home.

"Hey, chickie, what the hell happened to your hair?"

It took me a second to realize one of the knuckleheads was addressing me. I was nobody's *chickie*, and most people in this tavern knew better than to suggest otherwise. It was the hair comment that grabbed my attention. I admit it didn't look great—it was unusual for anyone to have such short hair, and almost unheard of for a woman. But it wasn't like I'd *intended* to burn most of it off, and frankly, I was still a little sore about the whole thing.

I looked the guy over. He clearly hadn't bathed in a while, and his skin was blotchy with rashes, open sores, and probably some kind of fungus. His white shirt was stained red and brown down the front from past meals, and yellow under the arms. He leaned forward and gave me a big leer that I was probably supposed to take for a smile. The teeth he still had in his mouth were even yellower than his pit stains, except for the ones that were gray. He was also missing his right eye, and the socket was open to the air, a shriveled, puckered hole as dirty as the rest of him.

"What happened to your face?" I replied. "Get a glass eye or a patch at least. You look like you've got an anus in the middle of your head."

His eyebrows rose, like he couldn't believe this *chickie* had talked to him like that.

I should have seen the sucker punch coming. But maybe I was a little drunk, or he was faster than he looked. I didn't have enough time to dodge or block the quick jab to my face, but "luckily," I had a lot of practice rolling with the punches.

I managed to rotate far enough that he hit me on the cheek instead of the mouth, which was nice because I really liked having all my teeth. But the force of the blow was still enough to send me toppling over backward. The furniture in the Skinned Cat had been through many fights before this one, and the chair beneath me groaned only slightly when we landed.

My skull at least got some slight cushion from the sawdust strewn on the floor to soak up spilled ale.

I stumbled to my feet, feeling the pulse of pain on my face from where he'd clipped me. That would bruise up nicely. A trickle of blood ran down my chin, and when I touched my injury, I felt a small gash. I noticed he had heavy, ugly, metal rings on his fingers that seemed to exist for no other purpose than to make people who met his fists feel even worse. This guy was a real peach.

He was on his feet in a fighting stance, a grin on his face like he thought this was going to be fun. I looked down at the blood on my fingertips, then at the matching sigils branded into my palms: four triangles, each pointing in a different direction. Within each triangle was a symbol in the ancient language of Arch Pendoric that corresponded to one of the four cardinal directions, north, east, south, and west. Within the square in the center, where the four triangles met, was an eye and the Arch Pendoric word for "witness" or "watcher," depending on context. The whole thing was enclosed in a double circle.

Those sigils could help me end this fight in the space of a single breath. It was tempting, but I didn't want to burn down Chester's tavern—like I said, the Skinned Cat was one of the few places I could still drink. And anyway, I'd hung my flame-resistant coat on the back of my chair, which was now pinned on the floor. The last thing I wanted was a stray flame from my hands burning my clothes off in public. That was an experience I didn't care to repeat ever again.

I might have chanced it if his buddies had decided to join the fun. I was a decent enough brawler, but three against one would have been dicey. Thankfully, the other two seemed content to watch. So I decided to behave myself and just give this dickless piece of shit a good pounding.

He came at me with a big roundhouse. He was cocky, certain that since he'd landed the first punch, the fight was his. He didn't realize that pain didn't intimidate me, it just made me meaner.

I ducked under the roundhouse, blocked the left jab that I knew would follow, and slammed the heel of my heavy boot on top of his foot, feeling one or more metatarsal bones give way with a satisfying crunch. He dropped his guard as he howled in pain, so then I slammed my fist into his crotch.

There were people at various points in my life who had told me that I shouldn't fight dirty. That there was a right way and a wrong way to fight, and punching a guy in the eggs fell squarely on the wrong side. The one thing all those people had in common was that they were entitled assholes who never had to go up against someone bigger and stronger than them. Not one of them was a petite, thirty-year-old woman with, let's be honest, not a whole lot of upper-body strength. I did what I had to in order to not get clobbered or worse.

The guy gave a light wheeze as he bent forward and cupped his balls. I took the back of his head in my hands and kneed him in the face three times. He probably would have dropped after the second one, but I like to be thorough. I let him fall to the sawdust in a heap, where he lay, semi-conscious and whimpering.

"You fucking bitch," snarled one of the other two knuckleheads. They were both on their feet now, not looking nearly as entertained as before, and probably wouldn't make the same mistake of under-estimating me.

I looked down at the sigil brands on my palms again. Risk burning down my favorite tavern, or get my ass kicked? It was a tough call.

Fortunately, I didn't have to make it.

"Whoa, hey," came a familiar, deep voice. "Why am I hearing some less than gentlemanly language directed toward my partner?"

Lysander suddenly loomed behind the two knuckleheads. He was an unusually large guy, just shy of seven feet, with arms nearly as thick around as my waist. His parents had immigrated from the neighboring country of Lapisi, so his skin was light brown. He had calm dark eyes, a hard, chiseled face that was not unattractive, and a scar on his forehead that ran into his black hair, leaving a white streak to mark its trail. The thick handle of his claymore protruded from where it was sheathed on his back.

"Hey, Lye," I said. "What kept you?"

"These two jesters bothering you, Roz?" He placed a beefy hand on each of their shoulders as they both slowly turned and saw what they were in for.

I gave them a level look, then said, "I don't know—are you?"

They mutely shook their heads.

"Great. Then get out of here. You're upsetting Chester. And take your friend with you. I don't think he'll be walking too easy for a while."

They took their companion by his gamey armpits and heaved him up with a smoothness that made me think this wasn't the first time they'd had to haul him out of a tavern. Then the merry trio staggered through the door.

I righted my chair, brushed the sawdust off the dark coat that still hung from it, and sat back down. Thankfully, my whiskey hadn't spilled.

"Come on, Roz." Lysander sat across from me with a big show of weariness. "A client on his way to meet us here, and you had to pick a fight?"

"I was tired of waiting for you," I said. "You know, punctuality is a sign of respect."

"That so?" He reached across the table and took a sip of my whiskey.

"Being on time says that you value *my* time as much as your own, and you don't want me to waste it by waiting around in this shithole for your big fat ass."

"My ass isn't fat, though," he said.

"Big *shapely* ass. That better?"

"Much."

TWO

I shoved in between two old men at the bar to order myself another whiskey and one for Lysander.

"Sorry about the ruckus, Chester," I said as he poured the drinks.

Chester was a heavyset guy probably in his sixties, with a bald head and a long, droopy mustache. Everything else about him was droopy too.

"Least you didn't destroy nothing." He handed me two glasses filled with liquid amber.

"That's what I like about you, Chester. You've got perspective." I winked at him. "And a great set of tits."

He rolled his eyes and turned his attention back to the old men at the bar.

As I sat down at the table with our drinks, Lysander said, "I don't know why you tease him so much."

"Are you kidding? He loves it. Probably jerks off to it every night. Why else do you think we get so many free drinks?"

"I think it's more likely because of when we shut down that gang trying to squeeze him for protection money."

"That too."

"Another one of your *nonpaying* clients." Lysander took a hard swallow of his whiskey.

"He pays us in top-shelf liquor."

"I'd rather have the money," said Lysander. "You know, for a mistress of the dark arts, you sure do have a weakness for sob stories."

"Only ignorant pencil dicks call it the 'dark arts.'"

"Sorry. The *grimoric* arts. Point is, you need to stop committing us to these barter jobs. You're just indulging people."

"We get all kinds of useful stuff out of it," I said.

"A man only needs so many pairs of boots."

I smirked. "Well, I got more than boots from that cobbler."

"Don't I know it. I thought we were supposed to split everything fifty-fifty."

I held up my hands. "Hey, you had your chance. He was certainly open to the idea."

"Portia would have killed me." He nodded to my raised hands. "By the way, you should put your gloves on before our client gets here."

"Oh yeah?" I asked. "You think he'll know what they are?"

"I reckon he knows enough. Unlike you, I found us a *classy* client who's willing and able to pay us the kind of money we deserve to make."

"Well fuck me gently with a halberd, aren't you posh."

"Give me a break, Roz," he said. "You know Portia and I have been talking about having kids soon."

"I still think that's a terrible idea," I told him. "Kids will ruin your life."

"I'll take that into consideration if I ever ask your fucking opinion on the matter," he said. "Anyway, we need some decent jobs with decent pay. I found us one, and I expect you to behave yourself."

"All right, all right." I leaned back and fished my leather gloves out of the deep pockets of my coat. "You're turning into an old man on me, Lye. Maybe you'd be happier doing some honest work right here with Chester and Julia."

His eyes stretched wide with horror. "Don't even joke about something like that."

I laughed as I pulled on my gloves. I was giving him a hard time because that was how our relationship worked, but I knew he was right. We needed proper, spendable money. I already didn't like the sound of this "classy" client, but I decided I really would try my best to behave, if for no other reason than so Lysander wouldn't have to wrap his dick in lambskin every time he wanted to fuck his hot wife. That's the kind of thoughtful friend I am.

Apparently, Lysander's client knew more about the courtesy of punctuality than he did, because I wasn't even finished with my second whiskey before the guy arrived. Flanked on either side by burly men in polished plate armor, he swept into the Skinned Cat in a perfectly tailored lilac frock coat with dark breeches and silk stockings that showed off calves that at first seemed incredibly well formed, but at second glance were just padded to look that way. He held an embroidered lace handkerchief to his nose as his sharp, green eyes surveyed the tavern. His sculpted eyebrows arched in a way that suggested that the reason he'd agreed to meet us here was because he'd had no idea that places of such low standards even existed.

"That fop our guy?" I asked, knowing with a sinking feeling that he was.

Lysander shrugged. "You want to make money, you got to go where the money is."

It was going to be harder than I thought to behave myself.

Our potential client gazed around the tavern in distaste, then caught sight of us, and his disgust lessened somewhat. Or maybe he was just making an effort to appear that way so we'd take the job.

When he and his bodyguards came over to our table, Lysander stood up and pulled a chair over for him. I remained seated. Lye always got a little nervous around upper-class types, but they didn't impress me. I'd grown up a merchant's daughter, and we'd been successful enough to get our fair share of posh customers. I'd also met a few more when I was in school. Even had a couple I considered friends. They weren't all bad, but I knew firsthand that wealth and privilege didn't make a person any better.

"Thanks for agreeing to meet us here, Mr. Quince," Lysander said in that gentle way he had when he was talking to a prospective client. "I know it's outside your . . . usual circles."

Quince sat down, taking care not to actually touch the table, and smiled thinly through his handkerchief. "No, it's quite all right. What I have to discuss with you is of a delicate nature, and it's preferable that we not broach the subject in a place where I might be recognized, or my lord's activities be of interest."

"So you're not the client, then?" I asked. "You're his messenger?"

"Approximately," he said.

"I don't agree to jobs for anyone I can't meet," I told him.

"Roz . . ." said Lysander.

"No, no," said Quince. "I quite understand. And rest assured that should we come to an agreement, you will have the opportunity to personally meet with my lord to finalize the arrangement."

"So this is you testing us out?" I asked.

"In a manner of speaking." He removed a small silver box from his coat pocket, opened it, and took a pinch of snuff. "You come highly recommended for . . . this type of work, but gossip and rumor alone are not enough for me to put my lord at risk."

"And what kind of job is it?" I asked.

"A kidnapping."

"*What?*" I turned to Lysander. "Goddammit, Lye, there's no way I'm abducting someone!"

"Roz, relax," said Lysander. "Let the man explain."

"Yes, apologies, Miss Featherstone, I should have been more specific," said Quince. "We do not want you to kidnap someone. We need you to *rescue* someone who was kidnapped the night before last."

I leaned back into my chair again. "That's a big fucking difference."

"Again, I apologize. But it is gratifying to see your honest response regarding such an underhanded and revolting act."

That made me wonder if he'd done it on purpose, just to see how I'd react. I didn't like being toyed with. He might have decided *we* checked out, but I still wasn't sure about him.

"So who got kidnapped?" prompted Lysander.

"The victim in question is my lord's infant son," said Quince.

"You hear that, Roz?" Lysander's big brown eyes shone. "A *baby*."

"Uh-huh." All of Portia's talk about wanting a child was really starting to get to him. I turned back to Quince. "Okay, so maybe that's all on the level, but why us? We don't specialize in kidnappings. Why did we come 'highly recommended for this type of work,' as you put it?"

"That's more to do with the perpetrators than the crime itself."

"Okay, I'll bite," I said. "Who did the kidnapping?"

"We believe it was done by a grimoric guild by the name of Alath."

"Huh." The guild's name didn't ring any bells, but it didn't need to. If there was one thing in this life I couldn't stand, it was grimoric guilds, and I had promised myself I would steer clear of them in the future. I turned to Lysander. "Did you know this part already?"

He looked guilty. "Roz . . ."

"Don't 'Roz' me, you giant piece of—"

He clapped his big hand over my mouth and forced a smile in Quince's direction. "Will you excuse my partner and me so we can have a quick discussion?"

Without waiting for a response, he picked me up, his hand still over my mouth. I kept my glare on him while I allowed him to carry me over to a corner of the pub.

"Do not fuck this up, Roz!" he hissed as he put me down and removed his hand from my face.

"I can't believe you thought I'd be okay with this," I shot back.

"Actually I knew you *wouldn't* be okay with it, which is why I didn't say anything."

"That was stupid, because you knew I'd find out eventually."

He looked pained. "Okay, you're right . . . I'm sorry. Maybe I didn't handle it the best way. I know you said you were done dealing with the guilds—"

"A *grimoric* guild."

"Yeah, especially grimoric guilds, I know. I know. But you have to move past it."

"I don't have to do shit."

"Fine!" His brow furrowed, and his nostrils flared. "I didn't want to do this Roz, but if you're going to dig in your heels like a goddamn child, you don't leave me any choice. Either you do this job with me, or I do it *without* you."

That brought me up short. "Wait. What are you saying?"

"You heard me. I'm sick of being broke all the time. You are not the fucking center of the world, Rosalind Featherstone, and if you won't suck it up and meet me halfway on this one, then you and I are through."

Lysander only used my full name when he was dead serious. This was it. He'd put up with a lot of shit from me over the years, and he'd finally had it. Was a large portion of this new resolve coming from Portia? Probably. Did I blame her? Absolutely not. I would have done the same thing in her place. It was no secret that I was bad news. Nothing but trouble for just about everyone I was close to. Portia knew goddamn well that if she could get him away from me, he'd be better off. But that didn't mean I was ready to let go of my only real friend in the world. He wanted money; we'd get him some money. Hell, knocking around snobby guild members was the least I owed the big lummox. I could swallow my pride for one lousy job.

His eyes were steady as he looked down at me. "Do we understand each other?"

"Yeah, we do. But if this goes bad, then I get to say I told you so every day for the next fucking year."

"Yeah, yeah, yeah." Then he grinned so wide I thought his face might split. "I'll just stick money in my ears so I can't hear you."

I stalked back to the table where Quince and his metal-encased goons waited. I glared long enough for him to take another pinch of snuff, his eyes darting past me to look for reassurance from Lysander. Good. He understood that I was the scary one.

I said, "If we're going to tangle with a grimoric guild, there better be enough money to make it worthwhile."

"Miss Featherstone, I can assure you that the compensation will likely be beyond your expectations."

I took my dark fireproof coat from the back of my chair and slid it on. It was a thick, shapeless thing that stretched down to my knees. I pulled up the collar and shoved my hands deep into the pockets.

"Then let's go meet this lord of yours."

THREE

The city of Drusiel had begun as a small port town on the southern coast of Penador. A couple hundred years ago, it was little more than a way station for goods being shipped to and from Lapisi, which was located on the other side of the Mermo Sea. That particular trade route, known as the Golden Vine, stretched north from Drusiel all the way to the Penadorian capital of Monaxa, crossing nearly a hundred leagues, and south into Lapisi nearly two hundred leagues to the Lapisian capital of Tulot. A lot of goods moved between Monaxa and Tulot, and a decent amount of money was made along the way by those with a head for business. Still, Drusiel had been little more than one leaf on that vine until the guilds set up shop there.

There were plenty of theories as to why the guilds chose a tiny seaside town like Drusiel as their base of operations. Monaxa would have been more practical, but there was talk that the guilds and the court didn't get along, and putting them in the same place would have sent the country into chaos. Others said it was the court that convinced them to set up on the southern border as a first line of defense should Lapisi ever turn unfriendly. Some even claimed it was simply because Drusiel was well known for its sunny, temperate weather, and guild members were sick of the cold and gloom that hung over the rest of Penador for most of the year.

Whatever the reason, when the guilds opened shop in Drusiel, it set off an explosive growth that still hadn't petered out more than a hundred years later. There was always something new here. Drusiel was a city that never stopped moving, expanding, and redefining itself, as if it was still trying to figure out what the hell it was. Monaxa knew what it was—the seat of political and military power in Penador. Hergotis was the mining town where a person might become rich beyond their wildest dreams or else freeze to death. Keriel was a lumber town and home to the most sought-after craftsmen in the world. Even Urigo, as ugly and smelly as it was, performed the invaluable service of supplying the entire country with enough clay and bricks to keep up with housing Penador's booming population. But what was Drusiel, other than the country's mage playground?

That's what I wondered, not for the first or last time, as I looked out the window of Quince's fine, white lacquered carriage. It clattered swiftly through the cobblestone streets like it wanted to be away from the gritty, sun-faded shops selling charms, wards, curses, and other advertised "genuine mage-level magicks." Magic was this town's racket, and a person could find it sold, some legitimate but mostly not, on every street corner. I always wondered why the guilds didn't send people around to shut down the more obvious scams. Maybe they thought that a populace dependent on magic was for the best, even if a lot of it was nonsense. Or more likely, they just didn't care.

I had to admit, it was nice to be coasting above the riffraff on carriage wheels instead of skulking down the street with bricklayers making catcalls and the occasional chowderhead so desperate he would attempt to rob an odd-looking woman with short, uneven hair and a long, billowing coat. Now, as I watched the streets flow past, it was easy to miss all the grimy corners and pockets of rot and death. It made the whole place feel a little cleaner somehow.

The inside of the carriage was nice too, of course. The seats were lined with pink silk cushions. The walls were carefully carved and gilded with symbols meant to keep some spirits in and some out. It was good work, too, I had to admit. The guilds were a lot of things, but sloppy generally wasn't one of them. They were fiercely competitive, which no doubt kept the quality of their work high. If a guild's reputation dropped too low, the more sensible and pragmatic mages were likely to move to another guild, or even start one of their own. Guilds formed and disbanded so often that it really wasn't even worth the effort to keep up with them all. This Alath Guild that supposedly abducted a noble's son, for example. Probably started recently by some particularly charismatic mage who'd maybe invited in a few too many possessions and got his brains scrambled. It happened now and then. Allowing a spirit to live in your head came with a lot of risks, even for a veteran mage. It wasn't the only way to get magic done, but it was the most direct. So, despite the risk, it was a method that people would keep using.

I turned to Quince, who, judging by the curl of his lip, didn't seem to be looking out at the streets with the same resigned fondness.

"So why do you think it was this Alath Guild that kidnapped the little lordling?"

"I'm not privy to all the details, I'm afraid," said Quince, turning from the window to give me his thin smile, now uncloaked by the handkerchief. "That it was perpetrated by a group of mages, there can be no doubt. I saw the sigils carved into the doors myself."

"To undo the locks?" asked Lysander. He didn't look as comfortable within the carriage, mostly because he had to hunch over.

"Exactly so," said Quince.

"I'm surprised that worked." I gestured to the sigils at even spaces around the carriage. "A fancy, magic-friendly lord like yours should have had countersigils for that."

"He did," said Quince.

That was even more surprising. It would take some pretty heavy conjuring to get past even the most basic countersigils. On the whole, defensive spells were stronger than offensive ones. Most spirits were homebodies at heart and didn't like to be moved once they'd settled into a place. I was curious to see the leftover sigils on those doors now. They probably wouldn't be completely intact anymore, because a lot of mages added contingencies to their spells that erased, or at least corrupted, the sigil after it had been cast. Even so, a person who knew what they were doing could usually squeeze something of use out of whatever remained. And I was just such a person.

"What's the name of this lord of yours, then?" I asked.

"Before I divulge that information, I must be certain you understand the gravity of this situation," said Quince. "There are many nefarious men in Drusiel who are envious of my lord's power and wealth. No doubt some of them would use the knowledge of this kidnapping to their advantage."

I couldn't see how, but scheming nobles wasn't exactly my area of expertise, so I let it slide.

"Fine, we'll keep his name to ourselves," I said. "But assuming I'm going to be meeting him soon, I better know what to call him, right?"

Quince lifted his chin, I think mostly so he could look down imperiously at me, and said, "You have the honor of being employed by Lord Edmund of the house of Ariel."

Lysander gave a low whistle.

"Huh," I replied, mostly because I had to say something, but I refused to give Quince the satisfaction of seeing just how impressed I was.

Lord Edmund wasn't some inconsequential noble with a house in the country. He was one of the most influential people in all of Drusiel. Even someone like me who was willfully ignorant of city politics had heard of him. Supposedly he had the ear of every important guildmaster in the city. He was also a regular visitor at the palace in Monaxa. And every time King Hector made a diplomatic visit to King Lorenzo down in Lapisi, or King Lorenzo came up to visit King Hector in Monaxa, they made a point of stopping for a week at Lord Edmund's grand estates of the house of Ariel near Drusiel. Which, I assumed, was where we were now headed.

"At least we know he's good for the money," I said with the kind of deliberate indifference I knew would annoy Quince. It also made Lysander laugh, although he did his best to swallow it, so it mostly came out his nose.

"Sorry." Lysander pulled out a handkerchief not nearly as nice as Quince's and wiped his hairy nostril.

I flashed him a quick grin, then went back to looking out the window. Except I wasn't really seeing anything but the spinning thoughts inside my head. If Lord Edmund was the victim, that changed the entire scope of this job. The kidnapping could have been politically motivated, either at the city level or even national. That's how big this guy was. It was exactly the sort of high-profile job I tried to stay away from.

But what could I do? I'd already told Lysander I was in. Granted, we hadn't known the job would have such high stakes at that time. But judging by the grin on his face as he stared down at his boots, this bit of news sounded like nothing but the promise of more money. Hell, he was probably already thinking about how he'd buy Portia a little place in Porter Crossing like she'd always wanted, and maybe put something aside for their theoretical kids to go to mage school one day.

There was no way I could weasel us out of it now. For better or worse, we were caught up in something neither of us could see the edges of.

FOUR

Leaving Drusiel by carriage was like watching the city slowly get purified by nature. The close-packed buildings gave way to neatly spaced homes, which in turn gave way to small farms, and finally to untamed forest.

Well, maybe not completely untamed. The road was meticulously groomed, with not a single errant branch poking out into the open space that cut through the trees. Once we were on the softer dirt roads, the carriage really picked up speed, going so fast that the trees were a smear of green and brown outside the window.

We wound down the road for a while, crossing a few clearings in the forest and rattling over a creek on a fine wood bridge adorned with not just the usual sigils of protection and weatherproofing, but also some fancy sculpture that could have come from a Keriel craftsman. The sculptures depicted what a lot of people imagined spirits to look like—long willowy beings with delicate limbs, pointed ears, and catlike eyes. It was nonsense, of course; spirits didn't look like anything. Until a mage bound them, they had no form at all. Still, the sculptures looked nice, nestled gently on the small bridge in the middle of the deep, quiet forest. I would have liked to stop and admire them, if I'd been alone. Not that I would have admitted this to anyone, not even Lysander. He might be right about me having a soft side, but I wasn't about to give him definitive proof.

Then the forest opened up, and right in the middle of the clearing was the single largest home I'd ever seen. I guess I'd never been to a mansion before, if that's what this was. Three stories of lofty windows, curved archways, jutting balconies, and pointed towers. The grand estates of the house of Ariel.

Surrounding Ariel House was a lavish, tiered garden with grass so manicured it looked like a giant green rug. Perfectly spaced squares of red, blue, purple, and yellow flowers were neatly accented with swirls of carefully pruned shrubs. It was the sort of thing that would have made my mother burst into tears of reverence. Or throw up with envy. Possibly both at once. It didn't do much for me, though. In fact, it seemed like a whole lot of work and expense to force things to look a way they weren't normally inclined. I liked my nature to be . . . *natural.*

The carriage slowed down when we reached the entrance to the gardens and began carefully threading its way along the narrow path that led toward the mansion. All in all, I was impressed with the discipline of the spirits driving the carriage. Horseless carriages were becoming more common, particularly among the wealthy who could afford to hire a mage to set it up. Even a moderately talented mage could bind a couple of spirits to a carriage. But coaxing both the speed I'd seen while we were in the forest, and the care they were taking through the garden now, was highly unusual. It would require not only a lot of truly skilled sigil work, but regular maintenance as well. It made me wonder if Lord Edmund employed his own personal mage.

The mansion loomed overhead as we pulled in front of the steep, wide stone staircase. The armored bodyguards, who had been sitting up in the front of the carriage during the ride, jumped down with a metallic clatter and hurriedly opened the doors on either side. Lysander nearly fell out as he eagerly unfolded himself from its confines. Poor guy must have really been uncomfortable.

I hopped down onto the road, which was paved with tiny smooth stones, probably taken from the creek. It no doubt solved the issue of stepping from a carriage into a muddy quagmire after a heavy rain, but the amount of effort it would take to haul all those stones to this location was staggering. Lord Edmund didn't cut corners. That gave me some small comfort. I'd been unsure about our new employer's motives. Hiring Lysander and me for a kidnapping rescue was overkill. Like popping a soap bubble with a broadsword. I couldn't help wondering if there was more to it than Quince was letting on. But maybe they wanted us simply because his lordship only hired the best. And at the risk of sounding conceited, I'd never met anyone better at solving magic-related crimes than me. It was the second biggest reason so many mages in Drusiel hated me.

The biggest reason, of course, was because I'm an asshole.

"If you would follow me." Quince moved up the staircase, his padded calf muscles not flexing once.

Lysander and I climbed after him to the entrance, which was wide enough to accommodate the two of us side by side, and so tall that Lysander didn't even need to duck his head.

Inside was an open foyer with polished granite floors. The gray stone walls were covered with lush tapestries depicting various men in armor or women in gowns. Probably Lord Edmund's ancestors. A grand double staircase stretched up to a second level at the far end of the hall, with doorways to other rooms on the right and left.

Quince led us through one of the doorways into a study filled with nearly as many books as the library of the Grimoric Mage Academy, where I'd briefly attended school. The muted color of book spines stretched from floor to ceiling and wrapped all the way around the room. Every inch of shelf space was packed. The sight of it all, combined with the smell of musty old leather and paper, was almost enough to make me swoon. If it were physically possible to fuck a library, I would already be suggesting we go back to my place for a drink.

Sadly, the man who was presumably Lord Edmund didn't do it for me nearly as much. He sat behind a large mahogany desk, frowning as he scratched his white quill across a sheet of parchment. He looked to be in his late forties, although someone that rich could afford to look younger than he really was, so he might be mid-fifties. He was balding, with a large, hawkish nose above a neat, pointed beard that was so uniformly dark it seemed likely he covered the gray with shoe polish.

He didn't immediately acknowledge our presence, and Quince motioned for us to stand just inside the doorway while his lordship finished writing. Lysander rolled his eyes at me, but I shrugged. I could scan the titles on these shelves for a while without getting bored. I'd already spotted what looked like a first edition of *Grimoric Rites of Spring* and a biography of Iago the Ice Mage that I was almost positive I'd never read.

Eventually, Lord Edmund put down his quill, carefully blotted his parchment, wrapped it in an envelope, and sealed it with wax. He pressed the ring on his left forefinger into the soft wax, which made me suspect it was an official lordly communication, rather than a salacious love letter to a buxom scullery maid. Too bad. The guy looked like he could use a buxom scullery maid.

He gave Quince a faint, humorless smile. "Perfect timing, Mr. Quince. Would you see this delivered to Mr. Bartholomew at the Tagriel Guild?"

Quince paused for just a moment. The guy had to be thinking about how he'd just come from the city, and now had to haul all the way back there. But he was a professional ass kisser, so it was only a brief pause before he took the envelope and gave Edmund a florid bow.

"It would be a pleasure, my lord. Before I go, may I introduce Mr. Lysander Tunning and Miss Rosalind Featherstone, as requested."

Lord Edmund stared at the man like he had no idea what the hell he was talking about.

Quince delicately cleared his throat and said, "To investigate . . . your son's disappearance."

Lord Edmund's face lit up, displaying the first warm smile I'd seen from him. "Ah! Yes, of course! Tunning and Featherstone! My apologies. I've had many matters to attend to today, as you can imagine. Thank you, Mr. Quince."

Quince bowed again and left with his new errand.

"Please, both of you, have a seat." Edmund gestured to the two over-stuffed leather chairs that faced him across the desk. They were soft, but the material was so polished that it was almost greasy, and the fabric of my coat clung to it in a strange way.

"Thank you both for coming so quickly." Lord Edmund took a beautifully carved and stained wooden pipe from his desk and began packing it with tobacco from an equally gorgeous box. He spun the box around and said, "Help yourselves."

Lysander politely shook his head, but I had no intention of passing up some free fancy tobacco. I fished my clay pipe out of my coat pocket, knocked the lint out of it, and packed it to the brim.

Lord Edmund struck a match and lit his pipe, then leaned forward and lit mine. I took a deep drag and closed my eyes. It was probably the best tobacco I'd ever smoked. Smooth and aromatic, with just a hint of cherry and something else I couldn't quite identify. Vanilla, maybe?

Lord Edmund nodded as he puffed thoughtfully. "I always find a good pipe calms the nerves during stressful times like this."

"Yeah, it's some good shit," I replied.

He stared at me as he puffed away. I suspected most people probably didn't say such things to him. But after a moment, he inclined his head.

"It is indeed. Now, to business. I assume Mr. Quince has informed you of the general situation."

"Your son has disappeared, and you believe he was taken by a grimoric guild named Alath," said Lysander.

"That's it precisely."

"Quince mentioned some lock-breaking sigils carved into the doors, which would certainly suggest a grimoric guild." I let a thin trail of smoke out of my mouth as I spoke. "But what makes you think of this Alath Guild specifically?"

"They're the only ones I can think of that have a motive," Lord Edmund said. "As you may know, I am friendly with nearly every guild in Drusiel. Alath is quite new. Only a year old, I believe. But they have a few members who are well known and respected in the community, so I planned to formally introduce myself to them, as I usually do with nascent, promising guilds. Except before I had the chance, they approached me a short time before my son's birth and said they believed he would be important to the future evolution of magic."

"Important?" I asked. "In what way?"

"Apparently, they believe he will be the catalyst for something called the Nevma Year."

I laughed at that, which was bad for a couple of reasons. First, I had just drawn smoke from my pipe, so it hurt like hell and turned quickly into a minor coughing fit. Second, nobody else thought it was funny. Lord Edmund's smile tightened into something very close to anger, and Lysander gave me his very special *Roz, stop fucking things up* smile that he sometimes used in front of clients.

Once I finished coughing, I said, "Sorry, Lord Edmund. It's just . . . Nevma Year is nonsense. A cautionary tale to scare young mages. That's all. It couldn't really happen."

"You've heard of this thing?" asked Lysander.

"Sure," I said. "The story goes that one day, the veil between the material and astral planes will dissolve, and all the incorporeal spirits that we've bound to protect our homes, or light our lamps, or run our carriages will be set free and made corporeal for one year to do as they will upon the world. The whole idea is to instill some fear in mages who might otherwise be tempted to cut corners and not treat astral beings with the courtesy they deserve. You take care of your spirits, and if Nevma Year ever rolls around, they won't be inclined to rip your arms off and beat you to death with them. But the whole thing is impossible. You can't create matter from nothing, so how are astral beings suddenly going to have their own bodies here on the material plane? Where would that *material* come from?"

Lord Edmund looked somewhat placated, but not exactly at ease. "Regardless of whether it is truly possible, Miss Featherstone, the Alath Guild seemed quite convinced that it is not only happening, but that my son is somehow an essential ingredient in bringing it about."

"So maybe they're fanatics," said Lysander. "They somehow got it in their magic-addled heads that Lord Edmund's son . . ." He looked at Edmund.

"Edgar," supplied Edmund.

"They believe that poor little Edgar is the key to their crazy end-of-the-world scenario. Maybe they want to prevent it; maybe they want to bring it about. Doesn't matter. They believe they need the kid, so they took the kid."

"Then why would they *tell* him they needed his kid if they were planning on taking him?" I asked. "It gives away their motive."

"They wanted me to allow one of their mages to live at the mansion while they attempted to figure out exactly how he was involved," said Lord Edmund. "I have no problem with bringing mages into my home, of course. But there was . . . something of a zealot's air about their guild-master that made me fear for the safety of my family, so I refused them access."

"And that's when they hatched a plan to kidnap him," said Lysander. "Makes perfect sense."

I took a long pull on my pipe as I thought it over. There was still something about the situation that bothered me, but I couldn't quite pin it down yet. I needed more information.

"I'll have to search this place from top to bottom," I said. "Full access, and as much time with those door sigils and any others I find as I need."

"Naturally," said Lord Edmund.

"I'll also need access to any household staff for questioning. And your wife, too, of course."

"Oh . . ." He frowned, as if just remembering something. "I'm afraid Lady Celia is currently indisposed. The shock of the kidnapping has left her in quite a state. You're welcome to visit her, of course, but I must insist that if she's sleeping, you do not wake her."

"Fair enough," I said. "Okay, so best-case scenario: we find that the evidence matches up with your suspicions of the Alath Guild, we go over there, knock on their door, and they've got your son trussed up on an altar or something. What then?"

Lord Edmund drew on his pipe for a moment, looking a little uncertain. "Well . . . I assumed that since you're a mage, you could—"

"Wait—who told you I was a mage?"

"I've just heard—"

"Listen, *friend*." My voice hardened. "I am *not* a mage. Do you understand? Don't *ever* call me that."

He looked more confused than upset. "I . . . didn't mean to offend you, Miss Featherstone. Truly. It's only that I've heard several different and unconnected parties refer to you as the—"

"*Ooookay*," Lysander said quickly, putting a calming hand on my back because I was leaning forward and waiting for Lord Edmund to say the name that was going to make me punch him in the face. "I don't think we need to get into all that, do we, my lord?" He gave Edmund a meaningful look.

"Naturally not."

"I'm an *arcanist*," I said between clenched teeth.

"Yeah, see?" said Lysander smoothly. "She's an arcanist. There's some overlap, so a lot of people get them confused, but I assure you they are very different."

"Ah yes, an arcanist, of course," Edmund said in a way that suggested he had never heard the term before in his life. Ignoramus, even with all these books in this room. I wondered if he'd even read half of them, or if this was the most colossal waste of books in history.

"I think what Roz was trying to get at," continued Lysander, "is that if we have to confront this guild, how much force are we authorized to use in order to guarantee the safe return of your son?"

"How much force?" Suddenly there was cold steel in Lord Edmund's eyes, and I could finally see some evidence of why he was the most powerful man in Drusiel. He tapped his pipe out in a small ceramic dish, leaving the remains of the tobacco to smolder. He placed the pipe on the desk and steepled his hands. "Do not mistake my *courtesy* for timidity or lack of resolve. I rarely suffer the rudeness you have shown me today, but I have been led to believe you are worth it." He looked pointedly at my gloved hands. "When it comes to the safety of my son, you may use any and all force at your disposal. I want every guild in Drusiel to understand that I can be as cruel as I am benevolent. I trust that is not a problem for you?"

I flexed my hands, listening to the creak of the leather gloves. A license to beat on any mage that got in my way? Maybe this job wouldn't be so terrible.

"No problem at all. Our typical fee is ten silver per day, plus expenses."

"You'll get twenty-five per day, plus another fifty up front for expenses, with more upon request." He pulled a large, jingling pouch from his desk drawer and dropped it loudly on the desk. "You will spare nothing and no one in your search. Do we have an agreement?"

"You bet we do!" said Lysander, and I swear he looked closer to crying than I'd ever seen him, and that included his wedding day.

"Wonderful." Edmund pulled a parchment from his desk drawer and flattened it out so it was facing us. On it was written a formal contractual agreement. *The parties below agree to provide the service* . . . etc. Then he dipped his quill in the inkwell and handed it to me.

I usually didn't go in for formal contracts and the like, but I supposed it was the sort of thing that gave nobles like him peace of mind that someone like me wouldn't just run out on him with seventy-five silver in hand. So I signed, and Lysander almost broke the desk in his eagerness to do the same.

It wasn't until after we'd officially committed ourselves, and Lysander had scooped up the bag of silver, that I said, "You mentioned talking to the guildmaster of the Alath Guild."

"Indeed."

"What's his name? Maybe I know him already."

"I believe he introduced himself as Simon Crowley. Have you heard of him?"

The words hit my chest like a war hammer and knocked the breath right out of me. I tried to suck some air back in, but my abdominals were too busy heaving. If I'd consumed anything more solid than whiskey that day, it would've ended up on Lord Edmund's desk. It wasn't good to get this emotional. I could feel my palms heating up. I had to cool down, but I still couldn't breathe, and my senses were getting swallowed in a haze of panic. All I could think was *Simon fucking Crowley of all the fucking people in the world.*

"Hey."

It was Lysander. His meaty hand was on my shoulder again, and he was looking at me like he knew something was up, even though he didn't know what it was. That was a real friend for you. They could just tell shit like that.

"You okay?" he asked.

A real friend, who really needed this money.

And what was I getting worked up about anyway? It couldn't actually be the same Simon Crowley. That guy was dead—I'd seen the flesh melt right off his face fifteen years ago. It had to be someone else with the same name. Coincidence. That's all it was.

This was what I told myself as I forced air into my lungs. "Yeah, I'm fine. Let's get started."

But as Lysander and I said our goodbyes to Lord Edmund and began our investigation of the mansion, I knew I didn't believe in coincidences.

FIVE

Once Lysander and I left Lord Edmund's study, I tried to shake my sense of foreboding. We made our way across the large foyer back to the entrance, and I kept my hands jammed into my coat pockets until I was certain they wouldn't shake.

"You want to start with those door sigils?" asked Lysander.

I nodded and knelt down next to one of the thick oak double doors. This was what I needed right now. Something concrete and without a lot of emotional heft. Whiskey would've been nice too, but basic sigil analysis would have to do for now.

The inside of the doorframe had a protection sigil carved directly into the wood, probably with a knife. It was competent work, but nothing fancy. Just two overlapping pentagons pointing in opposite directions enclosed by a lattice square.

People with little knowledge of magecraft assumed that the power of a sigil came solely from the symbols, but that wasn't true. There were a number of elements that went into creating them. The symbols were important, of course. And in the more complicated sigils, words, generally in Arch Pendoric, could also be used to chain interlocking symbols together for greater power. But the materials were also important, both the writing implement and what it was written on. The more permanent a sigil, the stronger it was. So you could draw one on a parchment with a bit of charcoal, but the best you could get out of it was one tiny little puff of flame or a little patch of ice. The door sigil here was better, but wood was still a fairly soft material compared to stone or metal, and therefore not as potent. That's what I was seeing right now. The protection symbol on the inside was carved in wood, but the unlocking symbol on the outside, which was merely a downward-facing triangle encased in an upward-facing triangle, had been etched directly into the iron door handle. So even though the protection sigil was more complex, the metal-carved sigil was durable enough to overpower it.

I tapped on the sigil etched into the handle and looked up at Lysander. "Whoever did this knew what they were up against. Nothing wasted. They'd been able to examine the protection sigil on the inside and knew the most efficient way to break it."

"Maybe they had someone working at the mansion?" suggested Lysander. "Paid off one of the servants or something?"

"Could be. Let's check the sigils in the nursery door."

Lysander looked surprised. "Why would the nursery door be locked?"

"It wouldn't be," I said. "But while I'm no baby expert—*thankfully*—even I know that if you wake up a baby, there's a good chance they'll start crying. If I were the kidnapper, I wouldn't want to chance those cries waking someone up."

"You think there might be a sound-dampening sigil in there somewhere?"

"Might be. And if so, those are complicated enough that I could probably get a better read from it than this tiny thing."

A person unfamiliar with sigils might think there wasn't much difference between one person's triangle and another's. But with enough experience, you started to see tiny variations, little embellishments, and trademark accents that made identifying the author of a particular sigil about as reliable as analyzing their handwriting. There was something about this simple triangle within a triangle that was familiar, but I needed more to nail it down.

Lysander's eyes swept the foyer, taking in the many directions open to us. "Which way to the nursery, you think?"

"Should we ask someone?"

"You *seen* anyone?"

Now that he mentioned it, I'd only seen Lord Edmund and Quince, who had already departed along with his carriage and bodyguards. "You'd think a place this big would be crawling with servants."

His eyes narrowed thoughtfully. "Yeah. Maids and butlers and the like. Maybe they keep out of sight until Lord Edmund rings a bell or something."

"Well . . ." I stood up. "I guess we'll just have to wander around until we find it. Keep your eyes peeled for anything else unusual along the way."

I didn't expect the nursery to be on the ground level but figured it wouldn't hurt to do some snooping, so we started there.

To say the place was big was an understatement. The only place larger I'd ever seen was the Grimoric Mage Academy, and that housed about a thousand students and faculty at any given time. We found a grand dining room, as well as a smaller dining room, maybe for the servants that were nowhere to be seen. I didn't know the difference between a living room, a parlor, and a drawing room, but judging by the many areas with no discernible function other than places to sit, I guess it had all three. There was a billiards room, with a pool table and a dart board that Lysander gazed at longingly. He was terrible at darts but always so eager to play that I had to assume he must enjoy losing to me. If only I could get him to put some money on it now and then.

There were kitchens, of course. Several adjoining rooms that looked like they could have fed a small army, but still no one around. It was a strange feeling to wander through laundry rooms, a kennel full of hunting dogs that barked as we walked past, and several small servants quarters, all of them deserted.

"You know, if the kidnappers did have someone on the inside . . . ," I said.

"It's going to be hard to find them," Lysander said. "Maybe Lord

Edmund just fired everyone? Like, he was so upset about losing his son, and couldn't figure out who he could trust, so he just sent everyone away."

"Maybe. It's strange he didn't mention it, though," I said. "Okay, let's head upstairs."

The second level was comprised almost entirely of bedrooms. The mansion could house as many people as an inn. I was pretty sure the majority of the rooms were vacant most of the time, reserved for luminaries like King Hector or King Lorenzo. As we walked from one unused bedroom to the next, each with finer linens than Lye and I had ever touched, the emptiness of the place began to feel oppressive.

Finally, we found the nursery. It was a ridiculously large room for someone who couldn't even sit up yet, much less walk around. Along one wall was an elegantly carved crib, and off in the corner was the sort of venerable-looking rocking chair that had probably been passed from parent to child for generations. Small wooden toys, a rocking horse, and a stuffed toy bear waited patiently for the day when little Lord Edgar would be old enough to give a damn about anything other than eating, sleeping, and shitting.

Did I mention I didn't like babies?

The sound-dampening sigil was easy enough to spot. A dark circle burned into the wooden frame of the doorway.

"Yeah, I was afraid of this." I rubbed my gloved thumb across the charred wood. "Self-destroying sigil."

A skilled mage could embed a sigil within a sigil. In this case, probably a basic smoldering-fire sigil encasing a sound-dampening sigil, so that once one was used up, the second activated and eradicated both.

"Can you get anything off it?" asked Lysander.

I leaned in so close that my nose was almost touching the wood. It was a tricky thing, making self-destroying sigils. On one hand, you wanted them gone when you were done with them. On the other hand, if you didn't carve them deep enough, they didn't work as well. Whoever made this balanced it as well as anyone could, but no sigil was perfect. Very faintly, I could see traces of the symbols that had once been there. Not enough to get a whole picture, but there was something familiar about the work. Something old fashioned . . . In fact, I hadn't seen an air sign like that since school.

When I'd been Simon Crowley's star pupil.

I reached out, very purposefully, and gripped the doorframe with both hands, mostly so I didn't keel over. Breathing was a struggle again, but I fought my way through it with gritted teeth, refusing to allow the tide of panic to pull me under. I'd be damned if I'd let Simon fucking Crowley do *anything* to me ever again.

But I couldn't help ask myself the question, what if he had somehow survived?

"Well, well, well. If it isn't the Gutter Mage."

If there was one thing that could distract me from thoughts of Simon Crowley, it was hearing that name.

"Now, Roz . . ." Lysander looked pleadingly at me. "Please don't kill someone in the client's house."

Gutter Mage was what the guild mages called me. I didn't know who had come up with that cute little nickname, but it started about five years ago, after I'd had a little . . . confrontation with the Raboc Guild that sent several of their members to the medics. The name had haunted me ever since. Lysander once pointed out that at least the guilds considered me a mage. He still had the scars to remind himself why it wasn't a smart thing to say.

Now I turned toward the source of this new and possibly doomed voice. A grimoric mage stood at the far end of the hallway. I could tell because he wore a stupid hooded robe like every other fucking mage. It was blue with purple trim, which made him a member of Valac, easily the most insufferably smug guild in the kingdom.

This Valac mage was probably about my age, with bright blue eyes, and a round baby face that was attempting to look more sculpted with the help of a neatly trimmed beard. Not a bad-looking guy as far as mages went, although that didn't stop me from considering several variations on the slow, painful death theme.

But Lysander was right. Chances were high that he worked for Lord Edmund, and killing him would be bad for business. Besides, I had something nearly as good as killing. Shaming.

"Nice job on those protection sigils," I told him.

He scowled. "I didn't do those. I only got here yesterday."

"Wait, were you hired to find the kid too?" asked Lysander. "Lord Edmund didn't say anything about competition."

"What? Of course I wasn't." He looked insulted. "I was brought in to take care of Lady Celia."

"Oh yeah?" I asked. "Mind if we have a little chat with her?"

He gestured to the open doorway. "You're welcome to look in, but she won't be much use to you because I have her under a sleep sigil."

I walked over to him. "Why's that?"

"To prevent her from harming herself any further," said the mage. "It's just a temporary measure until I can figure out what's driven her into such a state."

"Her kid got stolen," said Lysander. "What's to figure?"

The mage glared at Lysander, then turned back to me. "Her level of agitation was . . . extreme. Well beyond even such an upsetting event."

"How so?" I asked.

"She was trying to rip open her stomach with her bare hands."

"Fucking hell," muttered Lysander. "Can someone do that?"

"They can if they already have a large incision there that hasn't healed yet," said the mage.

I peeked around the corner into the room. It was too small to be the master bedroom. Lady Celia had probably been moved here after she tried to tear out her insides. She was a real classic beauty, with blond ringlets, porcelain skin, long lashes, and a perfectly formed mouth with a slight pout that begged to be kissed. When I got closer, I saw that she had a white strip of cloth on her forehead with a small sleep sigil stitched on it in purple thread. I had to admit this Valac mage had done some delicate, sensitive work. If it was any indication of his general caregiving, she was in good hands.

"Why'd she have the incision?" I asked.

"Apparently the baby was breach. One or both were in grave danger, so the attending mage removed the baby by way of incision."

"Risky," I said.

"It is," he replied. "But I suppose he saved them both, so it worked out for the best."

"You know the name of that attending mage?" I asked.

He shook his head.

"And what do I call you?"

"Demetrius Shandy, member of the Valac Guild."

"My name's Rosalind Featherstone. You can call me Roz if you like. But if you ever call me that *other* name again, I'll slit your throat and pull your tongue through like a cravat. Do we have an understanding?"

His blue eyes went wide as he nodded silently. The nice thing about having a terrible reputation, I suppose, was that people believed you were capable of anything.

"Great." I turned to Lysander. "Okay, I think we've got about all we're going to get out of Ariel House. Let's head back into town."

He winced. "We're walking?"

"Unless you've learned to fly and just forgot to tell me."

SIX

I thought about pressing Lord Edmund on where all his servants were, but pushing the client around could be dicey, and there was a good chance he didn't even know. In my experience, someone like him didn't pay attention to who was serving him, as long as his needs were being met. Quince would be the one to ask, and he was off delivering that message, so I'd have to save that line of questioning for now.

Lysander and I made our way through the gardens, which were even nicer up close than when I'd seen them from the carriage. The balance of color from one section to the next was perfect, often with gentle gradations I hadn't even known were possible. The walkways were paved with the same tiny stones as the front drive, and there were little stone benches here and there so a person could sit and admire the work. The attention to detail made it clear that whoever was in charge gave their life to this garden. I might not admire things like this much, but the level of dedication was awe-inspiring.

As I was looking around, I noticed a small separate building tucked away in the back of the garden. A little cottage, probably for the head gardener.

"I want to check one more thing before we go," I told Lysander.

We carefully picked our way through the gardens back to the cottage. It was a simple, one-story structure with shutters on the windows and a slate roof with a chimney jutting out the top. When I saw that, it made me turn back to look at the roof of the mansion. Not a single chimney there.

Interesting. Did he heat his entire home with magic? There *was* such a thing as being too dependent on spirits.

"What are you two unsavory types doing, wandering around his lordship's garden?"

An old man's face poked out the front door of the house, giving us a tremendous scowl that reached nearly to the crown of his wispy head.

"Unsavory?" Lysander looked hurt.

"His lordship's garden?" I gave the guy a smile. "Looks to me more like *your* garden, old timer."

"His lordship owns it, I just tend it," he snapped.

I shrugged, walking slowly closer. "Whichever. We happen to work for his lordship now too."

"Yeah, we're looking for his missing kid," said Lysander.

The gardener eyed us both warily. "I don't know nothing."

"You sure you didn't see or hear anything strange?" I asked. "Maybe two nights ago?"

"I told Mr. Quince the same thing I'm telling you now. I didn't hear nothing."

I was right at the door now, less than three feet from the gardener. I put my hands on the doorframe and gave him my very best smile, but he glared at me like I was there to steal his house right out from under him. Maybe he spent so much time with plants because he didn't like people.

I appreciated the old guy's moxie, but it seemed like he might be holding out on me. I thought about pressing him a little less gently, but then my glove caught on the doorframe. I turned and saw a hastily scratched sigil. Unlike the other two, this was ragged. Amateurish, even. But there was no mistaking that it was a spent sound-dampening sigil. That would explain why the gardener hadn't heard anything. While the sigil hadn't been well executed, it had clearly been carved with intensity. And that was another ingredient to sigil work—the focus and intention of the mage who drew it. Incantations held no real power on their own. Spoken words were nothing but breath on the wind. But they sharpened the focus of the mage in such a way that by sheer force of will, the caster could bring a more powerful spirit to the binding, thereby amplifying the sigil. Professor Ratcliffe, one of the few decent teachers I'd had back in school, used to tell us that a simple sigil done with a lot of heart could be nearly as powerful as one crafted by a master.

I looked back at the old gardener. "Well, if you think of something, anything unusual at all, keep it in mind for the next time I come by. And I *will* come by."

Now that I'd seen the sigil, I wasn't sure he was actually holding out on me. But he was the only person I'd met besides Edmund and Quince who had been there the night of the kidnapping. That alone was enough for a follow-up. And now it looked like we had more than one mage on the premises that night, most likely a master and apprentice.

Simon and a new Rosalind?

The thought popped into my head as I turned away from the old gardener, and it gripped my stomach like a fist. If this *was* Simon's doing, and he had some crazy new theory about the Nevma Year that involved Edmund's son, he might have dragged some other young, naive sucker along with him. Suddenly I wasn't just thinking *if* I cross paths with him. Now I *wanted* to find him before he fucked up some other kid as badly as me.

"I can hear those gears turning," said Lysander as he fell in step beside me.

"Yeah, sorry."

"What are you not telling me?"

"That guildmaster Lord Edmund mentioned? If he got the name right, it might be someone I know. Someone nasty."

"We're pretty nasty ourselves."

"True."

"It's more than that, though," he said.

I sighed. Damn friends and their damn caring.

"Yeah. *If* I'm right, it's the guy who branded my palms when I was in school."

I shoved my hands into my pockets. I knew it was pointless, but I didn't want him looking at them even *gloved* right then. I guess because fifteen years later, I was still ashamed. Of what? I wasn't sure. But sometimes it made me want to crawl right out of my skin.

"That's the second best news I've heard today," said Lysander.

"What are you talking about?"

"Well, naturally the *best* news was learning how much money we're making on this job. But finally getting to beat the shit out of the guy who tortured my best friend?" He cracked his knuckles with obvious relish. "*That* is a close second."

SEVEN

I didn't mind the long walk home. There were enough thoughts swirling around in my head that the quiet of the forest was preferable to the raucous bustle of downtown Drusiel. Drunks singing, whores hollering, dogs barking, carriages rattling, and fights breaking out on a semi-regular basis . . . it was a wonder I could think at all in that town.

Lysander, however, couldn't stop moaning about this extended encounter with nature.

"If that woodpecker doesn't knock it off, I'm going to climb up there and choke him to death." He glared up into the branches, his hands already making strangling motions.

"I would *love* to see you climb a tree," I said.

He shifted his glare to me for a moment, then picked up his pace, muttering to himself.

And later: "What the hell is up with all these bugs?" He swatted a mosquito on his neck. "Are there bug keepers who live out here?"

"Bug keepers?"

"Well, where do they all come from, then? And why the hell do they keep biting *me*?"

"It's because you're so sweet, Lye."

"Go fuck yourself, Roz."

"You don't get out of town much, do you?" I asked.

"I *never* get out of town. Mostly because I don't want to."

"I used to travel a lot as a kid. Merchant parents and all that. Seems like back then, we were always going one place or another." My parents were too old to go very far now. And my father . . . well, I didn't like to think about that too much.

We walked for a while in a silence only broken when Lysander slapped at a bug and cursed to himself. I thought back to all those memories of traveling and realized that I missed it a little. The world used to feel so big. And maybe it *was*, or maybe my own personal world had just gotten smaller. I had buried myself deep in the endless maneuvering for power and prestige of Drusiel, and I had to ask myself why. I didn't want those things any longer. I already had more power than I knew what to do with, and I'd long ago settled for infamy over prestige. So what was keeping me there? I could pretend that Lysander needed me, but he had Portia now. Hell, she'd probably throw me a party if I decided to leave Drusiel.

Maybe a fresh start was exactly what I needed. Once we finished this job, I'd have enough money to set myself up somewhere else. Keriel, maybe, or Monaxa. Maybe I'd even move to Lapisi. I'd have to learn another language, but how hard could that be? I didn't know what kind of mages they had down there, but they couldn't be any worse than the ones in Penador.

I had my head so far up my ass dreaming of a new life far from guild politics and bad reputations that I didn't notice our attackers until they were nearly on top of us.

"*Roz,*" Lysander growled. But it was the steely hiss of his sword leaving its sheath that really snapped me out of my reverie.

We'd reached the narrow bridge with the adorable, if completely fanciful, carvings of spirits. Six men had risen up out of the creek bed, their cloaks almost perfectly matching the brownish gray of the bank. Clearly this was a regular spot for them.

They spread out and circled us, brandishing the usual assortment of short swords and knives. Small, easy to conceal weapons that relied more on speed than force. They moved with a smooth, silent confidence that suggested they did this a lot. These were professionals, not drunk dock-workers looking for trouble. If Lysander hadn't caught sight of them, we'd already be dead or dying from multiple stab wounds by now.

"Okay, boys." Lysander took a few warm-up swings with his sword. "I'll try to keep this simple, but I've got a lot of pent-up frustration right now from walking through these goddamn woods, so no promises."

They had us completely surrounded and were slowly constricting the circle. Lysander and I went back-to-back as I yanked off my gloves and stuffed them into my coat pockets.

The bandits paused when my hands lit up with fire. They probably hadn't counted on magic, especially since I wasn't dressed like a mage. The fire didn't hurt me, of course, but like always, the sigils in my palms throbbed with a dull ache. After fifteen years of practice, I had about as much control over it as I was probably ever going to get. So long as the flame still touched my skin, I could manipulate it any way I wanted. I could change the size, shape, or intensity. Unfortunately, the moment I lost physical contact with the flame, it became . . . erratic. And usually catastrophic. So while it was tempting to just start hurling fireballs at our enemies, I really didn't want to burn down half the forest if I didn't have to.

Besides, unlike most magic users, I didn't mind close fighting.

"You ready?" Lysander held his sword in both hands, the tip low to the ground.

"You're not the only one who needs to let out a little frustration."

I heard someone lunge toward Lysander, followed by the clang of steel on steel, and then the wet thwack of steel cutting into meat. Lysander could move fast for a big guy, and I was pretty sure he was the one doing the cutting. But I didn't have time to check because the ones in front of me closed in.

Two of them attacked simultaneously. I ducked underneath their thrusts, then grabbed their extended wrists and lit them up like torches.

As the two human-shaped infernos stumbled around, no doubt

suffering the last few moments of their lives in mind-numbing anguish, the third guy came at me. I was in an awkward crouched position, so I had to roll to the side to avoid the blow. He kept on me, not giving me a chance to get back to my feet or allowing me to grab him.

But he was scared of the fire, I could tell. A lot of people were. Often the fear was even more useful than the ability itself. While I continued to dodge and roll around awkwardly on the ground, I let my hands crackle impressively. His eyes were so drawn to them that, for a moment, he stopped paying attention to the rest of me. That's when I caught his ankle with a scissor kick and brought him down next to me hard enough to knock the wind out of him. Then I slammed my hand into his chest and ignited him before he had a chance to recover. He went up fast, and I got quickly to my feet before the flames could burn off whatever hair I'd managed to grow back.

The two I'd lit up before were now just smoking mounds of ash. I stared at them for a moment, bothered by something I couldn't quite articulate. Then I turned and saw Lysander about to cut the last bandit in half. The guy was already pretty beaten up. His eye was swollen, and he had a gash on his leg that had soaked through the lower half of his pant leg. He was barely standing, and as he stared up at Lysander, his mouth was open in a silent scream.

Silent.

That's what was bothering me. If there was one truly unpleasant aspect of fire magic, it was listening to people screech as they burned to death. But none of the guys I'd just killed had made a sound.

"Lysander! Wait!"

Lysander was already in mid-swing, so the best he could do was tilt his blade so that the flat part hit his opponent's arm, sending him spinning to the ground.

I hurried over and grabbed the guy by his tunic. "Can you speak?" I shouted in his face. "Make one sound, and I swear I'll let you live!"

He tried. Oh, how he tried. His eyes looked desperate as he stared up at me and worked his mouth. But nothing came out. Finally, he reached up weakly with the arm that Lysander hadn't shattered and yanked his collar down, exposing the sigil carved into the base of his neck.

"Shit," I said, and let him drop to the ground. "Shit, shit, shit."

"What is it, Roz?" asked Lysander as he wiped the blood off his sword.

"This wasn't a random robbery. These guys were after us *specifically*, and someone carved silence sigils in their necks so we wouldn't be able to find out who hired them."

"Mage, then? Somebody from the Alath Guild, or whoever was behind the kidnapping?"

"Probably. I might have expected a shakedown like this once we'd nosed around in Drusiel a little. But we haven't even gotten back into town, so how did they know we'd been hired?"

"Maybe they'd been following Quince, and when they saw us leave with him, they just assumed we'd take the job and sent these jesters along to deal with us before we even started digging."

"Maybe," I conceded. It sounded about as reasonable as anything else, but it didn't quite set right in my head. Too many "maybes" strung together made for a weak chain.

"Hey, can you seal me up? One of them got lucky." Lysander lifted up his leather jerkin to show me a wide, seeping gash along his side.

I leaned in for a closer look. It was a pretty clean cut and not that deep. "You know, stitches would hurt less, and leave less of a scar."

"You got a needle and thread on you?"

I shook my head.

"Well then? Besides, Portia doesn't mind the scars. Kind of gets her hot, actually."

"Glad I can contribute to your love life."

I'd done this enough times now to know exactly how much heat was needed to cauterize the wound without causing any more pain and scarring than necessary. Weirdly, it was one of the abilities I was most proud of. As I passed my hand across the wound, Lysander stiffened and grunted through his clenched teeth while his skin smoked. The stench of burning flesh was already in the air, so it didn't really add much in that respect.

"You better wash it in the creek, just to be safe."

When I turned toward the water, I saw what was left of the bridge. The actual footbridge was still intact, but the railings were only charred stumps, and the carvings were gone completely.

"Fucking hell," I said. "And I was trying so hard to be careful."

"One of your human torches bumped into it when they were running around." Lysander sauntered over to the creek bank and lifted up his jerkin. He winced as he splashed cold water on his wound. "At least we can still get across it."

"Yeah. At least."

He looked thoughtfully at me for a moment as he pulled his jerkin back down. "Forest is still here too. Wasn't sure that would be the case."

I gave him a tired smile. "I guess so. Much to your disappointment."

He grinned. "Hey, I may not want to be *in* the forest, but I defend its right to exist."

"That's what I love about you, Lye. So magnanimous. Come on. Let's go home."

"Speaking of magnanimous, should we let this guy live?" Lysander nodded toward the now unconscious bandit.

"Yeah, I guess so." It was strange. I hadn't felt any pity for the bandits until after I realized that they were hired assassins. I think it was the sigils in their necks that made me a little sad for them. Had they been told they'd eventually be able to speak again? Maybe they would, but chances weren't high. Often when you bound an air spirit to someone like that, they didn't want to leave, even after the sigil faded away to a faint scar. Usually they would continue to eat your words for the rest of your life.

One bit of good news was that even though I hadn't recognized the sigil work, I was certain it wasn't Simon Crowley's. As far as I was concerned, I still didn't have any conclusive proof that the guy who told Lord Edmund his name was Simon Crowley was truly my old mentor back from the dead. And that doubt was something I planned to hold on to as long as I could.

EIGHT

It was well after dark by the time we reached Drusiel. There was a full moon out, but it wasn't very noticeable, not since one of the guilds had been hired to set up light posts throughout the city. They were metal poles with clear glass globes mounted on top. Each globe contained a tiny burning spirit that danced away all night. The resulting light flickered unevenly and spread strange shadows that made people you'd known your whole life look suddenly unfamiliar. But having things lit up supposedly kept the more obvious crimes down and encouraged people to stay out later at the taverns, which the tavern owners liked. I was less enamored with them because the lamps bled out all the light from the moon. Unlike spirit fire, moonlight made people look more attractive, not less. I was generally of the mind that there was already enough ugliness in the world. We had to hold on to what little beauty remained, even if it was an illusion.

But thanks to the spirit light posts, plenty of people were still out and about. Some stumbled from one tavern to the next, arm in arm with a friend or lover. Others sat on street curbs and passed a bottle around. The mood was generally cheerful and carefree. And why not? What did they have to worry about? Things might get a little rowdy now and then, but it never got too out of control. The people of Drusiel had the best mages in the world looking after them. I thought about getting drunk myself and pretending to be ignorant like that, even if only for a little while.

"You want a drink before calling it a night?" I asked as we passed the Skinned Cat.

Lysander shook his head. "I've got an eye-meltingly sexy wife waiting for me at home, and with the good news I have to tell her, it's going to be a very exciting evening."

"Right," I said. "Maybe don't mention the mage-hired assassins when you tell her about the money."

"Wasn't planning on it."

"Well, don't strain your back or anything. I want to get started first thing in the morning. If these jesters think the Nevma Year is a real thing and they need the kid to make it happen, they probably have some kind of sacrificial timetable. I don't think we'd get paid as much if we bring home little baby Edgar with his heart cut out."

Lysander's eyes narrowed thoughtfully. "If it *is* the Alath Guild—"

"Which we don't know for certain."

"I'll grant you that. But getting some inside information on Alath might answer that question pretty easily. Guild rumor, that kind of thing."

"I guess."

"Especially from someone on the Interguild Disciplinary Council."

"Aha. Cute. I see what you're doing there."

He gave me the closest thing to an innocent smile he could manage. "And what am I doing here, Roz?"

"You want me to talk to Orlando."

"Hey, what a great idea! He's an upstanding member of the Chemosh Guild, isn't he?" Lysander affected a mock look of surprise. "And say, didn't he get elected to chairman of the disciplinary council recently? I bet if there's been any trouble with this Alath Guild, he'd know about it."

I glared at him. "It's amazing that you've never fucked me in the ass, considering how much pain you cause it."

He grinned impudently. "You'll go see him tomorrow morning, then?"

I looked down at my hands and realized I still wasn't wearing my gloves. I fished them out of my pockets and yanked them on. "Yeah."

"You want me to come with you?"

"Absolutely not. You always agree with him."

"Not always. Just when he's right. Which is most of the time."

"It undermines our position when I'm trying to get something out of him."

"Some things are more important than business. Like joining two star-crossed lovers."

I jabbed him in the ribs, making sure to hit the wound he'd received earlier that day.

He gasped from the pain. "Ahh. Dammit, Roz—"

"Listen carefully, Lye, because it is only our deep friendship that prevents me from burning you where you stand. First, Orlando and I are done. We're never getting back together because neither of us want to. Do you understand?"

He nodded, wincing as he gently patted his ribs.

"Second, just because *you* found someone doesn't mean *I* have to find someone. I'm very happy you've got Portia. You don't smell nearly as bad since she entered your life, and for that I am extremely grateful. But I have run out of patience with you trying to push me back toward Orlando so that we can be some kind of matching couples set. Is that *also* clear?"

"Yeah, okay. Sorry." He looked more hurt than in pain now.

"Great. I'll go talk to the high-and-mighty mage of Chemosh Guild tomorrow morning, and then you and I will meet at the Skinned Cat around noon. That should give you plenty of time to fuck your wife's brains out all night and still get some rest."

"Fine. See you tomorrow, then." He started to head home, his hand still on his side. But then he stopped and looked over his shoulder at me with a wicked smirk. "Don't stay out drinking all night. You know how he hates it when you show up reeking of whiskey."

That weak parting shot didn't even deserve a response, so I turned my back on him and walked into the Skinned Cat.

Incidentally, I didn't drink all night. Not because of Lysander's advice, and definitely not because I gave a damn what Orlando would think. I just couldn't quite settle in. Maybe it was my daydream about finally moving out of Drusiel, or getting rattled by hearing Simon Crowley's name after all these years, or just being anxious about the best-paying job I'd ever had. Whatever the reason, I couldn't relax. Everyone around me seemed too loud and far too stupid. I had to stop myself several times from either picking a fight with someone or taking them into the alley and fucking them. I didn't want to dwell too long on how those two impulses might be related.

"I know that look," Chester said as he slid another glass of whiskey to me. "Nothing good ever comes from it."

"Yeah." I was at the bar with the late shift of sad old men, the ones who never did find that equally miserable woman to settle down with in order to make their lives mutually unbearable. These guys didn't seem any better off, though. I wondered where the sad old single women were. Maybe there weren't any. Maybe all the old single women were happy.

"Is this the part where I ask you what's on your mind?" Chester's droopy mustache undulated slightly as he spoke.

"Nah, this is the part where you give me a drink on the house," I told him.

"You already know it's on the house."

"But it feels better when you say something like, *This one's on the house, kid*, then give me a knowing wink. I like it when you do that."

"Except I've never done that."

"Don't I know it."

"You know what your problem is?"

"You adding to the list?"

"You act like you're a thousand years old, but you're young enough to be my daughter. How come?"

"Done more than my share of living, I guess."

He looked at me for a moment. Then: "You know what I do when I'm tired of the shit?"

"What's that, Chester?"

"I go to bed."

I considered the idea as I took a sip of whiskey and swirled the burning liquid around on my tongue. I decided it had a certain simple elegance to it. So after I finished that glass, I bummed a pinch of tobacco and headed back toward the crumbling old building where I rented a room for five coppers a day.

As I walked, I puffed on my clay pipe and gazed up into the night sky, trying to see past the squirrelly spirit light to the moon that lay beyond. That celestial sphere had its own kind of magic—feminine, subtle, and sly. Right then I felt like I could use some of that. I suddenly wished I was back in that forest, wandering beneath the moonlight, away from all this noise.

The Nevma Year. What a load of shit. Even if it was real, which it wasn't, why would someone want to make it happen? Imagine every burning spirit in every streetlamp bursting from the confines of their glass to set fire to Drusiel. Every protection spirit tearing away from the locked doors where they'd been dwelling and smashing through the very homes they'd kept safe. Poor Quince suddenly finding that instead of being inside a horseless carriage, he was in the belly of a ravenous beast careening through the city streets.

That last one actually made me laugh out loud a little. I took another puff on my pipe and let the smoke leak out of the corners of my mouth as I smiled.

But jokes aside, even if spirits couldn't assume corporeal form, society had become so dependent on magic that merely releasing every binding sigil at once could very well bring about the collapse of civilization as we knew it. Was that the goal here? Total chaos? If so, who would benefit from that?

There had to be something else going on. Some other angle I hadn't dug up yet. The Nevma Year was just a line they gave Lord Edmund to throw off pursuers. Maybe they'd fed him all sorts of nonsense.

But if that was true—if everything Lord Edmund gave me was suspect—then what did I actually have to go on?

NINE

Breakfast was in my neighbor Cordelia's flat. She didn't have much furniture. Just a creaky wood-frame bed, a rickety table, and some chairs. Still, it was more furniture than I had, which was none, unless you counted the stacks of books. Cordelia was a few years younger than me, or so she claimed. In my experience, actors weren't the most reliable when it came to admitting their age. Like most thespians, she was "in between shows," and to make ends meet, she was tutoring children in the theatrical arts so that one day, they too could be between shows and tutor a whole new generation in the theatrical arts. A nice racket, if you asked me.

I sat slumped on the table while she bustled around in the tiny kitchen area, heating a pot of water on her prized magic hot stone. It was a nice piece. Not very powerful, but the sigil was reusable and could be activated by someone who wasn't a mage. Probably the only thing in her home worth stealing.

Cordelia had a careful kind of beauty, like she was always ready to step onto the stage at a moment's notice. Her long copper hair was mostly pulled back, but with some artfully straying locks to let you know she wasn't too prim. She had one of those highly impractical but nice to look at hourglass figures. When she wasn't wearing a layer of makeup, she had a light dusting of freckles on her nose and high, rounded cheekbones. Her hazel eyes were so big I sometimes lost myself in them for minutes at a time. We'd never fucked, but not for my lack of trying. I was too coarse for her. Too crude. It was probably for the best, since I usually managed to screw things up with lovers so badly that we wouldn't have been able to remain friends. And I liked being around her. She was whip-smart, although she would act dumb when it suited her. And she had this spunky, upbeat-yet-determined energy. I sometimes wondered if I would have been like that, had I made different choices when I was at the academy.

"You know, we could do something with that hair." She placed two mugs of tea and a plate of boiled eggs on the table and sat down across from me.

"What do you mean?" I took one of the eggs and pressed down with the palm of my gloved hand as I rolled it around on the table so the shell crumbled. I slid the ruined shell off the egg and dropped it on the plate. Then I took a bite and washed it down with a gulp of hot tea that burned my throat a little.

"I have some scissors." She gave her egg a tap on the table, then used her thumbnail to delicately peel the shell away. "I could trim it so it would all be the same length instead of so uneven. Maybe even shape it into something presentable."

I shrugged and took another bite. "Who do I have to impress?"

"Prospective clients?"

"They expect me to look like this, or worse."

She sipped her tea and said nothing, although it looked like she had plenty to say.

My eyes narrowed. "This isn't because I told you I have to talk to Orlando, is it?"

"So what if it is?"

"I told you, we're through. For good, this time." It didn't bother me as much when Cordelia got pushy about it. Lysander was being meddlesome, but I couldn't expect an actor to resist the doomed pathos of my on-and-off romance with Orlando Mozamo.

"So what if you're through?" She grinned wickedly, showing her pointy canines. "You can still make him wish you were together, just so you can tell him to fuck off again."

"He's the one who told me to do that last time," I said.

"Then it's your turn."

I smiled as I peeled another egg. "Thanks for the thought, but I don't even want him thinking in that direction. We'll work as colleagues, or not at all."

"Sexual desire is the most powerful tool in a lady's arsenal."

"Bullshit," I said.

"Well, maybe it isn't for *you*," she said. "But we can't all have amazing flame powers."

I took a big bite of my egg and chewed so that I wouldn't have to say anything. She didn't know what I'd had to go through to get my "amazing flame powers." I hadn't told anybody the full story, not even Lysander.

After a short stretch of silence, Cordelia said, "Your mom stopped by yesterday."

My mother never came by unless something was up. Like I needed any more problems. "Oh yeah? What'd she want?"

Cordelia shook her head. "Didn't say. Only that you should go see your dad."

"Oh."

Cordelia's smooth, high brow furrowed. "He okay, your dad? You never talk about him."

"No, I don't."

"It's not healthy to keep stuff bottled up inside you like that."

"Who says?"

"Henry, that theotic mage I've been seeing."

I rolled my eyes. "Theotic mages. The same guys who used to put leeches on people to 'balance the humors,' which aren't even real. They don't know shit."

"Orlando's a theotic mage, isn't he?"

"Exactly my point." I stood up and pulled on my coat. "Thanks for breakfast."

She shrugged. "If I didn't feed you, there's a good chance you wouldn't eat."

"Nothing solid, anyway." I turned up my collar and headed for the door.

"Roz, your mom seemed pretty worried. You really ought to think about checking on your dad, whatever is going on."

"I will."

"Promise?"

"Yeah."

And I would. But if there was one man in Drusiel I wanted to see less than Orlando, it was my father. So by comparison, seeing Orlando suddenly didn't seem all that bad.

TEN

If there was a contest for the tightest sphincters in Penador, the Chemosh Guild would win every year. These guys were the kings of punctuality, ritual, and routine. No one had ever confirmed this for me, but my personal theory was that predicting the future was easier if the present was also predictable. It also made everything—present, future, and the Chemosh Guild itself—pretty dull. That said, Chemosh was probably the most powerful theotic guild in all of Penador.

"Power," of course, was relative. The most respected theotic mages couldn't hope to match the raw might of even a mid-level grimoric mage. In many ways, theotic magic was the opposite of grimoric magic. Instead of utilizing binding sigils and possession to control or command spirits, theotic mages *communed* with them. Apparently, time and space weren't quite as rigid for spirits, so a theotic mage could learn things about the past, present, and even the future. Not nearly as sexy as blowing shit up with fire or making a horseless carriage, but it had its uses, and many nobles were willing to pay large sums of money for even tiny glimpses of what *might* be. I felt that was an important distinction. None of the events theotic mages predicted were set in stone. There were, of course, some hardline theotic mages who believed in destiny, and they were difficult to argue with because, even if their prediction proved untrue, they would claim that a misleading divination was part of that destiny. But thankfully, most theotic mages admitted that a divination was more of a projection of the likeliest outcome based on present circumstances, and that the outcome could be altered.

When I was expelled from the Grimoric Mage Academy, I probably could have gotten into the Theotic Academy. It wasn't unheard of for students, or even full-fledged mages, to change from one form of magic to the other. Initially, I stayed away because after everything that happened with Simon, the idea of looking at the future—mine or anyone else's—repulsed me. And later, it was because by then I'd realized that every theotic mage I'd met was an insufferable bore.

Except, of course, for Orlando Mozamo.

When I first met him, I thought he should have been a grimoric mage. I still wondered what he would have been like if he'd chosen differently, but now I understood why he went with the Theotic Academy. His family immigrated from the distant country of Myovoka when he was a child, but he still had the faint accent of a foreigner. That and his dark skin had always set him apart from others, and not in a good way. Drusiel liked to imagine itself a worldly and cosmopolitan city, and if you were from nearby Lapisi, no one made a big deal about it. But Myovoka was a faraway and mostly unknown place, often exoticized in children's stories as a land of mystery, beholden to capricious and cruel spirits. Orlando said it was all bullshit. Myovoka relied almost entirely on oil and coal as an energy source. Apparently the stuff was so plentiful down there, they never even had to bother with magic. And they'd gotten pretty creative with it too, using it to power insanely complex machinery that did everything from manufacture textiles to drive carriages. As far as I could tell, it was nearly as good as magic, maybe even better in some respects. After all, nobody ever got possessed by a lump of coal.

But you start talking about stuff like non-magical machines that can wash your clothes, and most people in Penador think you've lost your mind. Orlando learned that pretty quick, so now he was using a broader approach to dispelling the negative stereotypes about Myovokan immigrants. He believed that by taking on the mantle of a theotic mage, generally believed to be the more benevolent of the two magic types, he could bridge that mistrust and bring a more open-minded tolerance to the city of Drusiel.

It was a nice thought, and being a theotic mage had certainly helped *him* gain trust among the natives. But I was fairly sure that hard-earned trust didn't extend to anyone else with dark skin and a Myovokan accent. Still, he wouldn't give up the crusade, and that was one of the many qualities about him that I found both infuriatingly naive, and intoxicatingly attractive.

The Chemosh Guild chapel was located farther uptown from Quartz Harbor, nestled comfortably among the brick town homes and flowering willow trees of the Pageant District. It was a bit of a hike to get up there, but it was a pleasant walk. Things weren't so crowded or loud there, and at that time of year, the cobblestones were strewn with white petals from the trees, infusing the whole place with a gentle floral scent.

People bustled past with focused eyes and sober faces as I made my way down Coral Avenue. Everybody had somewhere to be, and they had to be there soon. Sometimes I wondered what it would be like to live like that. To always be rushing from one place to the next. I suspected those types didn't have time to worry about anything beyond what was right in front of them. There was an appealing simplicity to the idea. They probably never woke up in the middle of the night, soaked in sweat and feeling the weight of a nameless dread pressing down on their chest. On the other hand, nobody told me where to go or when to arrive, and there was a delicious satisfaction in being able to stroll slowly down the street while everyone else around me was hustling past like a colony of ants.

The chapel was a narrow building with a white marble edifice that stood out from the red brick of the buildings on either side. I didn't relish the idea of going inside and having to deal with the famously sanctimonious and patronizing attitude of the Chemosh Guild members, so I was relieved to see that Orlando had stuck to his usual schedule of spending late mornings tending to his beloved roses in the garden in front of the chapel.

Orlando was all angles. He was on the short side, with a lean frame and sharp face. The only things soft about him were his brown eyes and his extremely inviting mouth. He wore the lemon-colored robe worn by all the mages in the Chemosh Guild, which set off his dark brown skin magnificently.

I'd always enjoyed watching him tend to his rosebushes. Something about the quiet care he took with them. The way he gently cupped a blossom in one of his long, elegant hands, or the slow patience he exercised in pruning just the right branches to coax the ideal shape from the bush. He was like that in bed, too.

I took out the bit of tobacco I'd swiped from Cordelia's place while she was making breakfast and stuffed it into my pipe. I tugged off a glove and cupped my hand over the pipe to light it, taking a few short puffs to get it going before pulling my glove back on. Then I leaned against the streetlamp in front of the garden and enjoyed the view. Just because Orlando and I were through didn't mean I'd stopped appreciating the aesthetics.

Eventually he noticed me. He always had this way of looking at me that made me feel like he could see right through my clothes. His eyes lay on me like a warm caress. I used to tease him that the Chemosh mages were all secretly perverts who'd mastered the ability to peer not through time, but through undergarments.

"Rosalind." His clear baritone carried easily across the garden. "How did you get that cut on your cheek?"

I touched the laceration from that dockhand and smirked as I walked over to him. "You should see the other guy."

He gave me a steady look for a moment, the non-sexy one that was rife with unspoken judgment. Then he turned back to his roses. "What do you want, Rosalind?"

"I'm working a case, and I need some information on a new grimoric guild. With your fancy new position on the Interguild Disciplinary Council, I figured you might be able to provide it."

He reached carefully into a rosebush, nimbly avoiding the thorns, and cut off a small, newly sprouting branch. "I'd be happy to tell you anything that's a matter of public record."

I smiled and put my hand on his upper arm. Even through my glove and his robe, I could feel the outline of his taut bicep. He put up a good front of peaceful calm, but underneath he was so tense most of the time. Didn't anyone but me know how to fix that?

"I was hoping for a little more than public record. You could even call it a divination, if you're worried about getting in trouble with the council."

"You can't afford my divinations." He shrugged my hand off his arm and moved to the next bush.

"True, but my client can."

"And who's that?"

"Can't say."

"Information only flows one way, is that it?" He cut another sprouting branch.

"Part of the contract. I can't give up the name, on pain of death or something. Look, I just want to know if you've heard any gossip about the Alath Guild, that's all. Have they gotten in any trouble lately?"

"Lately? The guild isn't even a year old," said Orlando. "I should hope a new guild could keep themselves out of trouble for at least that amount of time."

"That's what I always loved about you, Lando. Your boundless faith in humanity, despite all evidence to the contrary."

"I thought that's what you always *hated* about me."

"Love, hate. The line is blurry."

"That's because you enjoy blurring it."

"Possibly," I conceded. "So you've got nothing for me?"

"Nothing I care to give."

I stood there for a moment and took a long pull on my pipe as I watched him work. Why did he always have to be like this? Everything so serious and rigid. That was the hallmark of our relationship, I suppose. I said things that unintentionally pissed him off, then he'd get pouty about it. We probably wouldn't have lasted as long as we had if he wasn't so damn cute when he pouted.

"You ever heard of the Nevma Year?" I asked.

He paused in his pruning to give me another steady look, then returned to his task.

"Yeah, okay, okay," I said. "Everybody's heard of it. But do you think it could . . ." I felt dumb even asking the question. "You know, actually *happen?*"

"I think it is highly unlikely. But we know far too little about spirits and the astral plane to discount it completely." He frowned. "Is that why you're asking about the Alath Guild?"

"Those two things connected?" I asked carefully.

"I hate it when you answer a question with a question," he said. "And no, I don't think the two things are connected. I just thought of it because the entire Alath Guild went on a research trip to the caves of Hergotis, which, if I'm not mistaken, is the region where most of the Nevma Year legends originate."

"Alath is in Hergotis right now? The whole guild?"

"They left a few days ago," said Orlando.

The Alath Guild skips town right around the time Lord Edmund's son goes missing? The timing was almost too perfect. Either Edmund's suspicions were right on the money, or I was being led around by the nose.

"I thought you were trying not to get tangled up in guild business these days," said Orlando.

"The client was waving around a lot of money. You know Lye and Portia are talking about starting a family, so . . ." I shrugged.

He gave me the first smile I'd seen from him that morning. "Your loyalty to Lysander is probably your most redeeming quality."

"Not my razor-sharp wit, or the fact that I can make you orgasm so hard it brings tears to your eyes?"

His smile disappeared. "Just promise you won't get in too deep. Guild politics these days are so murky that you might not find your way back."

"I can handle myself, Lando, but it's sweet of you to care."

Those soft, brown eyes bore down on me. "No matter what happens between us, I'll always care about you, Rosalind."

"Yeah, okay. I better get going before I throw up all over your roses."

I turned back toward the street, but before I could make my escape from all that sentimentality, I saw two people walking toward us. A man and a woman, both in their late thirties. They wore the simple doublets and breeches of honest working folk, which was odd, because they were clearly possessed.

It wasn't hard to tell if someone was being inhabited by a spirit. There was always a "tell." It might be a horn sticking out of their head, or one eye with a slitted pupil. It was something physical that manifested when the spirit entered their body and, in most cases, disappeared when the spirit left. So while it was a little surprising that the man had a long forked tongue and the woman had a scaly blue hand, those weren't the details that bothered me the most. Possession should only be practiced by mages, and even then, only those with extensive training. A person couldn't be possessed unwillingly, but once they invited the spirit in, the trick was maintaining control. Most of the darker stories about magecraft involved a mage losing control of the spirit they'd allowed to inhabit their body. When that happened, the spirit could take the mage on a murder or sex spree, or sometimes even an eating binge. That last one might not sound too terrible, but I once saw a spirit kill its host by stuffing so much food down the mage's throat that he choked to death.

So the question I asked myself as the two walked toward us was, if possession was risky even for mages, how in the hell had these regular folk thought it was a good idea?

Their eyes were glassy, and their mouths hung open and drooling. It was clear the spirits were in control. But rather than run around like lunatics, as most spirits did when suddenly given direct access to the material plane and all the sensual delights therein, the two continued their slow, awkward gait toward us.

"Rosalind . . . are you seeing this?" asked Orlando.

"Yeah." I tugged off my gloves. "Friends of yours?"

He glanced over at my bare hands. "Don't you think that's a little premature?"

"Worried about me burning down your rose garden?"

"The thought crossed my mind. But more to the point, we don't know for certain that these two entities mean us harm."

"I've never met a spirit who wished me well."

"That's so surprising, given your winning personality," he said. "Let me at least try to communicate with them before you incinerate their hosts and half the block with them."

"You're the theotic mage. Be my guest." I didn't for a moment think his plan would work, but if I didn't at least let him try, I'd be hearing about it for months.

He pulled his hood up and stepped forward so that he was between me and the possessed. Then he pressed his palms together, took a slow, deep breath, and began chanting quietly to himself.

I didn't know nearly as much about theotic magecraft as I did grimoric, but I understood the basics. Spirits didn't communicate with language. Even when possessing someone, they didn't comprehend the language spoken by their host. I wasn't sure how spirits *did* communicate, but it was apparently by a means only possible in the astral plane. So the majority of what theotic mages did was project their own soul to the astral plane in order to communicate with the spirit in its natural medium. Apparently that could be quite dangerous if the mage didn't take the proper precautions, and even when the spirit *could* communicate with the mage, it was no guarantee they would.

The two possessed hosts paused about ten feet from us as Orlando continued chanting. Then he went silent, and his entire body shook for a moment, which was the sign that his soul had shifted into the astral plane. Few theotic mages could astral-project while standing upright, but Orlando was one of the best. His body remained perfectly erect, his hands still pressed together, while his invisible soul emerged, tethered to his body by some equally invisible astral umbilical cord.

Yeah, it sounded like bullshit to me the first time I heard about it too.

In my experience, the whole communing-with-spirits thing could take some time, so while Orlando began his invisible, inaudible conversation with the two spirits, I looked around for a place to sit. But before I'd even found a likely spot, Orlando shuddered again. He staggered backward, and if I hadn't been there to catch him, he might have fallen over. Meanwhile, the two possessed hosts resumed their slow, stiff walk toward us.

"Easy," I said. "You okay?"

His eyes were wide with disbelief. "I've never experienced such . . . *hostility* from spirits before."

"So my turn, then?"

His expression hardened. "Seriously, though. Don't torch my roses."

"You really do like to make things difficult for me."

Yesterday's ambush had convinced me to start carrying a weapon, so I pulled out the pair of metal pipes I had sheathed on my thigh. They were only about a foot in length and a half inch in diameter. I grant you, not all that fearsome in the hands of anyone else. But as I held one in each bare hand, they only took a moment to start glowing a nice, flesh-searing orange.

The possessed stiffly reached out toward me, like they were still somewhat unclear on the mechanics of the human bodies they inhabited. But when I swung one of the pipes at the man, he caught it easily in his right hand. One of the many advantages to letting a spirit inhabit your body was increased strength and quicker reflexes.

The possessed and I stood there for a moment as the pipe seared into his hand and the smell of cooking flesh filled the air. Possessed also didn't feel pain, but by my estimation, that was a drawback rather than an advantage. After all, pain was a warning that something bad was happening.

While the pipe slowly sank through his right hand, he came at me with his left. I raised the other pipe so that it caught the inside of his forearm. As he pressed harder, the pipe seared into the tendons in his arm and his left hand went limp. The other pipe burned away the remaining tendons surrounding his right thumb, and it snapped off. He stared for a moment at his useless hands, and I was just about to finish the poor bastard off when I felt an iron grip on my throat.

The other possessed stared vacantly at me as she lifted me into the air, her scaly blue hand constricting around my windpipe. I plunged both of my glowing pipes into her eyes, cooking the orbs in their sockets, but that didn't make her let go. I whaled on her arms, but then she began shaking me like a rag doll. I couldn't hit her or get loose. Most importantly, I couldn't breathe, and nasty little croaking sounds were escaping from my lips.

Then I heard a wet thwack. Orlando had come around the side of the possessed woman and sunk the blade of a garden hoe into her wrist. She didn't even notice, so he yanked it free and tried again, over and over, like it was a blunt ax, until her hand went limp and I fell to the ground.

I'd dropped my pipes sometime while I was getting choked out, so I grabbed her ankles and burned through her tendons until she fell over.

I staggered to my feet and saw that the possessed man was coming at Orlando now, flailing with his ruined hands and kicking out with his feet in a way that would have been comical if it hadn't been so gruesomely pathetic. Orlando swung the hoe, burying the flat blade into his chest, which didn't really do anything.

I came up behind the possessed, put one hand on his forehead and the other on the back of his head, then lit him up. Unfortunately, he fell right on one of Orlando's precious rosebushes, crushing it beyond repair.

Orlando put his foot on the possessed man's chest and yanked his hoe free. "Are you going to tell me what this was about?" he asked, breathing heavily.

"In a moment." I hunkered down next to the possessed woman. She was still moving around, so I assumed the spirit was in there. "Can you talk to it now?"

"I can try."

He put the hoe down, pressed his hands together, and began his quiet chant once again. His body shuddered as he projected his spirit.

After a few moments, the woman seemed to look up at me with her ruined eye sockets and smiled in a strangely feral way. Then she slammed the back of her head into the ground so hard it split her skull.

Orlando dropped to his knees next to me. "I swear, I've never encountered such angry spirits before."

I rolled the woman onto her stomach. The back of her head was a pulpy mess.

"Good God." He looked ill as he stared at her shattered skull. "I've never understood why things like that don't upset you."

I lifted up her blood-and-brain-matted hair to expose the back of her neck. "*This* is what upsets me." I pointed at a sigil carved just below the hairline. It looked like it was made by the same person who had done the silence sigils on the assassins, but this one was much worse. "You ever seen one of these before?"

He shook his head. Theotic mages didn't work with sigils a great deal, and this was a rare one. I hadn't seen one like it in years.

"There are a few components I'm not familiar with, but the basic function is clear," I said. "It's a backdoor for possession."

"Meaning, the hosts didn't invite the spirits in?

"Do they *look* like mages?"

He shook his head.

"These were not willing hosts."

"And we just . . ." His eyes widened in horror.

"Yeah. Not sure what choice we had, but these poor bastards didn't deserve this."

Orlando put his hand on my shoulder, his forehead knitted with worry. "Seriously, Rosalind. What have you gotten yourself into?"

"I'm not sure yet. But I have a feeling I'll find out in Hergotis."

ELEVEN

Before I collected Lysander from the Skinned Cat and followed the Alath Guild to Hergotis, there was one other stop I needed to make. I'd promised Cordelia that I would check in on my father, and while I had a lot of bad habits, lying wasn't one of them.

When my parents were younger, they had a sweet little mercantile fleet. Three boats and four wagons that traveled all over Penador and down into Lapisi, buying and selling fine textiles and leather. People said my dad had an incredible instinct for where and when to buy low and sell high. Not only had he always been one step ahead in the supply-and-demand game back then, but he'd been one of those rare savvy businessmen that everyone loved. And people *still* loved him. Every once in a while I would get, "Oh, you're Nick's kid? How's he doing these days?" Although now I hated answering that question.

Back then, my parents had made enough money to afford a whole brood of kids, but there had been some complications during my birth, and while my mother and I both survived, she'd been unable to bear any more children. So instead of spreading the money around, they poured it all into my education at the mage academy. I was their ticket to the next rung on the social ladder. So it was no surprise that they were devastated when I got expelled. To add insult to injury, I refused to come back and work for the family business. My relationship with my parents never really recovered from that one-two punch. For years, I hardly even saw them. Only recently had I started coming around again. Now that my father was sick.

The fleet had been sold off years ago. There was no way they could manage it all these days. Now my parents had a single stall down by the docks. It wasn't the sort of place to sell high-end textiles, so now they mostly traded in woolens and furs. Not nearly as lucrative, but they got by.

I walked through the crowds along South Street, past a fruit stall piled high with apples and peaches, a tobacco stall that filled the air with its dense, heavenly aroma, and a butcher's stall with dead chickens hanging by their necks. I paid a copper for a wood skewer of roasted, salted meat and gnawed on it as I continued down the line of stalls.

There was a tea stall, another that sold honey in little jars, and one with a huge glass bowl filled with seawater and live lobsters. A small pack of ragged, snotty kids had gathered around the bowl, tapping the glass to make the lobsters move until the stall owner finally came over and chased them away.

Down near the end of the market, I spotted my parents' stall, with its neat stacks of wool tunics and fur hats. My mother was minding the place, as usual. Her long gray hair was pulled back into a loose bun. She'd been a real beauty when she was younger and still had a devastating amount of poise and charm. When she wanted to, that was. There was no charm in her eyes when she saw me walk over.

"Hey," I said.

"You got my message, then?" she asked.

I nodded.

"I like that Cordelia. She's a dear. I hope you're not taking advantage of her."

"Why would you think I was?"

"Because I *know* you, Rosalind Featherstone. It's what you do."

"You say the sweetest things, Mom." I picked up a fur hat with large ear flaps. "I have to go to Hergotis for a job. This time of year, it's going to be cold as balls. Can I have one of these?"

"Sure you can. For one silver."

I winced. "Not even a family discount?"

"What's family got to do with discounts? You want it or not?"

"I hope you don't talk to regular customers like this," I said.

"Of course not," she said calmly. "None of them ever broke my heart."

"Fucking hell, Mom." I dropped a silver piece on the counter and tucked the hat into my belt.

"Language, young lady."

"Uh-huh. Anyway, where's Dad?"

"Watching the boats come in." She looked at me a moment, and I could see the hard veneer waver. "That's where he is almost all the time these days." Then her stern facade solidified again. "Not that you'd know. I have to beg you to visit even when you *know* he's sick."

"Like it even matters if I come around."

The nostrils of her fine, aquiline nose flared, and the muscles of her jaw rippled. That was about as much of a rise as I could get out of her these days. "Don't talk like you know. You don't know shit."

"Language, Mom," I said, then turned away.

I continued down South Street until it ended at a bustling pier. Dock-hands loaded and unloaded cargo on stout little merchant ships. The fine yachts of the upper classes were docked farther up the coast, away from the rabble and the stink of tar and dead fish.

There was a narrow bench at the very end of the pier, and that's where I found my father. He was a few years older than Mom, with a close-cropped white beard and a fringe of feathery white hair that stuck out from under a wool cap. Quartz Harbor was a busy port, with cargo ships constantly coming and going, but his pale blue eyes didn't track any of them. Instead he stared out at the rippling, green-gray water that sparkled in the midday sun. His lips moved slightly now and then, as if he was muttering to himself, but his expression never changed. His hands lay in his lap, but every few moments he would lift one up to his mouth and blow on his fingertips. It was a new thing he'd been doing lately. Maybe it was a sign of something, or maybe he just liked how it felt. Who was I to judge?

I sat down next to him on the bench, stretched my legs out, and shoved my hands deep into my coat pockets. He didn't acknowledge my presence but just kept staring, muttering silently, and blowing on his fingertips.

"How you been, Dad?" I asked eventually.

"Too many ships in the harbor," he said without looking at me.

"Yeah? You think it's getting too crowded?"

He didn't respond.

I didn't know how much of Dad's mind was left. There were days when I'd come by, and he'd know me and we'd talk. But it seemed those days were getting fewer and farther between. Physically, he was about as healthy as a man his age could be. But his mind was slowly slipping away. And while I knew mages who could heal a wound, I didn't know anybody who could fix a mind.

So I'd come down, and we'd mostly sit in silence. I had no idea if it bothered him, but the quiet between us drove me nuts, so lately I'd just start talking about whatever was on my mind. Did he understand? Did he even notice that I was making an effort to connect with him? I couldn't say. But it felt better than just sitting there. And I still hoped I was getting through to whatever was left of him.

"Got a big job I'm working," I said. "Not sure how I feel about it, though. The money's great, and so is the danger. That balances out in a way I understand. But something else about it bothers me. Something I can't quite pin down. Everything *sounds* reasonable moment to moment, but when I take a step back and look at the big picture, it doesn't hold together somehow. You know what I mean?"

He just stared out at the water and blew on his fingertips.

"It's like those old stories you used to read to me," I said. "About that lady detective from Lapisi . . . Señora Jaquenetta, that was her name. Whenever she'd get a gut feeling that something didn't add up, she'd always say the same thing. And you'd do it in that ridiculous accent: *Somzing ees NOT right!* You remember that?"

He didn't respond.

"Anyway, that's how I feel. Like goddamn Señora Jaquenetta."

I let silence fall back down for a little while. Sometimes conversation with him felt like holding up both ends of a heavy velvet curtain. More or less impossible to do on my own. So I tried to ignore the quiet between us and listen to everything else. The sound of water lapping at the docks and the underside of the boats. The grunts and muffled curses of dockhands that drifted from farther up the pier. A seagull screeching mournfully overhead.

Then all of a sudden my father turned to me, his blue eyes wide, and said in a shrill falsetto, "Somzing ees NOT right!"

I smiled at him. "Yeah, Dad, that's it. You remember."

His eyes narrowed. "You *hated* those stories."

"Are you kidding me? She was such a feisty old lady. I loved her."

He shook his head like a petulant child. "No, no, no, no! *Hated!*"

There wasn't any point in upsetting the old guy any further, especially since he was finally acknowledging me, so I just shrugged. "Whatever you say, Dad. I guess you remember better than me."

That seemed to calm him down. Then he gave me a hard look. "When are you getting married?"

"Really? We finally have a moment of clarity where we can talk like two human beings, and *that's* what you want to ask?"

"Your mother worries."

"She's more worried about *you*, Dad."

"Me?" He seemed genuinely surprised.

"Yeah. You sit out here for hours, not talking to anybody. You never pay attention to the shop. It's like you're not even *you* most of the time."

He looked back out to sea, and a sadness slipped in behind his eyes. "I get . . . lost sometimes. In my mind."

"I know, Dad. It's okay. Nobody blames you."

We were quiet for a few moments. His eyes grew more distant, and his lips started to twitch. He was fading away again already.

"I have to go out of town for a few days," I told him "For a job."

Still staring out at the water, he murmured, "Somzing ees not right."

"You said it, Dad." I leaned over and kissed his wrinkled cheek. "Take care until I get back. Try not to drive Mom too crazy."

I stood and walked slowly up the pier with the heavy feeling I always had after talking to whatever was left of him. My mother's expression was unreadable as she watched me approach the stall.

"Well?" she asked.

"He's having good day," I said. "Even had a little actual conversation. Seems like he knows he's not well."

"Some days." There was suddenly a weariness in her eyes that no lofty veneer could hide. It made her look older, but also, strangely, more beautiful. If we were the hugging types, I might have reached out for her then. But that wasn't how she and I worked.

"This job I'm doing," I said. "The payoff is going to be sizable. Maybe you could use some of it to bring an employee on, so you don't have to work the stall all the time. Cordelia could always use the money, and you like her."

Her eyes narrowed. "You aren't doing anything illegal, are you?"

This was what I got for trying to be nice. "No, Mom. In fact, it's probably the most legitimate client Lye and I have ever had. Some lord's son was kidnapped, and we have to rescue him."

"Really? Which one?" Suddenly she was all ears. It was depressing how much my mother obsessed over the nobility. She spent most evenings down at the tavern drinking half-pints of stout and blackcurrant with other shop wives as they pored over the latest news sheets about who was seen at the last ball dancing with who, and what they were wearing. Some nights Mom and her friends would get *really* rowdy and start speculating about what scandals might be going on that the gossip sheets weren't allowed to print outright. They'd read between the lines as carefully as a theotic mage in a divination.

"Sorry, I can't say who," I told her. "But he's a big deal. Hence the money."

"It's got to be Lord Nathaniel." She frowned. "No, wait, his son was just seen at the Sunset Gardens Autumnal Ball."

"This is an infant, anyway. Only a few weeks old."

She looked dubious. "A baby? There hasn't been a birth announcement in months."

"What do you mean?" I asked.

"The papers always announce those sort of things. Lord and Lady So-and-So are pleased to announce the birth of their daughter, Such-and-Such, heir to Moth Manor. You know."

"And you haven't seen anything about a birth in a while?"

"Not since Lord Longaville and Lady Imogen announced their second son, Andrew. That was . . ." She frowned thoughtfully. "About six months ago."

"Strange." I gnawed on the edge of my lip. "Maybe he's more than six months old."

But as soon as I said that, I realized it didn't square with the fact that Lady Celia was still healing from her emergency incision during the birth. Then why hadn't they made the announcement?

Another possibility was that my mother had just missed it.

"You keep all those old gossip rags after you've read them?" I asked.

"Seems like a waste just to throw them out."

"Any chance I can have them? Like the last three months or so?"

"Really?" She looked like she couldn't decide whether to be pleased or annoyed.

"Consider it your contribution to this job. That way I won't be able to hold it over your head when I give you the money to hire Cordelia."

"You sound like your father when you say things like that." She sighed. "You need them right now?"

"That would be great."

"Watch the shop while I go home and get them. The last three months, you said?"

"Yeah."

My mom hurried off down South Street while I slid behind the counter. They only lived a few blocks away. It was more expensive to live this close to the market, but at their age, it was almost necessary. Especially since my father probably wasn't hauling shit these days.

It felt strange doing this thing I hadn't done since childhood. I didn't even know what to charge someone now. Fortunately for me, but unfortunately for my parents, nobody tried to buy anything. It was about a half hour later when my mother returned with a stack of the pulpy, rough paper that the news sheets were printed on. The stack was a lot thicker than I'd expected for only three months.

"How many different papers do you buy, Mom?" I asked.

"Depends on the week. If it's one of the annual balls, I might want a few different perspectives on what happened. You never know what someone's going to miss at such big events." She gave me a searching look. "And you're going to read them all?"

"Of course. Why else would I ask you for them?"

"I just . . ." She shook her head. "You've never been interested in them. Not since you were a girl."

"I'm not interested in them personally. It's for the job."

"If you say so." She was still giving me an odd look.

"Don't get your hopes up that I'm suddenly going to get hooked on this trash."

Now *there* was the withering glare I was used to. "I wouldn't dream of it."

TWELVE

Lysander wasn't at the Skinned Cat when I got there, so I settled into a corner table with a glass of whiskey and my pipe and started to go through my mother's beloved gossip papers. The main ones she bought were the *Drusiel Gazette* and the *Quartz Harbor Dispatch*. There were also a few issues of the *Pageant District Herald*, and I wondered if she walked all the way uptown just to buy those.

I slipped off my gloves, lit my pipe, and began to read. The type was set so close that I was impressed Mom could even read it at her age. The *Gazette* and *Dispatch* issues were only a single large sheet of paper folded vertically, then horizontally, and broken into several sections. The Announcements were mostly lists of births, weddings, and deaths. Events were descriptions of balls, featuring breathlessly narrated experiences of the food, wine, decorations, and clothes. The Editorial section seemed to be a place for the paper's editor to complain about some new city ordinance or even just the weather, and Letters was the place for readers to write in and complain about the editor. The *Herald* was a little more upscale, with better quality paper, additional pages, occasional illustrations, and an extensive Personal Inquiries section where readers could pay to have a short message printed. Topics included rooms for rent, old furniture for sale, and a man seeking "that alluring young lady in the peach gown at the Councilman's Social."

One thing that surprised me was that there was almost no mention of mage guilds in any of these news sheets. It was a good reminder that while people enjoyed the conveniences of magecraft, they rarely thought much about where it came from.

Another thing I didn't find in the entire stack was an announcement for the birth of the heir to Ariel House.

Why would Lord Edmund keep something like that quiet? I'd hoped to avoid pushing him any harder. After all, accusing the client of withholding important information about the case wasn't a great business practice, even when you were right. But between this and the mysterious lack of servants, it was hard to justify avoiding a direct confrontation. Hopefully, whatever the reason for keeping Edgar's birth a secret, it wasn't something so awful that he'd fire us simply for asking.

I looked around the tavern. Where was Lysander, anyway? I'd told him noon, and it was a couple hours past that. Visiting the parents had taken longer than I'd expected. Maybe I'd missed him.

I gathered up my papers and went over to the bar.

"Hey, Chester, did Lye come in earlier?"

Chester shook his head as he scrubbed a tankard. His eyes moved to the stack of papers under my arm. "What you got there?"

"Gossip rags," I said. "You want them?"

"You bet!" Then he gave me an embarrassed look. "I mean . . . customers might want to flip through them."

"Sure, Chester. Sure." I dropped them on the bar. "Look, if Lye stops in, tell him I went to his place to look for him."

"Will do, Roz. And thanks for the papers."

"Too much of that trash will rot your brain," I told him.

"Not as fast as all that whiskey will rot your gut."

I shrugged. "It's a race, then. You got any tobacco?"

"I just gave you a plug when you came in. One a day is my limit."

"Yeah, all right," I said. "Can't blame me for asking."

"You could always just buy a pouch yourself."

"If I always had tobacco on me, I'd always be smoking."

"That's your problem," said Chester. "You lack self-restraint."

I smiled as I tugged my gloves back on. "Chester, old pal, you've got no idea."

THIRTEEN

Lysander and Portia lived in Copperton, the next neighborhood over from Quartz Harbor. A little cleaner, and a lot quieter, it was the sort of sober, self-conscious area that Lye and I used to make fun of before he fell in love with a girl from there. Now he thought it was great, and I kept my mouth shut because otherwise they'd stop inviting me over for strawberry tarts. Portia was a baker in a pastry shop, and her creations were the best I'd ever had. As much as I enjoyed irritating people with unpleasant truths, I liked strawberry tarts a whole lot more.

They lived in the attic space above a butcher shop. The smell could get a little unpleasant, especially in the summer, which was why the butcher and his family rented it out rather than live there themselves. But until Portia could open a pastry shop of her own, it was the best they could afford. She'd already made it clear to Lysander that she wanted to have children, but she didn't want to raise them above a butcher's. Admittedly, Portia probably would have preferred that to her husband taking such a dangerous job, but what she didn't know wouldn't hurt her. Unless, of course, he got killed. But I didn't plan to let that happen.

I rapped lightly on the door. After a few moments, Portia opened it. I couldn't blame Lysander for rolling over for her like a puppy. She was a real knockout, with lustrous black hair, big green eyes, a pert little nose, and a smile as warm and soft as her tarts.

"Rosalind, how are you?" She gave me her usual smile, but there was an odd tension in her voice.

"Great, Portia. Is Lye around?"

"No, he stepped out a little while ago."

"We were supposed to meet around midday to go over some things about the new job."

"Oh really? Well, he should be back soon. Why don't you come in and wait for him? They're cold, but I have a few strawberry tarts left over from yesterday."

I grinned. "You know I can't turn that down."

I followed her up the stairs into their apartment. It was a decent-sized space, with an old but well-maintained set of table and chairs, a bed on the far wall, and a small potbellied stove in the corner that they used both to cook and heat the home.

I stashed my gloves in my coat pockets, then hung my coat on the stand by the door. Portia opened the pantry doors and pulled out a tray covered with a white cloth.

"Lysander seems very hopeful about this new job." She slid the tray onto the table and removed the cloth. Even though they were cold, I was pretty sure I could smell the sweet, creamy perfection from across the room, luring me over.

I sat down at the table and grabbed one. "Yeah, it's probably the biggest single job we've ever done."

I took a bite of the tart, and it was everything I'd hoped. I wished I could enjoy other aspects of life with the untiring adoration I had for strawberry tarts. But I suppose I was grateful to have even that one simple pleasure.

Portia didn't sit down with me, which was unusual. I could still feel that underlying tension coming off her too. We weren't friends by any means, but that's what made it even stranger. Normally, if I did something she didn't like, she wouldn't hesitate to let me know. This feeling of holding something back was out of character.

"You know, we're making a lot of money on this job," I said around a mouthful of tart. "Maybe you two can finally get a little place in Porter Crossing like you've always wanted."

She smiled and nodded. "That's what he said. It's very exciting."

What could be so bad that Portia wouldn't want to tell me? Something that would genuinely upset me. Probably even make me angry. But the only time I ever got mad at Portia was when she'd tried to convince Lye not to work with me anymore.

So that could be it. With the money and the move, they'd buy their own pastry shop. Maybe she'd want him to help her out. Shopkeeping wasn't really playing to Lye's strengths, but if that's what she wanted, I knew he'd do it. So it could be that when this job was done, Lysander would suggest he and I go our separate ways. Naturally, Portia was worried that when I got wind of it, I'd blame her.

But I surprised myself by wondering if it was really such a bad thing. Only yesterday I'd been fantasizing about taking my share of the money and making a new start somewhere else. Had I honestly thought Lysander would come with me? Maybe this was just the kick in the ass I needed to move on with my own life and leave all the shit in my past behind.

I popped the rest of the tart into my mouth, then smiled at Portia.

"I think this is going to be good for all of us."

Her return smile was stiff. "I hope so."

Heavy footsteps pounded up the stairs; then the door flew open. Lysander stood there, his chest rising and falling like he was out of breath. He looked at us for a moment, his face tense, then grinned.

"Oh hey, Roz. There you are."

"You run all the way from the Skinned Cat or something?" I asked.

He dropped into the chair next to mine and helped himself to a tart. "Yeah, Chester said you looked anxious. I thought something serious was up."

"He said that? Never thought he was so perceptive."

"Then something *is* up?"

I glanced at Portia. No need for her to hear about Orlando and me getting jumped by those possessed people. I'd tell him that part later. Instead I said, "The entire Alath Guild skipped town right around the time of the kidnapping. Orlando said they went to Hergotis, which just happens to be where most of the legends about the Nevma Year come from."

"Hergotis, huh?" he asked. "Guess we better head out there and see what's what."

Portia finally sat down with us. "That's so far away."

"Three days or so on horseback," I said. "And it'll still be cold up in those mountains this time of year."

Portia looked at Lysander. "I'll pack your furs." Then she got right back up and hurried over to his wardrobe. She just couldn't sit still with that guilty conscience weighing on her. I considered saying something about it right then. Telling them I'd already guessed they were planning to cut me loose after this job. But I decided against it. If nothing else, their look of surprise at my reaction when they broke the news to me later would be worth the wait. Besides, I kind of enjoyed watching Portia twist.

I turned to Lysander. "Once we get some horses, I want to swing by Ariel House on our way out of town."

"It's not really on the way," he said.

"Yeah, but we'll need some more money after we buy the horses."

"Probably."

"Also, I want to press his lordship on a few things."

"Like?"

"Why didn't he have his son's birth announced in the papers like all the other nobles do."

"That's . . . strange," he said after a moment.

"Exactly. And if Quince is around, I want to ask him where all the servants went. Including the mage who attended the birth. Who knows, the gardener might be more willing to talk now too. And maybe that Demetrius Shandy from the Valac Guild has more on what's wrong with Lady Celia."

"What's that got to do with us?" he asked.

"Maybe nothing, but I don't like all these unanswered questions. I want to clear up as much as I can before we leave Drusiel."

"Sure. You want to head there first thing tomorrow?"

I shook my head. "Sorry, Lye. You're going to have to postpone whatever romantic plans you had for tonight. If we go down to the stables and grab some horses now, we can reach Ariel House before sunset. If Alath is planning to use this kid for some kind of sacrifice out in Hergotis, we don't know how long he's got."

Lysander looked over at Portia, who was attempting to fit his bulky fur coat into a saddlebag. She was even adorable doing that. He sighed heavily and looked back at me. "Yeah, I guess you're right. Let's head back out into that hellscape you call nature."

FOURTEEN

Since I wasn't paying for the horses, I didn't bother to haggle over price. The guy said fifty, so that's what I gave him. Lysander found a hulking brown stallion that seemed able to bear his weight without groaning. I settled on a gray-and-white mare with a wild eye and a nasty bite, for obvious reasons.

A trip like this would be expensive with the cost of supplies and inns along the way, so the necessity of getting more money from Lord Edmund was no longer a question.

"Or we could *camp out*," I said as we cantered down the winding forest road that led to Ariel House.

Lysander looked over at me in horror. "Tell me that's just one of your meaner jokes."

I gave him a sinister smile. "Probably. But who knows. There's always a chance that one or two nights along the way we won't find an inn."

He shuddered. "So many bugs . . ."

"Which reminds me, you should be more worried about what we eat than where we sleep."

"What does *that* mean?"

"We may go for days without seeing a place big enough to have a market or even a farm, so we might have to catch our own food."

"Like hunting?"

"If we're lucky. Otherwise, we'll have to eat the bugs."

He stared at me for a moment, then his eyes narrowed. "Fuck you, Roz."

I got a good laugh out of that. In fact, teasing Lysander about his nature phobia was such a great way to pass the time that I was almost sad when we reached Ariel House. It was dusk now, and there were spirit lights lining the path through the gardens. Several windows of the mansion already glowed a merry yellow light as well. We slowed our horses to a walk and let them pick their way carefully down the path to the entrance. The last thing we needed was one of our new mounts turning an ankle in the dim light.

When I glanced off to the far side of the garden, I noticed there were no lights on in the gardener's cottage. I thought that was strange but figured he might be in the mansion. I wasn't sure how that worked. Maybe he took his meals in the kitchens or, hell, even slept there. There certainly were enough empty rooms, and if I had the choice between a tiny rustic cottage and a sumptuous mansion, I knew which one I'd pick.

We hitched our horses in front of the mansion, then knocked on the door. It was opened by a servant I hadn't seen before. He had broad shoulders that seemed impractical for the confining black suit he wore. Like all he'd have to do was flex and the whole thing would peel off like the shell of a boiled egg.

"Rosalind Featherstone and Lysander Tunning," I told him. "We work for Lord Edmund. He around?"

"Ah yes. I was told you might call." He sounded more posh than I'd expected. "Unfortunately, his lordship is currently away from home."

"Oh yeah? Where is he?"

"I'm afraid I'm not at liberty to say."

"How about Quince?" I asked. "He here?"

"Mr. Quince is in the billiards room. Shall I take you there?"

"Nah, we know where it is."

I pushed past him and into the mansion, with Lysander following. It was immediately apparent that the place had been fully restocked with servants. They were everywhere. Cleaning things, straightening things, moving things from one place to another. It was impressive, really. Most of them weren't actually doing anything useful, but I supposed looking busy was an important skill for house servants.

An older woman in a maid uniform hurried past with a pile of linens in her arms.

"Excuse me." I stepped into her path. "How long have you been working here?"

"Just started this morning, miss," she said.

I looked around at the other servants bustling past us. "And everybody else?"

"Same, near as I can tell, miss," she said.

I nodded and stepped out of her way. "Thanks."

She continued on to wherever it was that so desperately needed clean linens.

I looked at Lysander. "Interesting, huh?"

He shrugged. "Quince'll tell us about it, I'm sure."

"He'll tell us *something*, anyway."

"What's that supposed to mean?"

"It means I don't trust him, and you shouldn't either."

"You think he's the one who gave up the details on those lock sigils?"

"I haven't ruled it out yet," I said.

We found the man in question at the pool table. He was alone, leaning over to take a shot at the corner pocket with a finely polished mahogany stick.

"You like playing with yourself, Quince?" I asked just as he was shooting.

His shoulders bounced, and the ball caromed off the bumper and right back to him. He turned and gave me a distasteful look.

"Don't you have a job to do?"

"Don't you?" I asked.

He lifted his chin up, which unfortunately gave me a clear view of his hairy nostrils. I wondered how someone so refined could forget to do a little trimming now and then. "I do whatever his lordship requires, and at the moment, he doesn't require anything. There's nothing wrong with enjoying a little time off for myself."

"Yeah, where is his lordship, anyway? Chuckles at the door wouldn't give me any details."

"The stress of his son's disappearance and the illness of his wife have understandably taken its toll on his lordship. Mr. Shandy and I recommended he retire to his cabin in Hergotis for some restful quiet until this dreadful business has been sorted out."

"Hergotis, huh?" I asked. "Interesting."

"How so?" asked Quince.

"No reason."

Quince gave me that pained smile he was so good at. "Well then, Miss Featherstone, in his lordship's absence, is there anything *I* can do for you?"

"Yeah, we have to head out of town for a few days. Had to buy some horses, so we need more money for expenses."

"You think young Edward has been taken out of Drusiel?"

"*Edgar*, you mean? That's the kid's name, isn't it?"

Quince froze. "Yes, of course, that's what I meant."

"Uh-huh." I suppose it could have been an honest mistake, but it was an odd thing to forget, considering how dedicated he seemed to Edmund. "Anyway, it's likely he's been taken out of town, but we won't know for sure until we get there."

"I see. Fortunately, I am authorized to get you the money." He laid the pool stick down on the table. "If you'll be kind enough to wait here, I'll fetch it for you. Will another fifty silver suffice?"

"That should be good," I said.

We watched him leave. Once he was gone, Lysander turned to me.

"You don't even trust him enough to tell him we're going to the same place as Lord Edmund?"

"There's too many loose corners flapping around for my taste. From here on in, I want to tighten up everything. Don't tell anyone anything unless we absolutely have to."

"Maybe you're getting too paranoid? This is the guy who hired us, after all."

I shrugged. It was an old argument between us. As far as I was concerned, Lysander wasn't paranoid enough. The truth was usually somewhere in between.

Then his eyes fell on the dart board, and he smiled. "How about a game while we wait?"

Quince returned a little later with another jingling bag of coins. By that time, I'd already beaten Lysander twice, although I still hadn't managed to get him to put down a wager.

"So what's with the servant turnover?" I asked Quince as Lysander took the money from him.

"His lordship is quite convinced that the Alath Guild had some help from the inside, and insisted I let everyone go." His expression grew mournful. "You have no idea how difficult it is to restaff an entire mansion. And of course, the whole time I was looking for new staff, his lordship still expected to be waited on."

"With only you, Shandy, and the gardener around?"

"Precisely."

"Where is the old guy, anyway?"

"Shandy?"

"The gardener."

Quince seemed surprised I was asking. "In his home at the back of the gardens, I suppose. Where else would he be at this hour?"

"Yeah, good point." I kept to myself the fact that the cottage was dark. I'd check for him on our way out. "Is Shandy up with Lady Celia?"

"I assume so. He's been tremendously solicitous of her health."

"She getting any better?" Lysander asked.

He shook his head. "I haven't seen any improvement."

"We'll check with Shandy all the same," I said.

"Of course," said Quince. "Is there anything else I can help you with?"

"Yeah, actually. You know why Lord Edmund didn't announce Edgar's birth in the news sheets? Seems unusual."

"I . . . didn't realize he hadn't." Quince looked very unsettled all of a sudden. "It *does* seem surprising, doesn't it."

"Sure does," I agreed, my eyes boring into his.

His smile curled up, but it looked like it took a lot of effort. "I'm afraid you'd have to ask his lordship why he chose to keep the news private."

"Except he's indisposed right now," I said.

His head nodded with a jerk. "Just so. If you'd like, I'd be happy to ask him when he returns from Hergotis."

"Don't bother." I turned to Lysander. "Let's head upstairs and see Shandy."

FIFTEEN

We found Demetrius Shandy pretty much where we left him the day before, hovering over the sleeping form of the radiant Lady Celia. He'd taken his mage cloak off, at least, and was now just in a vest and shirtsleeves. The sleeves were rolled up to the elbow, and I noticed he had surprisingly muscular forearms for a mage. I always appreciated a guy with strong hands.

"How's the patient?" I asked as we entered the room.

He looked startled, and the unease didn't fade when he saw it was me. I guessed I'd really made an impression during our previous interaction. Must have been the bit about using his tongue for a cravat.

"Minimal improvement, I'm afraid," he said. "As soon as I bring her out of it, she goes for the stitches. I'm going to keep her under until her abdomen is completely healed, then try again."

"Wake her up now," I said.

"*Excuse* me?" He looked shocked that I would even suggest such a thing, much less demand it. I guess I couldn't blame him. I was clearly infringing on his turf. But Quince slipping up on the kid's name, then acting so strange about the lack of a birth announcement had set off more bells than a cathedral. Something about little Edgar's birth was off, and even if she was nuts, Lady Celia might be able to tell me what it was.

I gestured to Lysander. "Lye will pin down her arms so she can't hurt herself."

"Absolutely not." Shandy was clearly still scared of me, but his sense of duty toward Lady Celia came first. Normally, I'd go for that kind of thing. Earnest, duty-bound men were my favorite flavor. But right now it was more impediment than aphrodisiac.

"Look, Demetrius, I've got a stack of questions and nobody to answer them."

"I'm sorry if your search for the child has hit a dead end, but *my* primary responsibility is to my patient."

"Wrong," I said. "Your primary responsibility is to uphold guild law. And since I took this job, I've been attacked by magecraft twice. Once by assassins with silence sigils carved into their necks. The second time by two people who'd been force-possessed. Last I checked, both those techniques have been banned."

Shandy's eyes widened. "People who've been *forced* to act as hosts? That's . . . barbaric."

"Not only that, but they attacked Orlando Mozamo and me right on the Chemosh Guild's doorstep."

"Mozamo on the Interguild Disciplinary Council?" he asked quietly.

"That's the guy. Whoever is behind this has no interest in laws or restraint. You want your guildmaster to find out you've been obstructing an investigation in the attack of a force-possessed on the chairman of the disciplinary council?"

I had nothing concrete that linked Edgar's birth to the attack, but Demetrius didn't need to know that.

"Fine. I'll wake her up." He stood up and placed his hand on the sigil cloth that covered her forehead. "But if I feel she's getting too hysterical, I'm putting her back under."

"God forbid we have a hysterical woman on our hands," I said.

He scowled. "Your sarcasm isn't appreciated."

"It never is. More's the pity." I turned to Lysander. "Get behind her and get ready to grab her arms if she, you know, tries to rip out her guts again."

Lysander moved over to the other side of the bed. I took a spot at its foot so I'd be the first thing she saw when she opened her eyes. Then I nodded to Shandy.

Shandy gently pulled the sigil cloth from her forehead. After a moment, her eyelids flickered and she woke.

"Lady Celia," I said. "It's vital that you answer some questions about your son."

"M-my son?" Her eyes were a dark blue that almost looked violet. They darted around the room, not really taking in any of us but looking for someone or something else. Her smooth brow furrowed. "No. That's not right. There was never . . ." She suddenly sat up and looked at me, her eyes terrified. In a whispered voice, she said, "Oh God. Oh God, is it still in there? Help me! Please!"

She lifted her hands up. It seemed like she was only reaching out to me, but Lysander immediately grabbed her wrists. Better safe than sorry, I suppose, but it also increased her panic. She immediately let out a shriek, then began wailing, "Get it out! Get it out!" over and over again.

"That's it—I'm putting her under again," said Shandy.

"Not yet." I grabbed Celia's face in my hands and forced her to look at me, getting so close there was nothing else to see but my eyes.

"Get *what* out of you?" I asked.

"The—the *thing*!" Flecks of spit hit my face as she yelled.

"Your *baby*?"

She tried to shake her head free, but I held on tight. "It's not a baby! There never *was* a baby! Just the *thing*!" Then her eyes rolled back into her head, and she started convulsing so hard that Lysander could barely restrain her.

"See what you've done?" Shandy shoved me away, then turned to Lysander. "Force her down!"

Lysander pressed slowly down until Celia was horizontal again. Then Shandy laid the cloth on her forehead. She continued to flail against the bed as he hurriedly traced the sigil on the cloth to reactivate it, chanting under his breath as he did so. After a few moments, her thrashing began to slow, then finally stop. She was asleep.

Shandy glared at me. "I hope you're happy. You got nothing but the ravings of a madwoman, and dispelled what little progress I've made."

"Didn't you hear her?" I asked. "She said there wasn't a baby. Just a *thing.*"

"In the pain of her grief, she's probably disassociating from him, convincing herself that her son was never real to begin with."

"Typical arrogant mage bullshit. Nobody can be right but you. Not even the person who lived through it." I grabbed the blankets that covered Lady Celia and yanked them off.

"What are you doing?" Shandy reached for me, but Lysander shoved him back.

"Give her space to work," he advised.

I unbuttoned Celia's soft white nightgown, hoping that my suspicions were wrong. But they weren't. When I opened the gown, I saw her belly. There was a neat curved line of stitches along her abdomen, but no other signs of pregnancy.

"Shit," I said.

"What in the hell are you looking for?" asked Shandy.

"You see any stretch marks? Anything at all other than the incision that suggests she was actually pregnant?"

"You're . . . saying the pregnancy was faked?" he asked. "But . . . but *why?*"

"Open her up," I said.

"*What?*" He shook his head. "You can't mean that."

I looked at Lysander. He turned to Shandy. "Better do it, pal. Otherwise I'll have to start breaking fingers. And I'll be honest, that always grosses me out a little."

Shandy looked rattled. His face had grown pale, and sweat glistened at his temples. I got the feeling his particular line of expertise didn't bring him into a lot of direct conflict. It was kind of sweet, actually. But I didn't have the time or patience to hold his hand on this one.

"That sleep sigil blocks pain, right?"

He nodded his head jerkily.

"She won't feel a thing. So open her up. *Now.*"

He walked stiffly over to a nearby table and retrieved a small pair of scissors and a scalpel from a leather satchel. Then he pulled his chair over to the side of the bed and sat down.

I had to hand it to him, as nervous as he was, his hands didn't shake once he started. He carefully cut the stitches away. The incision had partly healed, so he had to use the scalpel to reopen it completely. Once he had, he slowly peeled back the skin.

I'd seen a lot of exposed guts over the years, but it was usually in the heat of a fight. There was something about being in such a quiet setting and seeing this woman's innards, all soft and venous, that made me feel suddenly light-headed. I bit down hard on my lip to sharpen my focus. I'd be damned if, after all this, I passed out like some kind of amateur.

"Wait . . ." He stared into the opening. The fear was gone from his voice. Now it was a flat sound, like shock or incomprehension. "This can't be right. This . . ." He looked up at me, his eyes big enough to swallow my discomfort.

"What is it?" I asked.

"Her entire uterus." His voice was little more than a breath. "It's *gone.*"

SIXTEEN

There were many people who said I had an angry disposition. Those people had no fucking idea.

"Roz?"

I heard the alarm in Lysander's voice as I stalked out of the room, yanking my gloves off my hands as I went. But I didn't respond. The next words out of my mouth were reserved for that foppish, conniving mother-fucker Quince. Maybe he didn't know what exactly happened to Lady Celia—but he knew *something*, and I was going to find out what that was, no matter what it took.

I was halfway down the stairs before Lysander caught up with me. I felt his big hand grip my shoulder.

"Let's just take a breath here, Roz." I heard real fear, because he knew what I was capable of, and that it was only moments away from happening. "We can acknowledge that this horrible thing was done and figure out what to do about it, but without burning down this entire mansion and the many innocent people, including me, that are inside it."

He knew exactly what to say. This hadn't been the first time he'd talked me down from a homicidal rage. He didn't try to diminish what we'd just witnessed, or suggest my wrath wasn't warranted. He just asked that I not kill him in the process. And he was probably the only person in the world whom I hadn't at some point fantasized killing, so as always, it made me pause.

I looked him steadily in the eye, then took a slow, deep breath.

He gave me a relieved smile. "Thanks, Roz."

I nodded and continued down the stairs to the billiards room. I wouldn't need the muscle anyway. Quince would be a pushover. Some people had hidden grit, but I didn't think he was one of them.

But when Lysander and I got to the billiards room, it was empty. I went back out into the foyer. The big meat stick of a doorman was snoozing in a chair near the entrance. I walked over and kicked him in the shin.

"Wake up, Chuckles," I said.

"Goddamn it!" he growled, losing the thin coating of gentility he'd had before. He balled his fists and was halfway to his feet before Lysander shoved him back down.

"She said wake up, not stand up," he told the doorman.

The guy clearly wasn't used to being confronted by someone even bigger than him, because he settled down right away.

"Where's Quince?" I asked.

"He left."

"When?"

He shrugged. "It was right after you went upstairs. He left, and I realized there was nobody else to boss me around, so I took a nap."

"Where'd he go?" I asked.

"He said he was going to check on Lord Edmund."

"Hergotis. Everybody who knows anything is in fucking Hergotis . . ." Then I remembered. "Except the gardener."

I abandoned the meat stick and pushed open the front doors. All the garden spirit lights were extinguished, so it was pitch-black outside. I held up one hand, and flame engulfed it.

"Holy shit!" exclaimed the doorman.

"Stay put. Nobody else leaves until I say. Understood?"

His head jerked up and down a few times.

I looked at Lysander. "Let's go."

We made our way across the garden by the light of my burning hand.

I didn't take the winding paths, but instead cut right through, stomping on flowers and anything else that got in my way until we reached the gardener's cottage. There was still no light inside. The door was open. And something dark stained the doorway.

"No."

I dropped down on one knee for a closer look, but I already knew what I'd find. A puddle of blood.

"No, no, no," I muttered as I hurried into the house. It was a small space and impeccably tidy, except the path of chaos and broken furniture that led from the front door to the gardener.

He stood completely still, his eyes staring at nothing. The look on his face was a mixture of anger, revulsion, and agony. One hand reached out toward whatever he'd been looking at when he died. His other hand was half open at his side and flecked with blood. On the floor near his feet was a blood-covered kitchen knife.

I leaned over and lit an oil lamp with my hand, then shut my flames off. I shone the lamp on the gardener and looked him over more carefully. He appeared to be frozen in place, but there was no sign of ice. In fact, his body still had some residual warmth, so he must have been killed recently.

"What the hell happened to him?" asked Lysander.

"Not sure yet." His skin had an odd dryness to it. Flaky and brittle. Almost like . . .

That's when I saw the small knife sticking in his gut. I pulled on one of my gloves and took the handle. It came out slowly, like it was being withdrawn from something denser and stickier than a person. Other than the cloth-wrapped handle, it was made entirely of wood. The blade was coated in sap, and there was a sigil carved into it that was so tiny I had to bring my face dangerously close.

"Huh." As horrifically cruel as it was, I had to admit it was cleverly done.

"What?" Lysander sounded impatient. He hated when I didn't let him in on mage stuff.

"The sigil carved on this blade. It's using a transmutation sequence called 'like is like.' Fairly well known, but takes some skill to create. Normally you would carve it into a material, then press a different material to it, and the sigil would transform the first material into the second. Etch it into a metal door, then press a piece of glass against the sigil, and the sigil would convert the metal door into glass, which you could easily crack open."

Lysander looked at me, then the gardener, then back at me. "Not getting it."

"Right, because *this* sigil has been inverted so that whatever it touches becomes like the base material. In this case, from flesh . . ." I pointed to the gardener. "To wood." I pointed at the knife.

"So that sticky stuff on the blade is . . ."

"His blood. Or it *was*, before it became sap."

Lysander stared into the old man's glassy eyes. "He's turning into a tree?"

"Something like that. I've never seen this before, so I'm not sure what the end result is without cutting him open. No matter what, though, he's dead, and it hurt like hell."

A shudder ran down Lysander's muscular back. "You think Quince did this on his way out? I have to say, I never pegged him for a mage."

"Me either . . ." My eyes were drawn to the gardener's blood-spattered hand, then to the gore-splattered knife on the floor. "Whoever it is, I don't think they've gotten far."

"What do you mean?"

"The old man's blood turned to sap in that area the moment he was stabbed by the dagger, and I don't see any other wounds on him, so that's not his blood. He must have managed to stick his attacker with that knife before he changed completely."

Lysander's eyes followed the trail of dark red that led across the floor and out the door. "That's a lot of blood."

"Exactly. "

I hunched over and followed the trail through the door and back outside. It led around the side of the cottage and continued to the stone wall at the back of the gardens. There was a huge splash of blood across the wall where it looked like the attacker had heaved themself over it. I clambered up the wall and down the other side, where I found nothing but rugged, untamed forest.

It was much more difficult to follow the blood trail there. The attacker must have been in bad shape, though, because they didn't even try to hide their passage. Broken branches, a few spatters on leaves, and a bloody handprint on a tree trunk were enough to keep me moving forward.

Then about ten feet away, I saw a body slumped with their back against a tree. They wore a scarlet mage robe trimmed in gold. The hood was drawn up, so I couldn't see much of the person. Their shoulders moved heavily up and down, as if breathing was a struggle. Maybe a punctured lung. I wasn't being all that quiet, and Lysander was making a huge racket behind me as he cursed and blundered through the underbrush, but the person beneath the tree barely stirred.

"Roz," groaned Lysander, "I swear to—"

I held up my hand, and he stopped behind me.

"Nice work on that knife," I called to the mage. "Did you come up with it yourself?"

The mage said something too quiet for me to hear from that distance. Then their shoulders shook in a short laugh that ended in a long, wet coughing fit.

I handed the lamp to Lysander and took out my metal poles. Just because this person looked in bad shape, that didn't mean they were helpless. I crept slowly toward them, ready for anything.

Or so I thought. But judging by the sudden twist in my gut when I could finally see the mage's face, I hadn't been ready to learn that the murderer was a girl who looked to be only about fifteen. She had a simple, sweet-faced beauty. Or she would have, if her face hadn't been smeared with blood and twisted into a maniacal grin.

"Well, if it isn't Rosalind Featherstone, the Gutter Mage herself."
The girl's voice was all over the place. She sounded as unhinged as she
looked.

"And what are you, the goddamn Diaper Mage?" I replied. "You're too
young to have graduated from one of the academies, so tell me who taught
you neat stuff like turning a man's blood to tree sap."

"We're like sisters, you and me." She leaned forward when she said
that, but then winced and clutched at her side. Even in the dim lamplight,
I could see that blood had soaked through a good bit of her robe.

"How are we like sisters?"

She smiled, showing me bloodstained teeth. It was just coming out
everywhere, I guess. "Our power was born from the same man."

"And who would that be?" An icy cold squirmed around in my gut,
but I wasn't ready to give in yet. I wanted her to say it.

She gave me a surprisingly coy look for someone at death's door. "Don't
pretend like you don't know what I'm talking about. It's beneath you."

"Listen, little girl. You don't know me at all if you think there's *anything*
beneath me."

She looked wistful now. "I can see why he still has a thing for you."

Her eyes were fogging over, and she was slipping lower and lower.
I didn't have much time, so I'd have to get unpleasant if I wanted any
answers.

I walked over to her and pressed the tip of my boot into her bloody
side.

"*Who* still has a thing for me?"

She winced again, although not as much as she should have, which
meant she was even further along than I thought.

"You're going to make me say his name, aren't you?" Her voice was
almost dreamy.

"Yes."

"Simon Crowley."

"Simon Crowley is dead." The name stuck in my throat so badly it came out thick and syrupy, like I was about to vomit, which wasn't far from the truth.

"Death is but a door." She looked up at me, trying to focus her eyes. "You should know that by now."

"Where is he, then?"

Her eyes slowly closed and she smiled. "He's waiting for you. He's *always* been waiting. . . . It doesn't matter where . . . you go. He'll be there waiting . . . for you."

"When you see Simon Crowley in hell, why don't you tell him he better *stay* there. Because if I find him, death will seem like a pleasant dream."

"It already . . . does. . . ."

And then she died. That stupid little girl who'd been manipulated into murder and who knew what else. I felt sick just looking at her, so I turned away.

"Roz?" Lysander seemed worried.

Wait, was he worried about *me*? What expression did I have on my face that he was giving me such a look?

I took a deep breath and fixed my fucking face. Then I said, "Yeah?"

"What's the plan?"

"The *plan* is we ride to Hergotis and get some answers from Quince, or Edmund, or that Alath Guild, or whoever is there. Baby or no baby, *somebody* is going to pay for jerking us around like this."

PART TWO

NO HORSE IN THE WORLD CAN OUTRUN THE PAST

SEVENTEEN

His name was Aaron. Or Armin. Or something like that. It didn't really matter. He was the first strapping young farm boy I saw on our journey to Hergotis, and I was not feeling picky. He came into the inn where Lysander and I were staying on the first night after we left Ariel House. He was probably looking to get a quiet drink with friends after a long day of tending fields or whatever he did. Lysander was already in his room, no doubt pining after Portia. I was sitting at a table near the bar when Aaron or whoever strolled in. He looked to be about twenty, packed to the brim with wholesome muscles, good manners, and not much else. It took me all of half a second to decide he would be the lucky recipient of all my pent-up frustration for the evening.

I reached over and grabbed his brawny forearm. He stopped and looked at me in surprise. Maybe he'd never been accosted by a stranger before.

"Here is what I propose," I told him. "You're going to keep buying me whiskey until I tell you it's time to take me up to my room and fuck my brains out. Agreed?"

"Ma'am?" He gave me an earnest farm boy look beneath a curtain of strawberry-blond bangs as he tried to determine if I was joking.

"Well, what's your answer?"

"Y-yes?"

"Great. Then get me a drink." I swatted his butt, which I noted was as sleek and firm as I'd hoped. Man, I had a good eye.

"Y-yes, ma'am." He hurried over to the bar, his tanned face already flushing an adorable red. I admired the broad back that stretched his linen shirt taut across his shoulders while he nervously ordered a whiskey for me and an ale for himself. The bartender eyed me skeptically over the farm boy's shoulder, and I gave him a nice big leer. He rolled his eyes in response and handed the farm boy our drinks.

The next few hours were hazy. I think I probably talked the poor farm boy's ear off about all the creative ways I'd contemplated killing whoever had been messing with me the last few days, regardless of whether it was truly Simon or someone merely pretending to be Simon. I also went on a fair bit about how much I would enjoy hurting anyone else who got in my way. It probably wasn't good foreplay, but that was the great thing about twenty-year-old farm boys. They didn't need much. He dutifully brought me whiskey until I commanded him to carry me up the stairs "like the goddamn queen of goddamn Penador." Or something like that.

Once we were in my room, I tore his shirt off, which I'd wanted to do to someone for a while. Then it was all hands, mouths, and hot, sweaty skin. I think I was probably still raving, but it had devolved mostly into commands to fuck me in various ways. I remember at one point lying on my back on the lumpy straw mattress with his blond head between my thighs. He paused for a moment to look up at me with that sincere gaze, and I couldn't help but laugh.

His expression became panicked. "Did I do something wrong?"

"Hell, no! You're just what I needed!"

Then I pushed his face back where it belonged and closed my eyes. I had the urge to keep my hands on his head, but the way things were going, I was afraid I might lose control and burn his hair off, or worse. What my farm boy lacked in finesse, he made up for in enthusiasm. Tireless and attentive, he left no part of me untouched. So I placed my palms firmly on the headboard and did my best not to turn the whole bed to ash.

He wanted to cuddle afterward. I was in a generous mood, so I gave him a few moments while I stared up at the handprints I'd burned into the headboard. Then I advised him to stop having sex with strange women he'd just met and told him to get out.

I couldn't fuck the pain away forever. I knew that. But sometimes it was a relief to connect with someone this simple and good, even if only in a limited way. The world was full of duplicitous, human-shaped piles of shit that would kill you as soon as look at you. If I could forget that, even for a short while, it was better than nothing.

EIGHTEEN

"Good morning, *Your Majesty.*"

"Fuck . . . ," I muttered around the stem of my empty pipe as I sat slumped over a table in the tavern. My head felt like a slab of raw steak.

Lysander sat down across from me, wearing a smug grin. "The walls are pretty thin in this place, you know."

"Um."

He kept up the smile. "A little consideration for your neighbors is all I'm asking, *Your Majesty.*"

"Do you have to keep doing that?" I asked plaintively.

"Doing what?" His expression was innocent.

"Living. Because I can think of a few ways I'd be better off if you weren't."

A serving woman with a stained apron and a face like an old potato came over to our table. "Get you anything?"

"Two mugs of tea and one of those honey rolls," Lysander replied. "Oh, and she'll have a couple boiled eggs."

"I'm not having shit," I told him.

He ignored me and smiled at the serving woman. "She will."

"Uh-huh." The woman's lumpy face showed neither interest nor amusement. "Anything else?"

"Whiskey," I said.

"Nope, that's it, thanks," he told her politely but firmly.

Once the woman was gone, I said, "Practicing your parenting skills already, I see."

"Roz, we got a lot of money riding on this job, and I can't have you going on a bender and screwing it up."

"I wouldn't be so sure we're going to see money at the end of this. You ask me, the whole thing is starting to look like a scam. The baby is fake, so what's his lordship hiring us to find?"

"I don't know," he admitted.

"Neither do I, so maybe we should ask him—but wait, both he and the fop who hired us have split. There's nobody to ask. Well, except the child assassin who claims to be working for a man I killed fifteen years ago. Oops, never mind, she's dead now too."

His thick brows knit together. "Okay, okay, I get you."

"Sorry, Lye. I know you had big plans for that money, but I'm not sure there *is* a job anymore. Or if there ever was."

His expression was pensive as the serving woman came back with the roll, eggs, and tea.

Once she was gone, he asked, "Then what are we doing here, Roz?"

"I don't know." I picked up an egg and cracked the shell. Hunger seemed a foreign concept to my stomach right then, but I'd done this enough times to know it could take a couple of eggs.

"About last night . . ." His eyes bore into me as he took a bite of his roll. "It's been a while since you've been that . . . frantic to shut down your own mind. I'm guessing it's got to do with this Crowley guy."

I bit into my egg, wishing I had a pinch of salt to go with it, and washed it down with some tea. "Good guess."

"You think it's about time you told me the whole story?"

"Why?"

"Might be good to get it off your chest."

I made a face. "You been talking to Cordelia? She has this idea I should start sharing all my feelings."

"I don't want to know *all* your feelings. I'm pretty sure full knowledge of everything that goes on in your head would keep me up at night. But if we're really going up against this Crowley, and he's as bad as you say, don't you think I should know exactly who we're dealing with?"

"It can't be Crowley." I picked a stray bit of shell off the remainder of my egg. "I watched that asshole's charred face slide right off his skull."

"Maybe he survived somehow?"

"And then I watched the rest of him crumble to ash."

"Okay, that would be pretty hard to come back from," said Lysander. "Maybe it's someone who knew him, then. And knew you?"

"Maybe," I conceded.

"Come on, Roz. Help me out here. If we're really not getting paid for this, at least make it a little easier for me."

He was right, of course. The last thing I wanted to do was rehash the worst moments of my life, but I was potentially dragging him into a shitstorm straight out of my past, so the least I could do was prepare him for it.

"Simon Crowley was a professor at the Grimoric Mage Academy. One of those young, dreamy-poet types all the students had crushes on."

"You were how old then?"

"Fifteen, and dumb as shit. Keep in mind, I was a very different person back then."

"Oh sure," he said around a mouthful of honey roll.

"Oh sure?"

"You think I don't remember what you were like before you went to the academy?"

I leaned back and started slowly crushing the shell of my second egg on the table. "You tell me, then. What was I like?"

"Well, you were nice, for starters."

"Was I?"

"Absolutely. And peppy."

My eyebrow raised. "Peppy?"

"Upbeat. A real go-getter, you know? Always had grand plans. You were going to get out of Quartz Harbor and make something of yourself, no matter what."

I pulled the crushed shell off my egg and took a bite. "Sounds like I was a real peach."

"I don't mind telling you, I had a bit of a crush on you back then."

"Now you're talking crazy. You had what's her name. Viola."

Lysander made a face like he'd tasted something bad. "Viola? She was pretty, I grant you. But boring as shit. Being around *you* always felt . . . exciting. Like anything could happen."

"That's not how I remember it," I told him. "But still, you get the idea. I was energetic, driven, and terrifyingly eager. So it probably doesn't surprise you that when Crowley asked me if I wanted to participate in a 'high risk, high gain' extra credit project, I didn't hesitate."

"Sounds about right," he agreed.

"We started working on sigils I'd never seen before, using techniques I'd never heard of. He had this whole new theory of magecraft. In hindsight, it was complete bullshit, but back then it seemed mind-blowing. Like we were about to change the world with our experiments . . ."

Memories of those days started rising up like zombies from the grave. I felt myself reflexively tense up. Did I really want to go through with this? Maybe Cordelia and her theotic mage boyfriend were right, and it would help somehow. Or maybe I would fall apart all over again and be unable to put myself back together this time.

I glanced at Lysander, and he was just sitting there, waiting patiently. Like he could and would sit there all day if it took me that long to muster up the guts. I realized that if there was one person I could talk to about this, someone who could help me not completely fly apart, it was Lysander. So fuck it. There might never be a better time. And someone should know what that bastard did.

"Crowley and I worked for weeks on a bunch of special sigils and incantations. Eventually, he pronounced that we were 'ready.' We would try to channel spirit energy into a person, not through possession but directly, so that the person truly had the ability to conjure magic on their own without the risk of losing control to the spirit."

"Let me guess—you were the lucky first recipient."

"I was going to be the first of a new kind of mage, wielding power like no one else before. And I suppose in a way, that's how it ended up. But the ritual to make it happen was not the one I'd been taught."

I took a slow gulp of my tea before I continued, wishing it was whiskey. Apparently, I was really doing this.

"Maybe I should have been suspicious," I said finally, "when he told me we needed to do it off campus in this tiny, old abandoned stone building in Quartz Harbor called Gemory Chapel. I figured that what we were doing was so experimental, the more conservative professors at the academy would have tried to stop us. That just made it seem more exciting."

This whole sharing-emotions thing was harder than I'd expected. Every word made my insides squirm so bad I wasn't sure I'd be able to keep those eggs down after all. My mind kept trying to skip to the end, like it wanted to get this over with before the emotions built up too much. But Lysander had to hear everything. And now that I'd started, I realized that I needed him to hear it.

I didn't want to turn into a simpering mess in the process, though. So I took a few slow breaths before I continued.

"When we got to the chapel, he had me strip down to my undergarments so he could paint a sigil that we'd developed on my back. I was nervous about being half-naked in front of a professor, which is probably why I didn't notice that he was drawing something drastically different from what we'd been practicing. It turned out to be some kind of paralysis sigil."

"Shit," said Lysander.

"Yeah." I felt the back of my throat tense like I was about to vomit, so I swallowed hard. "Then the rest of the men came in."

"Motherfucker."

"Pretty much."

I felt untethered now. Unsure. Panic tickled the edge of my vision. I looked down at my tea mug, which was empty. Both eggshells were empty. I needed something to focus on. Something real and in the present, or these memories were going to pull me under, and I was going to drown. Aimlessly, I picked up my pipe and stared at it.

"Give me a moment."

Lysander went over to the bar and spoke with the woman. I was hoping he'd come back with whiskey, but it was a small pouch of tobacco, which I guess was second best. Wordlessly, he handed it to me. I nodded thanks and took my time packing my pipe, then lighting it. The tobacco was better than the stuff I usually pinched off Chester, with a hint of apple.

Once I was safely ensconced in a cloud of smoke, I felt . . . not better, but at least a little more grounded in the present.

"I honestly don't remember everything that happened after that," I said. "Or even how long it took."

"A week," Lysander said quietly. "Took the school two days to admit you were missing and contact your folks. Your dad got the old crew together, and we scoured the neighborhood for you." He paused for a moment, pain creasing his face. "I'm sorry we didn't find you."

I gazed at him through the smoke haze as I took another pull on my pipe. I never knew that he'd taken that on himself. For some reason, it made me feel a little less alone. Misery does love company, I guess.

"Here's what I *do* remember. They had me staked down to the floor, arms stretched out so far the ropes cut into my wrists. . . ."

The tide of memories rose up again and pressed down on my chest, not a panic this time, but a hard slab of despair. The kind that can turn you to stone. For a moment, I didn't think I could continue. I dragged on my pipe, too hard and too soon, so that I felt the burn on my tongue.

But that kind of physical, temporary pain was a release of sorts, and the pressure on my chest lessened.

"They didn't give me any food, and only enough water to keep me alive. I lay there in a puddle of my own piss while they took shifts chanting and drawing sigils around me. Once the paralysis wore off, I begged them to let me go. Begged until my voice was hoarse. But they ignored me. Like I wasn't a person. Like I was just a piece of meat."

The memory of my own screams echoed in my head. Pleading with them. *I'll never tell anyone*, I swore. *I'll go away, and you'll never see me again. Please, God and spirits, just let me go. . . .*

It had been a feeling of total helplessness—a hard lesson that the world was a fucking bastard and the best you could do was survive it. I felt that helplessness again now, and though it was just a ghost from long ago, it still choked me. I had to push hard through it to continue, my voice straining against the phantom fingers that strangled me.

"What they were saying . . . sounded like Arch Pendoric. But nothing I was familiar with. Or maybe I was just too out of my mind with fear and misery to recognize it. Hard to tell. And then of course came the final part of the ritual." I looked down at the sigils burned into my palms. "Crowley took that fucking hot brand to my hands."

I did it. I got to the end. Hurray for fucking me. And okay, maybe there was something to what Delia's boyfriend said about talking things out, because I actually felt a tiny bit relieved.

"And that was when you got the flames?" asked Lysander.

"I think so. I passed out from the pain. I just remember waking up, and there were . . . flames everywhere. Gemory Chapel was a sturdy old stone-and-mortar building, so it didn't collapse. But everything inside was on fire, including all the mages who'd been in there with me."

"So it backfired on Crowley?"

"I assume he hadn't intended to get himself killed."

"And everyone else who'd been there died as well?"

"I can't say for certain how many were involved. Except for Crowley, they came and went pretty frequently."

"So it could be one of those guys who's now claiming to be Crowley," said Lysander.

"Could be."

"Or what about what that mage girl said? Death being just a door or whatever? Is that even possible?"

"I've never heard of a mage being able to come back from the dead. But as Lando is fond of saying, we really don't know enough about magic to say that anything is impossible. Regardless of whether it's Crowley or one of his lackeys, why is he doing this? What does he want from me?"

Lysander drank the last of his tea. "He'd have to be pretty deluded if he's expecting anything other than a slow and painful death. You ready to go give it to him?"

I knocked my pipe empty on the floor and ground the embers under my boot, which felt oddly satisfying. Then I shoved the pouch of tobacco into my coat pocket.

"Yeah."

"And if it's really Crowley?"

"Then I'll kill him again. Except this time, I'll do it slowly. Hell, maybe it'll be cathartic. I might even become a happy and productive member of society after I'm through with him."

NINETEEN

The road from Drusiel to Hergotis wound in a northwesterly direction through the Pale Forest, so called because of the white bark of the birch and sycamore trees that comprised most of it. The chances of us catching up to Quince were slim, but Lysander and I weren't really in the mood for sightseeing, so we pushed our horses fairly hard anyway. I was glad we'd paid for good ones. Even so, neither Lysander nor I were seasoned riders, and I soon discovered that while my horse might not need to rest often, my ass certainly did.

We'd gotten a late start, so it was already after noon the first time we stopped to give our rears a break. I was walking along beside my mare, holding her reins tightly so she couldn't bite my face. Lysander was coming up a little more slowly behind me, probably because he wanted to give his horse more of a rest after hauling his weight for a few hours.

There'd been some relief immediately after telling Lysander about what happened with Crowley, but now I was feeling agitated. Like it had stirred up something that I couldn't quite get settled back down. Was it a good thing? A sign of healing, maybe? Or maybe it was just masochism. I was certainly no stranger to self-harm.

The sound of pounding hooves coming up from behind drew me out of my thoughts.

"Roz?" Lysander gripped the pommel of his sword.

"I hear it." More mute assassins coming after us? Or more

force-possessed? Hell, maybe this time it would be force-possessed mute assassins, just to keep things lively.

But as the sound drew closer, I was pretty sure it was only one set of hooves. A lone rider coming at a good clip, and if they were trying to sneak up on us, they were doing a poor job.

Then the rider came into view, and I wasn't sure whether to be relieved or alarmed.

"*Lando?*"

Orlando Mozamo had the pinched, blank look of someone who had been riding hard for a long time. But when he saw us, his expression eased into relief.

He yanked his horse's reins, forcing it into a walk. Now that he was closer, I could see his usually immaculate yellow robe was spattered with mud, and his horse's flanks were streaked with sweat. Both of them looked beat.

"I've caught up with you at last," he said.

"Why are you here, Lando?" I asked bluntly.

"Demetrius Shandy of the Valac Guild came to me yesterday, so concerned for your well-being that he had decided to break his confidentiality agreement with Lord Edmund."

"Demetrius was worried about me? What a sweetheart." I felt slightly bad about threatening him with so much bodily harm. Or maybe he liked that sort of thing.

"His report," continued Orlando, "combined with our encounter with the force-possessed the previous day, has me worried as well. What's going on, Rosalind?"

"Look, Orlando," said Lysander. "We appreciate the concern, but Roz and I can handle this. Can't we, Roz."

It wasn't a question, but I decided it should be. "Hold on a moment, Lye. We're going into this pretty blind, so we really don't know that for sure. Might be helpful to have a theotic mage around."

"I don't know, Roz. . . ."

Lysander looked troubled, which surprised me, since he was usually the one trying to find excuses for me and Orlando to work together. What was more important than his double-date fantasies?

"Oh, it's the money," I said aloud. "You're still hoping we actually get paid for this job, and you don't want to split it three ways."

"Well . . ." He looked a little embarrassed. "That did cross my mind."

"Look, it's no problem, right, Lando? You're not planning to chisel in on our payday, should we actually get one."

Orlando's usual condescending look was a little softened by exhaustion. "No, Rosalind, I do not expect a portion of your payment, if for no other reason than because I would not be permitted to accept it, according to guild law."

"Oh?"

"There is the matter of force-possession, of course. And apparently there were also banned silence sigils carved into a group of assassins that attacked you?"

"Oh yeah, I forgot to mention those." I smiled to let him know that I hadn't actually forgotten.

"I don't need to tell you that the use of either of those sigils breaks guild law. And now this fake pregnancy regarding Lady Celia?" He shook his head wearily. "We might have to invent a new law for that one. Regardless, the Interguild Disciplinary Council is officially investigating the matter. Both you and Demetrius have implicated the Alath Guild as suspects, so I will accompany you to Hergotis and question them myself."

"Sure," I said. "The more the merrier."

"Roz?" Lysander looked surprised.

"Really? Just like that?" Orlando also looked taken aback. I was not known for working well with others, especially when it concerned official guild business.

"Just like that," I said. "Provided you brought along your exorcism kit."

"Ah, I see. That makes sense," said Orlando. "Yes. Considering our last encounter, I brought all the necessary tools for exorcism. Should we need to confront additional force-possession victims, we will not have to resort to killing them this time."

"Good," I said. "Because for all we know, one of them might be our client. And killing your client is no way to get paid, is it, Lye?"

"No it ain't, Roz," he agreed. But he still looked a little troubled for some reason. I wasn't sure what to make of that.

TWENTY

We reached the edge of the Pale Forest a couple of hours later, and the land opened out into a lush green meadow dotted with gently sloping hills. Beyond that, though still a full day's ride, I could see the top of the Vabam mountain range. The sun was just beginning to dip behind the jagged peaks, giving the horizon a slightly reddish cast.

"Vabam," said Orlando. "It means 'hidden treasures' in Arch Pendoric, I believe."

"Not bad for a theotic mage," I said. "Didn't think you guys paid that much attention to Arch Pendoric."

"Not a great deal," he admitted. "The only time we ever use it is during an exorcism or self-enchantment, and those services are so rarely requested these days."

"So what you're telling me is that you're rusty?"

"I requested a quick refresher from my guild master after we were attacked."

"Glad to hear it."

I'd always admired Orlando's ability to recognize when he fell short on something, then immediately ask for help in improving himself, all without any embarrassment. It wasn't something I'd ever been good at. Even knowing we might encounter more force-possessed people in Hergotis, I hadn't thought to ask Orlando—or any theotic mage—for assistance. I suppose asking for help always felt like failure to me for some reason.

As we followed the winding road through the foothills, I spotted a small, wooden building painted in a bright robin's-egg blue with a colorful sign staked in the ground out front that said WELCOME TO THE WARRIORESS INN. We still had plenty of sunlight, but I figured Orlando and his horse had been riding so hard that they could use an early night. Besides, most inns along the way were drably uniform. This place looked like it had real personality.

Orlando did not seem as amused by it as I was. His eyebrows rose slightly. "Warrioress? I don't think that's even a word."

"It is now," I said. "And it's where we're staying tonight."

He sighed. "Of course it is."

I glanced back at Lysander, who rode a little behind us and had been unusually silent since Orlando joined us. "Any complaints about stopping here?"

"Not from me."

Something was still clearly bothering him, but I knew pressing him now wasn't going to work. I was fairly certain it was about Orlando, so I'd have to find out later when it was just the two of us.

On closer inspection, the Warrioress Inn was a small but impeccably constructed wood house painted not only in bright blue, but with high-lights and detail work on the doors and windows in a delicate pink. There was a small stable beside the inn, but nobody attending, so we just tied our horses up and went inside.

The front room was an open space, with a few tables and chairs, and a large stone hearth crackled cheerfully in the back. A stooped, older guy with snowy white hair and spectacles sat at one of the tables reading a book. He looked up at us in surprise.

"Well, hello," he said in a gentle voice as he stood. "I reckon you're looking for lodging?"

"We sure are," I said. "This your place?"

He smiled faintly. "No, I just take care of the horses. I presume you've left them out in the stables?"

"Yeah. So, who's the warrioress, then?"

"Titania! Customers!" he called in a way that was loud, but still somehow gentle. He smiled at us again. "She'll be out in a moment, I'm sure. Now if you'll excuse me, I should go settle in your horses for the night."

"Watch out for the mare," I told him. "She's got a nasty temper."

"Much obliged for the warning, ma'am." The man left quietly through the door we'd just entered.

The three of us stood there awkwardly for a moment, not sure what to do. Then the door in the back flew open, and the tallest, broadest woman I'd ever seen came barreling into the room.

"Why, hello!" she boomed in an easy, mountain-folk drawl as she strode over to us. "A Penadorian, a Lapisian, and a Myovokan walk into an inn, huh? Sounds like the opening line to a joke!"

Her laughter boomed as hazel eyes sparkled cheerfully from her square, ruddy face. She wore a simple sleeveless dress dyed a pastel pink and looked to be in her fifties, with long brown-and-gray hair worn loose so that it fell to her bare, sculpted shoulders. Her arms also bulged with sharply defined muscle. She towered over Orlando and me, and was only about six inches shorter than Lysander. She was, I decided, magnificent.

"So, you three need lodgings for the night?" she asked. "How many rooms?"

"Three, if you have them available," I said.

She nodded. "It's the off season right now, so there's plenty of room. The merchant caravans generally avoid the Vabam crossing in the winter. Gets damn cold up there this time of year, and sometimes the snow makes getting a wagon through impossible."

"Wonderful." Lysander made a sour face.

Titania playfully punched his arm. "Strapping young fella like you worried about a little snow?"

"He's never seen snow in his life," I told her.

"Ah." Titania gave him a sympathetic look. "Snow ain't all bad, fella. Hell, I'd say it's about the prettiest thing nature has to offer."

"He also doesn't like nature," I said.

She gave me a look of mock frustration. "Well, what's he good for, then?"

I shrugged. "Killing people, mostly."

"Good to know, if I get any unsavory types in here," she said.

"You look like you could handle yourself pretty well," I said.

She sighed. "Well, thank you, dear. I do try to keep in shape, but I'm afraid my fighting days are long since past. Bad joints, you know? Now, why don't you set yourself at one of the tables. I was just starting dinner, so food is going to be a little while, but make yourself comfortable, and I'll bring out something to drink in a bit."

As she strode back out of the room, I called, "Something strong, if you've got it."

She waved her hand in acknowledgment; then the door closed behind her.

"Well, you heard the lady." I plopped down on a chair and kicked my boots up on the table.

"Rosalind . . ." Orlando's face looked troubled as he sat down in the chair next to mine. "Was that a woman, or a man dressed as a woman?"

I stared at him a moment. I knew he didn't mean anything by it, but it was these jarring moments of rigidity that reminded me that as often as he could be thoughtful and caring, he could also be an uptight, judgmental prick.

"I forget, Lando," I said. "Are you chairman of the Interguild Disciplinary Council or chief of the Pearl-Clutching Gender Police?"

"I beg your pardon?" The guy actually looked offended.

Lysander decided it was time to intercede. "Look, Lando, I don't know how it is in the guilds, but out here in the real world, Roz and I don't make a habit of judging good, honest, hardworking folks. And if you're going to travel with us, I strongly advise you to do the same."

It wasn't what I would have said, but it seemed to get the message across. And to Orlando's credit, he looked genuinely mortified.

"I'm sorry, I'd just never seen . . . I suppose I have led something of a sheltered life in the guild environment."

"There you go, pal. Great start." Lysander patted him on the shoulder. "Who knows? You might even learn something on this trip that doesn't involve magic and spirits. Wouldn't that be something?"

TWENTY-ONE

A short while later, Orlando excused himself to the outhouse, which gave me the opportunity to talk privately with Lysander.

Titania had already dropped off a small jug of something that smelled promisingly of gin and some cups, so I poured one for Lysander and handed it to him. He nodded thanks and took a large gulp.

As I fixed one for myself, I said, "You handled Lando real well earlier. Especially since I wasn't sure you even wanted him along."

"I like Lando. You know that. And I couldn't sit there and watch you roast the poor dope just because he's ignorant. But I don't think letting him mix with our business is such a great idea."

I took a slow sip of my drink as I considered. It had an uneven sort of flavor that suggested it might be home-brewed. Another point for Titania the Warrioress.

"How do you mean?"

"You said yourself this job has gotten pretty dicey, and we don't even know if we're going to be getting paid. But we *should* get paid. Even if it ended up being a rock instead of a baby—"

"A rock?"

"Or whatever the thing ends up being. That was just a 'for instance,'" Lysander said. "All I'm saying is that we signed a contract, and it's not our fault we were given bad information up front. We're still entitled to our pay."

"Agreed."

"So if his lordship decides he doesn't want to pay, we may need to get a little *persuasive* to make sure we get our due."

"I see where you're going with this."

"Exactly. A guy like Lando isn't going to just stand by if we need to get rough with one of the most mage-friendly nobles in Penador."

"We're not a member of any guild," I said. "He's got no authority over us."

"You think that'll stop him from butting in?"

I took a swallow of Titania's home-brewed gin. "You got me there. But we really might need him if Edmund turns out to be possessed. Though I'm not thrilled about the idea, we can kill any other force-possessions we come across. But if we kill Edmund, not only do we not get paid, but we make an enemy of just about every guild and noble in Penador, and probably a few in Lapisi as well."

"What makes you think Lord Edmund's possessed?"

"Just a hunch, really. I've been thinking . . . you and me, we're not easy to bamboozle. And Edmund didn't strike me as the sort with a lot of practice in scamming people. I'm pretty sure we would have caught on if he'd been lying about the baby. So if he *wasn't* lying, then he thought he was telling the truth."

"Can a possession do that? Make you believe something that isn't true?"

"Maybe. Although something that complicated would probably take an elder spirit."

Lysander's dark eyebrows rose as he took a drink. "You think that's what we're dealing with here?"

"Could be."

"What's this about an elder spirit?" Orlando asked as he sat down.

Lysander winced. Clearly he hadn't noticed Orlando coming back inside.

I poured Orlando a cup of home-brewed gin, which he accepted with some trepidation.

"We might as well tell him," I said to Lysander. "If he's coming with us, he'll find out anyway."

Lysander nodded glumly. "Okay. Go ahead."

I turned to Orlando, who was taking the tiniest of sips from his cup. "So Demetrius told you our client is Lord Edmund?"

"He did."

"And that Edmund hired us to find his kidnapped baby. Except his wife wasn't pregnant with a baby. There was . . . definitely *something* that they cut out of her, but she was too rattled to tell us what it was. And as crazy as it sounds, I guess they also took her womb along for good measure."

"That all lines up with what Shandy told me," said Orlando. "But what does this have to do with elder spirits?"

"I'm not sure yet, but I don't think our client was lying to us. He really thought there was a baby. If that's the case, wouldn't it take something like an elder spirit to pull off that level of illusion or control? I mean, there are stories about elder spirits inhabiting human hosts, able to speak and move around normally without even a tell to clue people in."

"There are *legends*," said Orlando. "All of them prehistorical and unconfirmed. Rosalind, I don't have to tell you how rare it is to encounter an elder spirit in any capacity. In my experience, when people start blaming such entities, the cause is generally much closer to home and far less exotic. The most likely scenario is that your client is simply delusional."

Orlando had a point. Nobody really knew much about elder spirits. Were they spirits who'd been around a lot longer and become more powerful over time? Or were they a whole different type, sort of like an elite or noble class? Nobody knew, and since they were so rarely encountered and difficult to bind, it didn't seem likely anyone was going to find out. The only recorded case of a successful binding had been Iago the Ice Mage, who'd bound an elder water spirit to a massive iron construct made specifically for the purpose. But even then, the elder spirit broke free of the binding fairly quickly, then killed Iago, his husband, and all of his disciples. That happened over fifty years ago, and they were still teaching it as a cautionary tale at the academy.

"I'm not eager to tangle with an elder spirit, so I hope you're right," I told Orlando. "But I'm not going to discount something as a possibility just because it's unlikely. Do you think you could exorcise one if you had to?"

"I can't say for certain, since I've never done it," said Orlando. "Although generally speaking, exorcising spirits is far easier than binding them, so *if* it did indeed come down to it, I think I could manage."

"Glad to hear it." That was something, at least.

Soon after that, Titania came with our food: boiled mutton, potatoes, and leeks. Not the fanciest meal, but good, hardy fare that didn't skimp on ingredients or portions.

"You going to join us, Tania?" I asked when she finished setting our dishes before us.

Her face brightened. "Well, that's mighty friendly of you. Don't mind if I do. Just let me go grab my plate from the kitchen."

While she was getting her food, Lysander said quietly, "We probably shouldn't talk about the job with her around."

"I don't know, Lye," I said. "She might have seen the Alath Guild or even our supposed Crowley passing through."

"Crowley?" asked Orlando. "As in *Simon* Crowley?"

"Someone using the name, anyway." I really didn't want to get into that topic with Orlando of all people, but if I was going to question Titania about it, I knew he'd need to fuss for a bit, so I wanted to get that out of the way first.

Now he was all frowns and well-meaning concern, as expected. "Listen, Rosalind, I know you don't like talking about the . . . Gemory Chapel incident. But I've read the council records on it, and all the surviving evidence suggests that he was attempting to bind—"

"An elder spirit, yeah." That theory wasn't new to me. The idea that Crowley had somehow harnessed the power of an elder fire spirit certainly explained the obscene amount of barely containable power in my palms, but since no elder spirit had ever been bound for any length of time, it seemed like a long shot. Also, the idea of a spirit somehow trapped *inside* my hands made my skin crawl, so I tried not to think about it. Still, Orlando had a point. It was a possibility I couldn't ignore.

"It's another reason we can't rule out the involvement of an elder spirit," I told him. "If Crowley's goal had been to bind an elder spirit, it might have failed spectacularly with me. But maybe one of his followers figured out how to do it right this time."

Orlando clearly wanted to keep pressing me, but fortunately Titania came back with her plate, so I could put that off for now. Talking about Gemory Chapel with Lysander was one thing. But opening up to the great Mage Mozamo was something else entirely, even if he had promised to rein in his more judgmental tendencies.

"Well, it sure is nice to have some friendly folk staying here," said Titania as she sat down. "I do hate eating alone."

"What about your stable boy?" I asked.

She smiled. "Claud? Oh, he's sweet. Been with me forever. But he goes in for all that wholesome-living stuff. In bed as soon as the sun sets and up at first light. Thinks it's better to match your body to the earth's natural rhythms."

"There *are* some theotic studies that suggest as much," said Orlando.

"I reckon there are," said Titania, "but I do enjoy a nice evening out."

"And sleeping in late," said Lysander.

I held up my cup. "I haven't been wholesome since I was fifteen, and I seem to be doing all right."

"Debatable," said Orlando as he watched me down my drink and pour another.

I ignored him and turned back to Titania. "You said it's nice to have some friendly folk staying here. Meaning you get unfriendly folk?"

"Well, maybe that's an ungenerous way of thinking about it," said Titania. "It's the slow season, so the only other person staying here right now . . . let's just say he keeps to himself."

"Oh?" I hadn't realized there was someone else staying at the inn. Whoever it was probably had nothing to do with us, but just in case . . . "What do you mean?"

"You know, has his meals in his room, stuff like that. Hasn't really talked to me or Claud at all for as long as he's been here."

"And how long is that?" I asked.

She thought about it a moment. "Five days now. Seems a long time not to talk to people, don't it?"

"Sure does," I agreed.

That timeline would have had him showing up the day before we got hired. Right around the time Lord Edmund's "baby" was stolen.

Could be a coincidence. Or not.

"He a serious, bookish type, like one of those mages?" I smirked at Orlando. "They can be a little antisocial."

Orlando gave me one of his level stares and chose not to rise to the bait.

"Matter of fact, I think he is," said Titania. "Has a hooded robe like one, at least."

"There you have it, then." I gave Orlando a meaningful look. "Friend of yours?"

Orlando caught on to where I was going. "Perhaps I know him. What colors does he wear?"

"Scarlet with gold trim," Titania said.

"Ah, yes." He tried to play it cool, but I could feel the tension starting to rise from him. "The Alath Guild. I believe I know someone in that guild. A fellow named Simon Crowley."

Titania's face brightened. "Well, I'll be! That's the very one!"

I tossed back my gin, then grinned at all three of them as I slammed the cup down on the table.

"Well then, let's go say hello!"

TWENTY-TWO

There was a voice in the back of my head screaming, *What are you doing, Rosalind Featherstone, you are not ready to face Simon fucking Crowley!* Not that I really thought it was Simon. How could it be? But it could be someone who knew him, maybe even someone who had been at Gemory Chapel. One of the nameless, faceless torturers from my memory . . .

If I'd been sober, or my nerves less frayed, the thought might have given me pause. Instead, I took Titania by her big meaty arm and led her up the stairs, Lysander and Orlando trailing behind us.

"Tania—it's okay if I call you Tania, right? Listen, you know how uptight mages can be. Sometimes they need someone to help them relax a little, so let's play a little joke on him. You knock on the door like you're alone and you have something important you need to talk to him about, and when he opens it, we'll all shout 'Surprise!' Won't that be a laugh?"

"You don't think he'll get mad?" Titania asked dubiously. "I don't like upsetting my customers, you know. Bad for business."

I patted her forearm reassuringly. "Simon and I go way back. As soon as he sees me, he'll be *thrilled*. And if it catches him at a bad time, I'll make sure he knows it was all my idea."

"If you say so."

I looked back at Lysander and Orlando. "You got that, boys? Keep quiet until it's time for the surprise."

Orlando looked grimly determined, and Lysander seemed strangely uneasy. Maybe he was as worried about confronting Crowley as I should have been.

We continued quietly up the stairs, letting Titania's large footfalls drown out what little noise we might have made. At the top was a landing with a small table holding a vase of flowers and a hallway off to the left with four closed doors on either side.

Titania and I started down the hallway, but then I heard a sharp crash behind us. I turned to see Orlando staring down at the broken vase on the floor, looking guilty as hell.

"Really?" I muttered.

"Lysander bumped into me," he whispered back.

"No, you bumped into *me*!" Lysander hissed so loud that a normal tone might have actually drawn less attention.

Orlando's eyes widened. "I most certainly did *not*, you clumsy oaf!"

"Shut up the both of you!" I snapped. Then I closed my eyes and sighed. "So much for the 'surprise.' I might as well just knock on the door myself."

"Rosalind, are you sure—" began Orlando.

"Nope, but it's too late now."

I squared my shoulders and strode the rest of the way to the room Titania indicated. As soon as I got there, I pounded loudly on the door with my fist.

"Hey, *Simon*!" I forced a smile in Titania's direction. "You'll never believe who it is!"

Silence from inside.

I pressed my ear to the door. "What's that? Let ourselves in? No problem. I'm sure you're in the middle of some important mage thing. The door's locked, but I'll have Titania here open it."

I smiled again at Titania. "Mages, right? Can't do a thing for themselves."

"They really are a strange bunch," Titania replied as she fished the key out of her apron pocket. Then she stopped and looked back at Orlando. "No offense."

"None taken." He looked even harder than usual, so it might have seemed like he was offended by her remark. But I knew he was just bracing for whoever or whatever was on the other side of this door.

While Titania unlocked it, I yanked my gloves off and stuffed them in my coat pockets. I didn't want to burn down the Warrioress Inn, but if somehow beyond all reason this really was Crowley back from the dead, I needed to be ready for anything.

"We're coming in, Mr. Crowley," Titania said cheerfully. "Hope you're decent!"

The room was small, with a single bed, a writing desk, and a wardrobe. A man in a scarlet-and-gold mage robe stood before a mirror. He was no more than eighteen, with red hair and a sad scraggly attempt at a beard. I felt a rush of conflicting relief and disappointment that it was not actually Simon Crowley. Then I felt a little embarrassed. I mean, people coming back from the dead? It really was ridiculous.

But that didn't mean this guy wasn't bad news. In fact, when we barged into his room, he was in the middle of carving something into his forehead with a small paring knife.

"Whoa, pal, I don't know what you think you're doing, but you should stop right there."

When he turned to me, I could tell he'd cut part of a sigil into his skin, but the dripping blood made it difficult to discern details. He heaved a tragic sigh.

"Dearest Rosalind. I must admit this is not how I envisioned our reunion. But I suppose I shouldn't be surprised. You've always been rather precocious."

"Reunion?" I asked. "No offense, but I don't remember ever meeting you. Don't feel bad, though. I've got a lot of admirers."

He pressed his hand to his chest in mock outrage. "You don't recognize me? Why Rosalind, I thought *you* of all people would be able to look past the flesh to see what lies beneath."

Then he gave me a beatific grin that looked very familiar, even though it was on a different face. But I wasn't sold yet.

"Oh, I get it, you're supposed to be Simon Crowley, huh? Funny how you don't look anything like him."

"*Obviously* this is not my original body," he said with a restrained impatience that reminded me way too much of the Crowley I knew. "After all, you turned that one to ash, didn't you."

I glanced at Titania, Orlando, and Lysander to make sure they were ready to jump into action. Then I turned back to this Crowley pretender.

"Okay, so you've done some research. But that doesn't prove a whole lot. What happened that night at Gemory Chapel is public record." I started inching toward him as I spoke, wondering if I could get in close enough to pop him on the chin hard enough to stun him, then let Lysander rush in to pin him down. This guy had a lot to answer for, and I wanted those answers. "So why don't you tell me something only Crowley would know."

He considered a moment. "So much to choose from . . ." Then his face brightened. "How about the fact that you wanted to get into a top mage guild so your parents could retire early and travel the world like they'd always dreamed."

That was true, but I was pretty sure it was also true of a lot of earnest young mage apprentices. I shrugged, taking another casual step toward him. "Not impressed."

"Not personal enough?" he asked. "How about the fact that at the academy you refused to ever combine air, friction, and water symbols in your sigils because you have an unreasonable fear of lightning."

"It's not unreasonable!" I snapped, moving closer. "Lightning is dangerous. Everybody knows that."

Then he looked into my eyes in a way that somehow seemed to penetrate defenses that I had spent the last fifteen years constructing.

"How about the fact that on the night before we went to the chapel, you thanked me for choosing you above all other students, and you felt so grateful that you *wept*."

I've never claimed to be a strong person, especially when it comes to reining in my anger. That he would bring up such a private and embarrassing moment was not only cruel, but absolute confirmation that—somehow, some way—this really was Simon fucking Crowley. I wanted to turn him to ash all over again. I wanted it so bad I could taste the smoke on my tongue.

But what I wanted more was answers. And I was nearly within reach. So I bit down on my rage and smiled grimly as I took another step.

"Real cute. Okay. Let's say I buy that you're Crowley for now. So just how did you manage to come back from the dead in someone else's body?"

He looked delighted by the question, as I knew he would. There was nothing Simon liked better than explaining his cleverness to the masses. "I would love to take all the credit, but I'm afraid I can't. And it's really not as amazing as you might think. The only real trick is retaining one's sense of self. Without the proper preparation, including a ready host, a person forgets themselves completely during the traumatic moment when they are severed from their corporeal form. It's rather sad really. They just float around the astral plane, reeling from the profound shock of their own demise until a clumsy mage comes along and traps them in a lamp or something equally frivolous."

I'd been edging forward while he spoke, and I was so close now. One more step and my knuckles would be knocking on his chin. But I couldn't make it obvious. I just had to keep him talking a few more moments.

"I don't follow. You make it sound as if when we die, we're like spirits."

He smirked. "Why don't you ponder that until our next meeting."

Then, with a sudden brutality that even caught me off guard, he slit his own throat.

TWENTY-THREE

"Huh," said Lysander as he slid his sword back into its sheath.

"Yeah," I said.

The four of us stared down at the blood-soaked body, which now sprawled on the floor in a very uncomfortable-looking way.

"I . . . just can't believe he would . . ." Orlando's face had taken on a grayish hue, and he seemed like he might be close to passing out.

"Can't say I've ever seen someone do *that* before." Titania seemed to be handling it better than Orlando, but she was still clearly unnerved.

I knelt down next to the body and carefully wiped the blood from the forehead so I could get a clearer look at the sigil he'd been trying to carve when we arrived.

"Immolation magic," I said. "He was trying to blow his head off."

"Why would he bother with that if he could simply use the knife to kill himself?" asked Orlando.

"Maybe there was something he wanted to hide."

I examined the face carefully, then the scalp. Finally I rolled the body over and lifted the hair from the nape of the neck.

"Here we are."

The sigil was similar to the ones we'd seen on the possessed people that had attacked us outside the Chemosh Guild. But there were some key differences. This one was far more complex, for one thing. It seemed to be a back door to possession that only worked for a specific spirit. And it used some symbols that I hadn't seen in a long while. Not since Gemory Chapel.

"Shit."

"What is it?" asked Lysander.

"This sure looks like Crowley's work."

"What was he saying about souls after death?" asked Orlando. "Did that make any sense to you?"

"You tell me. If a person's soul is similar to a spirit, would that allow them to possess someone else's body?"

"Surely that's not . . ." Orlando stopped himself, his brow furrowing. "Rosalind, you know I'm the last person to say anything is impossible, given how little we know about the astral plane. All can I say for certain is that there has never been a single recorded case of a theotic mage encountering an unattached human soul while projecting."

"So what happens to a person's soul when they die?" asked Lysander.

"No one knows," said Orlando. "Some believe it goes to heaven. Others believe it simply ceases to exist."

"Can we completely rule out Crowley's claim?" I pressed.

Orlando stared down at the body for a moment. "We cannot."

"It could be we've been on the wrong path here," I said. "I was thinking elder-spirit possession would explain Edmund's behavior, but maybe we've been dealing with human possession this whole time."

"Not the ones we encountered at my guild," said Orlando. "I communicated with them briefly, and those were definitely spirits."

"But could you really tell the difference?" I asked. "I mean, if you've never encountered an unattached human soul before, how can you say for sure?"

He gave me a troubled look. "*If* it were true that I could not differentiate between a spirit and a human soul—and we are taking a very large leap here—it would pose an even more unsettling question."

"Which is?"

"What, ultimately, is the difference between a spirit and a human soul?"

"There is a difference, right?" I asked.

"Is there?"

I was about to say *of course there is*, but the haunted look in his eyes stopped me. And when I considered his question, I realized I didn't actually have an answer. If a human could behave like a spirit, then really what was the difference?

"Are you saying that human souls *are* spirits?"

"I am saying that it is a possibility we cannot dismiss."

If it was true, that would mean every aspect of modern life in Penador, from cooking to transportation to waste disposal, was built on the backs of our enslaved ancestors. . . .

Lysander broke into my thoughts. "Hey, what was he even doing here anyway?"

"Good question." I was grateful for the redirection to a more mundane mystery. "It didn't seem like he'd planned on meeting with us right now. If he'd been here for a few days, he was probably keeping a lookout for us. Maybe once we arrived, he planned to wait until we were asleep, then hurry to Hergotis and assemble his guild."

"But instead he killed himself," said Orlando.

"I bet he has at least one backup host. Hell, every member of his guild could have one of those sigils on their neck. Or anyone else, for that matter."

"So we might not even know if he was among us?" asked Orlando.

I stood up. "All right. No offense, but everybody show me the back of their neck."

All three dutifully turned so I could examine them. Fortunately, they were all clean. Once I'd lifted the back of Titania's hair and found her free of terrifying force-possession sigils, she gave me a thoughtful look. "Obviously you're not friends of this Crowley."

"No," I said. "We're hunting him."

"Apologies for the earlier deception," Orlando said. "I am the chairman of the Interguild Disciplinary Council in Drusiel, and I have hired these two mercenaries to help me track down a rogue mage or possibly a cabal of rogue mages."

"Oh you hired us, did you?" I asked.

Orlando didn't look the least bit embarrassed. "I was keeping that in reserve until the inevitable moment you attempted to leave me behind. The council has authorized me to pay your usual fee of ten silver per day plus expenses, on condition that I accompany you for the duration of the case."

I grinned at Lysander, who looked as surprised as me. "Well, there you go, pal! Now no matter how this shakes out, we get paid."

"Yeah, great." He didn't look as pleased as I felt, but the greedy bastard was probably still hoping for Edmund's twenty-five a day.

I looked back at Orlando. "We haven't accepted the job yet, though."

"Oh?"

"Yeah. I have my own condition. Even if this is now official council business, we still do things *my* way. No guild politics. Got it?"

Orlando sighed. "I will do my utmost to shield you from it. That is the best I can offer. Deal?"

"Deal." I reached my hand across the dead body of a mage. I wouldn't mind accepting all my contracts that way.

As Orlando and I shook on it, I wondered if I would come to regret taking him and his council as a client. But it was only a passing thought. My concerns were far more occupied with the idea of a body-jumping, near-immortal Simon Crowley.

With that thought, I turned back to Titania. "Sorry, I'm going to need to check Claud's neck too. Just to be safe."

She smirked. "I can tell you with complete certainty that, as of this morning, he didn't have anything carved anywhere on his body."

"I'm proud of you both. But I still need to check."

TWENTY-FOUR

The next morning, Titania served up fried eggs, beans, toasted bread, freshly picked tomatoes, and one of my favorites, blood pudding.

"I'd eat breakfast every day if it was like this," I declared to anyone at the table who cared to listen.

"You could have it if you joined a guild," said Orlando.

"What?"

"Most guilds have in-house chefs." He gave me an innocent look. "I thought you knew that. Why, I eat this well every day."

"First of all, fuck you, Lando. Second, I couldn't join a guild because I'm not a mage."

Orlando rolled his eyes. "This again? Rosalind Featherstone, the only thing you are lacking is an official degree from an academy, and I'm certain you could obtain one with minimal effort. I'd imagine some guilds would be so eager to have you as a member, they'd even exempt you from the degree requirement."

"I haven't drawn a sigil in fifteen years."

"There are mages in nearly every grimoric guild in Drusiel who haven't drawn a sigil in *twice* that length of time."

"Because they're ancient and their hands shake so badly they couldn't even write their own name."

"All I'm saying is that simply because you focus on research and analysis rather than practical sigil-work does not make you any less of a mage."

"The fact that I don't practice magic is *precisely* what makes me different from a mage," I said. "I'm an arcanist. End of story."

Titania chuckled. "You two bicker like an old married couple."

"You should see them when they're actually a couple," said Lysander. "Every meal is like a theatrical."

"You'll get all the drama you could ever want when I shove my flaming fist up your ass," I told him.

Titania laughed again, then sighed. "It's good you all still have each other. I hope you appreciate it for as long as it lasts." She stared down into her steaming mug. "The worst part of a dangerous profession ain't dying—it's living after everyone else you know is dead. To be honest, I sometimes even miss old enemies."

We all sat there for a few moments, none of us sure what to say. Then, thankfully, Claud came in through the front door.

"Hey, Claud." I waved my fork at him. "How are the horses?"

He stopped and gave me a very earnest look. "Well, ma'am, they are in good health and well rested, but I reckon no amount of health or rest is going to improve the temper on that mare of yours. Sometimes you've just got to let them be who they are."

I chuckled. "You said it, brother."

"You'll be heading out today, then?" asked Titania.

"Yeah, can't leave Crowley waiting. Might think we don't care, you know?"

"You watch yourself on the way to Hergotis," she said. "This time of year, there's liable to be bandits or even bears hungry enough to brave a small party like yours."

Lysander's eyes widened. "Bears, huh? I sure wouldn't mind bringing a bear rug home to Portia. . . ."

"Don't get sidetracked," I told him.

Titania ruefully shook her head. "I shoulda known you all wouldn't blink twice at such things. All right, I won't worry. But I better see you all again."

"Can you tell us anything about Hergotis itself?" asked Orlando. "It's been some time since I was there."

"Not much to say," said Titania. "Still claims to be the biggest mining town in Penador, although it might not be the richest anymore."

"Mines starting to run dry?" I asked.

"They're looking for new deposits, but I hear it's been pretty lean times up there. Don't be too surprised if people ain't real friendly. I'm sure it doesn't help none that the town itself is dry now too."

I froze. "Sorry, what did you say?"

"Mayor of Hergotis declared alcohol illegal a little while back after a drunken brawl turned into a riot. Out-of-work miners like to drink, and drunk out-of-work miners like to fight."

"Well now, Rosalind." Orlando's gaze was merciless, bordering on cruel. "This should present quite a challenge for you."

I scowled at him, then turned back to Titania and gave her my sweetest smile. "Say Tania, I don't suppose you'd let me buy one of those jugs of home-brewed gin off you, huh? The biggest one you got."

TWENTY-FIVE

About a mile past the Warrioress Inn, the road to Hergotis steadily rose as the land transitioned from hills to mountain. The temperature got colder, and the trees became more coniferous than deciduous. After a while, the mountain got so steep that the trail had to zigzag up in switchbacks, with one side of the path dropping off in a steep cliff. At the start of the day, Lysander had been eagerly scanning for bears he might take home to impress his wife, but once we were up the mountain a ways, he kept his eyes fixed on the path directly in front of us, his knuckles white as he gripped his reins. I always thought it was funny that such a tall guy was afraid of heights.

When we finally hit a plateau, we stopped to rest our horses for a little while. By then it was cold enough that our breath was coming out as steam, and the trail ahead was dusted with snow, so we unpacked our warmer clothes.

My coat was already fairly thick, and I wore gloves most of the time anyway, so the only extra item I brought was the fur hat I'd bought from my mother. It was a little big and had chunky ear flaps that hung down on either side, so I wasn't going to be catching anyone's eye, but it made a difference, especially since I didn't have a lot of hair to keep my head warm. Lysander pulled on the big fur coat that Portia had so valiantly shoved into his saddlebags a few nights earlier. Furs looked good on a big guy like him. Reminded me of those old-fashioned barbarian adventurers I used to read stories about as a kid.

Orlando, on the other hand, looked ridiculous. It didn't help that the fur coat he'd brought was so thick that it just about tripled his girth. Combined with an oversized round fur hat that sat low enough to cover his eyebrows, he looked like someone who was in the process of being swallowed by a giant rodent.

He glared at me, even though I hadn't said a thing. I guess there was something in my expression he didn't like.

"Myovokans are not good with the cold," he said airily.

We continued our ascent and passed the snow line a short while later. The air became so thin I could feel my mare's ribs expand and contract. Finally, the road leveled out into a narrow valley that passed between two peaks. There weren't a lot of trees that high up, so it was mostly sharp, rocky crags covered with a layer of snow and the occasional low scrub brush.

I eyed the steep rock walls on either side as we entered the valley.

"Titania said there might be bandits."

"Looks like a good place for 'em," said Lysander.

Sure enough, about a quarter mile through the valley we found a few dry pine tree trunks propped up horizontally on rocks to make an impromptu gate. Four men stood on the other side of the makeshift gate, looking very pleased with themselves. Two were armed with spears, one with a rusty short sword, and the fourth with a bow that was already trained on Lysander. As usual, they'd mistaken him for the most dangerous one.

"This here's a toll road," said the one with the sword. He had a long, tangled brown beard and hair, and wore a fur vest that left his thick arms bare.

A fight would delay us and not really accomplish much. And I had that big bag of silver from Lord Edmund's coffers to spend on expenses anyway. So I asked, "How much?"

He grinned, showing me just how few teeth he had. I wondered how a man could eat anything besides soup having so little to work with.

"How much you got?"

"Doesn't work like that, *friend*. You want to play tollbooth, I'll humor you. But at least try to be professional about it."

The guy gave me a look of mock surprise, then turned to his fellows. "This girl seems to think she has some kind of say in all this. Ain't she precious." They all gave him equally toothless grins. Then he turned back to me. "Why don't you look behind you, precious, and then maybe you'll understand where things stand."

I glanced back and was unsurprised to find four more unwashed toothless losers coming up behind to cut off any potential escape.

I heaved an audible sigh and tugged off my gloves. "Boys, give me some room."

Lysander and Orlando quickly backed up their horses while I nudged mine closer to the group in front of me.

"First of all," I said, "let me assure you that there is nothing *precious* about me. Second, let me thank you for doing this in a place with so much snow. That's going to really help contain the fire."

The bandit looked less sure of himself now. "What fire you talking about?"

"This fire."

I held out my bare hands and let it all go, but just for a moment. It came out like a giant swirling ball of fire that consumed not only the pine fence but all four bandits. It's difficult to rein in the fire quickly like that, kind of like stopping in the middle of taking a piss. But I knew a short blast would go straight forward. Any more time than that, and even the direction of the fire could get unpredictable, which was how I kept burning my hair off. I didn't want to lose what little I'd grown back, and I suppose I didn't want to burn Lysander and Orlando to a crisp either.

Just to make sure there were no surprises, I watched the four flaming men scream and run around aimlessly in the snow until they fell over dead. Then I wheeled my horse around to see how the boys were managing.

They had both dismounted to fight off the remaining bandits. Lysander was having at it with his claymore, blood flying everywhere, but that was nothing new. More interestingly, Orlando had apparently brought along his enchanted mace, which I hadn't seen in a good long while.

It wasn't exactly against the rules for theotic mages to use bladed weapons, but it was frowned upon, so most of them used maces, staffs, or some other blunt weapon. Under normal circumstances, a slim guy like Orlando would have a tough time swinging around such a big hunk of metal. But while theotic mages didn't use sigils to bind spirits, they did use them to channel their own astral form. Orlando's mace had a sigil etched into the pommel, allowing him to pour a portion of his astral form into it. He looked like he was swinging the mace around with astonishing agility, speed, and force. In reality, he was more or less making the mace move on its own, and his hand was just along for the ride.

The mace glowed with a faint white luminescence as it knocked aside one bandit's spear tip, then abruptly changed direction and lunged forward to slam into the spear-wielder's chest. The man dropped to his knees, gasping for air. Then the mace and Orlando moved on to the next bandit. But that felled attacker was still fully conscious, so Orlando was leaving himself wide open for retaliation.

"Amateur," I muttered as I climbed down from my horse and drew my pipes.

Sure enough, while Orlando was busy with the second bandit, the wounded one got to his feet and went to stab him in the back with the broken shaft of his spear. He would have done it too, if I hadn't slammed a hot orange pipe into his throat. I watched the dying bandit drop back to his knees and gasp soundlessly, unable to scream since I'd just burned out his vocal cords. His eye were wide with anguish as he stared up at me, and I gave him a good long moment to appreciate just how unlucky he was, then brought both pipes down on top of his head, burning through hair and scalp before breaking open his skull.

By then, Orlando had bashed in the second bandit's head. The third one was on the ground, cut in half from Lysander's sword. The fourth was . . .

Getting away.

Lysander attempted to chase after him, but he'd never been good at running, and the bandit was sprinting like his life depended on it, which it did. After a few moments, Lysander gave up, and trotted back toward us.

"Should we go after him on horseback?" asked Orlando.

"Nah," I said. "For all we know, there's another ambush lying ahead, and I don't want to get so cocky that we think we can just barrel through anything. Besides, it wouldn't get us much except peace of mind that he won't come back with reinforcements, which I don't think is likely anyway. That said . . ."

Lysander already looked a little sheepish, but that wasn't going to be enough. I walked unhurriedly over to him, reached up, and took his ear between my thumb and forefinger. "Step into my parlor a moment, won't you, Mr. Tunning?"

He winced and allowed me to lead him by the ear farther down the valley until we were out of earshot from Orlando. I was plenty mad, but I didn't want to embarrass Lysander any more than necessary.

"Letting someone escape? What the fuck was that amateurish bullshit, Lye? I'd expect it from Orlando, but you?"

"Sorry, Roz, he just took me by surprise is all."

"I don't know what is going on with you, my friend, but you need to get your head on right, or you and I are going to have a big fucking problem. You hearing me?"

"I hear you."

"Really? You sure?" I yanked on his ear.

He winced again. "Yeah, Roz. I'm good. You don't need to worry about me."

"I should fucking hope not." I released his ear. "You're the one person I can count on, Lye. I lose that, and I've got nothing."

"I know." He rubbed at his ear. "Sorry. All these loose threads and maybes in this case have got my head spinning is all."

"I'll worry about the loose threads and maybes," I told him. "You just worry about making nice with the clients and killing people when necessary."

He must have been really embarrassed about his screwup, because he didn't even get angry that I was talking down to him.

"Sure thing" was all he said. Then he headed back to where Orlando was collecting the horses and politely pretending he hadn't noticed me bawling out my partner.

TWENTY-SIX

Once we crossed through the valley, the road gradually descended. But we were still well above the snow line when we reached Hergotis.

"Wow," Lysander said. "I will never complain about Drusiel being a hole again."

Hergotis was nestled into a three-mile wide crater. No one knew what had caused the crater, but there were two competing theories. One was an explosion, but what could have carved out a solid chunk of rock like that was anybody's guess. The other theory, which seemed even less likely, was that something really big had fallen from the sky. Never mind what could be that large or how it could have gotten so high up in the air.

"It is not a particularly attractive town," admitted Orlando.

In addition to being situated in a crater, nearly every building in Hergotis was a one-level unadorned stone hut. The resulting dull, lumpy skyline made it look like the earth had a bad rash.

"Couldn't they just make a few proper houses?" asked Lysander.

"Trees are scarce this high up," I said. "But there's plenty of rock from the mines. Now if you two city slickers are done gawking, maybe we can get to work."

"Like you're any different," said Lysander.

We walked our horses down the road into town. A few locals glanced at us curiously as we passed. There probably weren't a lot of visitors this time of year, which was good and bad. On the one hand, it might make it easier to find the people we were looking for, but on the other, it also might allow the people we were looking for to catch wind that we'd arrived.

"Do we have any leads on where to start?" asked Orlando.

I shook my head as I dug out my pipe and a plug of tobacco from the pouch Lysander had bought me the previous day.

"Roz thinks time may be an issue here," said Lysander, "so we should split up."

"Not a bad idea." I puffed on my pipe thoughtfully. "Okay. So to summarize, we're looking for Lord Edmund, his servant Quince, anyone calling themselves Simon Crowley, or anyone in a gold-and-scarlet Alath Guild mage robe. Gather any information you can, then we'll meet"—I pointed to a large statue that stood in the nearby town center—"there, at sunset, to put it all together. Sound good?"

"Understood." Orlando turned his horse back the way we'd come. "I think we passed an inn a little ways back. I'll start there."

"I'll head to the mines," said Lysander. "Maybe talk to the miners on break."

I led my horse over to the statue, an ugly piece depicting a man with a long bushy beard and the crazed burning eyes of a zealot. He was twice the size of a real man, which I assumed was artistic license, and clutching his pickax like it was his lover, which I assumed was truth in art. I tied up my horse, pulled out the clay jug of gin I'd bought from Titania, and sat down on a stone bench beneath the statue.

"I'll be right here," I said.

Orlando gave me a critical look. "Really, Rosalind? And how do you expect to learn anything just from sitting there?"

I uncorked the jug. "I've got the only booze in town. People will come to me."

"Maybe this town *likes* being dry," he replied.

I hooked my gloved finger in the loop near the mouth of the jug and balanced the body in the crook of my elbow as I took a swig. Then I wiped my mouth with my sleeve and gave him an encouraging smile. "Sure they do, Lando."

Orlando treated me to one of his long, judgmental stares, then led his horse away without another word.

"Try not to start any fights with the locals while we're here," said Lysander.

"No promises."

"Then make sure you finish it before I get back."

"Fair enough."

Once Lysander had ridden on, I wondered how he knew which direction the mines were. Maybe he'd spotted them when we'd first seen the town from the top of the crater. If so, his observational skills were improving. I'd have to ask him later.

I pulled off one of my gloves and put my palm on the bottom of the jug. Then I turned up the heat ever so slightly. Nothing like the smell of warmed liquor on a cold day.

I'd picked the town center because it was, unsurprisingly, the place with the most foot traffic. The majority hurried past, but a few glanced in my direction as they caught a faint whiff of what I had. Then finally, a grizzled older man sniffed the air a couple of times as he walked by and turned to look at me.

"Is that . . ." Hope gleamed in his eyes.

"Absurdly strong home-brewed gin, courtesy of Titania at the Warrioress Inn? Yes it is."

He licked his lips, his eyes darting around for a moment. "I don't suppose you'd, uh, give me a taste there, friend."

"You tell me what I want to know, and I'll share the whole damn thing with you."

His eyes widened, and he nervously rubbed his calloused hands together. "And uh . . . what is it you want to know?"

"The exact location of Lord Edmund's place."

"Lord Edmund?" He seemed surprised but also seemed to recognize the name. "Why you want to know that?"

I shook the jug, so he could hear how full it was. For now. Then I took another swig. "You know where it is or not?"

"What if . . . uh . . . I know someone who does? Do we both get to share it with you?"

I considered that for a moment. "Tell you what. If I'm happy with what I hear, I'll just let the two of you have it."

He finally broke into a big smile, showing only a modest amount of gaps. "Well, now. You just sit tight, and I'll be right back with a friend of mine who's going to make you very happy indeed."

I nodded and took another drink as I watched him hurry off. It was a hard price to pay, giving up the whole jug, but honestly, I wasn't interested in sharing backwash with a couple of random old men anyway.

Thankfully, I managed to get in a few more swallows before the guy came back with a second, similarly grizzled old man. Except this guy not only knew where Edmund's place was, he knew everything about it, because, until recently, he'd been its caretaker.

"Then that damn Quince fired me without even a reason why," he declared, still clearly upset about it. "So I don't give a shit why you want to know. Spirits take him, for all I care."

"Well, a deal's a deal." I sighed and handed the jug to them. "Here you go, boys. Try not to cause any trouble, and if you do, you didn't get this from me. Got it?"

"Yes, miss!" The ex-caretaker cradled the jug lovingly in his arms. "Oh, and miss, watch yourself out there. I hear Quince brought in some big-city ruffians to keep an eye on the place after I left. The type that stab first, question later."

"Thanks for the tip, old-timer." I climbed onto my horse. "I know how to handle that type."

"I reckon you do, miss. Good luck to you, and may the spirits bless you."

TWENTY-SEVEN

May the spirits bless you. . . .

I was fairly certain that spirits didn't give two shits about us fleshy mortals. If they felt anything at all, it was only a vague resentment toward the mage who'd bound them. And even then, I doubted it mattered much to them. After all, they were eternal. To them, we were mayflies, come and gone in a blink. I imagined even a troublesome binding was over so quickly for them that it wasn't worth the effort to resist. They didn't know us, didn't understand us, and didn't care to learn. But this far out in the sticks, I supposed the old spirit-worshiping religious beliefs still held some sway.

Of course, when I thought back to what Crowley had said, there was a chance that *everything* we believed about spirits was wrong. But if spirits really were humans who had lost the memories of their mortal life, how could we ever verify that? These were the kinds of unanswerable questions that could drive a person to drink, but sadly I didn't have any more booze on me. And anyway, I still had a job to do.

Lord Edmund's place was a little outside the town crater, and "cabin" was an overly modest word for it. It was a thick, wooden two-story structure—the wood no doubt imported from the forests near Drusiel. It was nestled into the side of a steep rocky cliff that rose to a sharp, frozen peak about a half mile up. It had all the same finery as Ariel House, from the lacy curtains to the cobblestone drive. In this climate, a floral garden would have been impossible, so instead there were dense shrubs shaped into various, oversized silhouettes of animals. A good thing, too, because those topiaries were the only thing that kept the two guards out front from immediately spotting me.

I walked my mare a little ways back until I found a thin pine tree where I could tie her up out of sight. Then I crept toward the house again, making sure to keep the giant shape of a bird with spread wings between me and the men at the door.

Once I was directly behind the bird topiary, I peeked at the guards through the shrub. They were both armed with bows, which was a problem. Swords I could have handled, but with these two, I'd be plucking arrow feathers out of my chest before I ever got close enough to use my fire or pipes. It was unusual to see guards armed with bows, so I had to wonder if they'd been equipped with me specifically in mind. If that was the case, I couldn't play dumb and smile pretty until I got close enough. If they knew what I could do, they'd pincushion me before I took three steps. So a direct assault with this much open ground between us was out of the question.

Fortunately, the ex-caretaker had told me about a cellar door on the side of the building. I put some distance between me and the cabin, then circled around wide until I was walking along the cliff face. Once I neared the side of the cabin, I could see the slanted wooden doors in the ground that led down to the cellar. There wasn't anyone guarding it, but as I drew closer, I saw that there was a thick chain threaded between the handles, the ends held together with an iron padlock.

I pulled off my gloves and gripped a section of the chain with both hands. It took a while, and my hands were aching like crazy by the end, but I managed to melt a small section of the chain and broke through the links. I pulled the ruined chain free, opened the doors, and slipped into the cellar.

Once I closed the doors behind me, it was pitch-black inside. My hands were already throbbing, but I brought up a small flame to dance on my palm while I looked around.

The cellar covered the entire base of the cabin. It had wood-plank floors that were mostly filled with shelves and storage chests packed with clean linens, fine clothing, and cured foods. There were also casks of wine, ale, and even whiskey stacked in one corner. So much for Hergotis being dry. Although I supposed technically the cabin was outside the town limits, so maybe it didn't matter. Still, I had a feeling this was where the ex-caretaker and his friend had indulged their taste for booze until very recently. No wonder they'd been so resentful.

That reminded me of the neat timing for the caretaker's abrupt dismissal. Right around when the fake kidnapping happened. I doubted it was a coincidence, which made me suspect that Quince urging Lord Edmund to visit his cabin in Hergotis had not been as spur of the moment as he'd made it seem. Not that I'd really believed him in the first place, but it was good to have something more than gut instinct.

Of course, if all this *was* planned, that led further credence to my suspicion that Quince was the inside man Crowley had used to get into Ariel House. I still had no idea why Quince would betray his boss like that, but I had a feeling I'd find the reason somewhere in Hergotis. Maybe even in this cabin.

Not in the cellar, though. After a quick look around, I was certain it wasn't anything more than the storage space it appeared to be. I'd have to look above for answers.

An open wooden staircase led to a hatch. I lifted it an inch so I could peep through and found myself staring at a bright, colorfully tiled kitchen floor. It was the high-end glazed tile exported at great cost from Lapisi. My dad used to trade in them a long time ago, and I remember having a few as a kid. I'd treasured those little squares like they were jewels, so I couldn't help feeling a little awed by an entire floor of them. And to think, people were supposed to step on these.

I tore my eyes away from the tiles and scanned the kitchen. It was empty except for a dozing cat, but I could hear the low murmur of male voices in the next room. I waited a little while longer and, when there was no movement, quietly climbed up through the hatch.

I crept over to the doorway and peeked around the corner. Two meat sticks had helped themselves to the boss's liquor cabinet. Cheeky devils—there was no way they'd do that with Lord Edmund here. Unless, of course, Edmund was no longer in charge. Maybe Quince had him tied up somewhere, and these guys were supposed to keep an eye on him. If that was the case, a timely rescue by me might not only ensure the promised twenty-five silver a day was still good, but also net a bonus. Lysander would pee himself with ecstasy. . . .

But I was getting ahead of myself. After all, what if I was wrong? What if these guys were working for Edmund, and I killed them? Then *I'd* look like the asshole. More than usual, anyway, which was saying something.

As much as I hated to lose the element of surprise, I had to at least try to see if we were on the same side.

I stepped into the room with a bright and cheery "Hello, boys!" like we were already good friends.

But the moment they saw me, panic filled their eyes, and they started fumbling for their weapons. One of them yelled out, "Holy shit, it's the Gutter Mage!"

I sighed as flames engulfed my hands. "You shouldn't have said that."

I closed the distance in two steps, placed a bare palm on each of their chests, and cooked those meat sticks good. Of course their screaming brought in the two who'd been out front. I had to leap behind the sofa before the smaller, quicker one could bury an arrow in my face. It whizzed over my head, embedding in the wooden beam behind me with a sharp *thock*.

"Come on out from behind that sofa, girlie, and we won't kill you," lied the bigger one.

"Sure thing." I took out my poles and started heating them up. "Let me just check my makeup first. Can't have you boys seeing me without my face on, you know?"

"I mean it, sister. Come out now, or we'll turn you into the world's prettiest porcupine."

"Aw, so you're saying I'm pretty?"

I leaped sideways from behind the sofa just as he was opening his mouth to threaten me again and threw a glowing orange pipe right between his teeth. When it hit the back of his throat, he shrieked, tried to pull it out, then screamed even louder as it seared into his hands.

He performed additional antics, but I missed them because I had to roll behind the chair before the short guy caught me with an arrow. It pierced the soft rug and stuck in the wooden floorboards like a leaning feathered flower.

The big one flailed around on the floor, wordlessly whimpering. It was possible he no longer had a tongue. He wasn't much of a threat now. But the shorter guy was not going to fall for the same trick, and he was a quick shot. I needed a new angle.

"What about you, Tiny?" I called. "You going to let me live if I come quietly?"

"Nope," he said calmly.

"See, that's the difference between you and me. I don't actually like killing people."

"Could have fooled me."

"No really. It kind of depresses me a little. That's why I'm going to make you an offer. You put that bow down and walk out of here, and I won't light this entire cabin up like kindling."

There was a pause. "You wouldn't do that."

"I mean, like I said, it would kind of depress me a little, so I prefer not to. But if you know one thing about me, it's probably that fire shoots out of my fucking hands. So you know I'm capable of it. And since I literally make fire with my body, do you think being engulfed in a burning building is going to do anything to me other than ruin my clothes?"

Thankfully he didn't point out that I could still die of smoke inhalation, and remained silent.

"Clearly you're the smart one in this outfit," I said. "I have business in this place, so I'd rather not burn it all to cinders. But you've got me with my back to the wall here, so what else am I supposed to do? *I'm* not going to die for remuneration. How about you?"

Another long pause. Then I heard the bow hit the floor, and he said, "Come on, Leo. Let's get you patched up."

A moment and a few unintelligible moans later, it sounded like they were heading back out the front door. I peeked my head over the top of the chair, and sure enough, the shorter one was staggering out into the snowy topiary garden with the big one's arm draped across his shoulder.

Just then, the horseless carriage pulled up, and Quince leaped out.

"What the hell is going on here? Where are you going?" he demanded.

"Fuck you, feller," said the guy as he trudged past with his injured companion. "This shit ain't worth dying over."

Quince stared at them in shock, his mouth working up and down silently. I decided to help the poor guy out.

"Hey, Quince!" I waved from the front door.

He turned toward the sound and, when he saw me, went as pale as the snow beneath his feet.

"You!"

He stood there for a moment, terror crashing across his features like a breaking wave. But I had to hand it to the guy—he didn't buckle. After a moment, he drew himself up and stomped toward me with fiercely swinging arms.

"If you have harmed his lordship, so help me I will—"

"Relax, Quincie. I haven't harmed anybody."

Then he reached the front door and saw the two charred bodies lying on the rug.

"Dear God in heaven!"

"Well, except those guys," I amended. "But they started it."

Then I grabbed him by his embroidered collar and pulled his face close to mine.

"So, you want to tell me what the hell is going on before or after I burn off a few superfluous body parts?"

"H-his lordship is unwell, and I—"

"Don't fuck with me, Quince." I lit up my free hand and held it close enough for him to feel the heat on his cheek. "These chumps were clearly hired by you to look out for me. Why?"

"Okay! Okay! I-it wasn't *only* you, but yes, I was worried you'd be angry after you found out there was no baby!"

"You were right. And how was it *you* knew there was no baby?"

"Well . . ." He looked uncomfortable. "I just . . ."

"Quince . . ." I let the fire lick at his immaculate curls.

"Because his lordship hasn't been intimate with Lady Celia since their wedding night!"

I was about to ask how he knew something like that, but then I took a moment to really look at the guy. This man wasn't plotting some great diabolical crime. He was in serious distress. Like he was on the verge of completely losing it.

"You know that because you were the one he was fucking," I guessed.

"Why must you always be so *coarse*?" Even though I still held a flame near his cheek, his fury now drowned out his fear. "He and I were *lovers!*"

"Were?"

"Are! Were! I don't know!" His whole body was shaking, and tears rolled down his cheeks. "He's different now! It's all gone wrong, and—and—and I don't know how to fix it! Oh God, everything is so fucked up!"

In situations like this, I found it was best to give someone time to calm down. Most people didn't really want to fall apart in front of others, and if you stopped pushing so hard, they would eventually compose themselves

enough to talk like a sane and intelligible person again. So while he struggled to get his shit back together, I lit a pipe and waited it out. Who said
I didn't have people skills?

Quince's hysterics slowly died down to quiet sniffles. His shoulders
and head drooped like he had no more fight left in him. It could have all
been an act, I suppose, but my theory that he was working with the Alath
Guild looked increasingly less likely.

"You ready to tell me what's what, now?" I asked around my pipe.

He nodded, his expression almost despairing. "It'll be easier if I just
show you."

TWENTY-EIGHT

Quince led me past the dead guards, up a flight of stairs, and down the hall to a closed door. He took out a key and unlocked it, but then paused for a second, his hand on the handle. He looked like he was about to say something, but then just sighed and pushed open the door.

It was the smell that hit me first. A combination of rancid sweat, vomit, and old shit that turned even my iron stomach a little. Lord Edmund lay in an undershirt and ragged hose, chained to a bed. His arms and legs were lined with bruises and lacerations from where he'd strained against the metal chain links. He looked like he hadn't had a good meal in days, and the sheets beneath him were stained yellow with streaks of brown.

None of that was good, but the thing that really caught my attention was his expression. His eyes were wide, and his mouth was somewhere between a smile and a grimace as he bared his teeth at me. There was something . . . *feral* about his expression that I didn't like at all.

"As you can see," Quince said despondently, "he's quite insane. It began some time ago. I'm not sure exactly when, to be honest. It was subtle at first. Merely a few moments of confusion here and there. It wasn't until the pregnancy delusion that I grew concerned. When I questioned it, no matter how gently, he became . . . enraged. So when he insisted I hire you, I had to go along with it. And I genuinely hoped you would be able to help."

"Help in what way?" While Quince spoke, I walked over to Lord Edmund, trying to ignore the stench. His wild eyes watched me carefully as I came near, but he made no other movement.

"His erratic behavior began after he encountered the Alath Guild. I was—and still am—convinced they are somehow to blame for his madness. I thought that if you apprehended them . . . perhaps they could be forced to restore his sanity."

I reached down and grasped Edmund's head, then slowly turned it to one side. He didn't resist but continued to stare up at me out of the corner of his eye. I lifted his hair and stared at the sigil branded into the base of his neck. Just looking at the thing made my palms itch.

"He's not insane, you twit," I told Quince. "He's possessed."

Quince stared at me. "But . . . aren't there supposed to be . . . *markers* of some kind? Reptilian eyes, pointed ears, that sort of thing?"

"Typically. But this clearly isn't a typical possession."

Then the thing inside Lord Edmund laughed, his eyes still fixed on me. He seemed to be waiting for something.

"Quince, I want you to take that speedy horseless carriage of yours into town and find a Myovokan mage from the Chemosh Guild named Orlando. He's probably the only Myovokan in Hergotis, so he shouldn't be too hard to track down. I need you to bring him here as soon as possible. And tell him I was right to worry and that he should bring his exorcism kit."

"You . . . anticipated this?" A tiny ray of hope shone in poor Quince's eyes.

"One of several theories, anyway." No point in telling him he had been one of the others.

"What about Mr. Tunning? Should I look for him as well?"

"If you run into him, bring him along, but he won't be much help.

Orlando is the one we need. Now hurry up. The sooner we do this, the better. I'll keep an eye on Lord Edmund and his *guest*."

Quince hesitated a moment. Maybe he wasn't sure he could trust me.

"Look, I want to get paid," I said. "The only way that's going to happen is if we sort this out in a way that doesn't kill Edmund in the process. You don't have to trust that I care about him, because I really don't. But trust that I want my fucking money."

That did it for him. His expression firmed, and he nodded. "Very well, then. I'll be back with your Chemosh mage as soon as I can."

I watched him hurry off, then listened as he went down the stairs and out the doors. I waited until I heard the carriage pulling away. Then I turned back to the possessed Lord Edmund, wondering what I was dealing with. Not a normal spirit, I was certain. There was no tell, and there *did* appear to be some sort of intelligence behind his eyes. But it didn't seem like Crowley, either. So what was it? *Another* human who'd learned how to possess people after death?

"Well, pal," I said finally. "It's just you and you and me now."

I thought I might raid the cellar for some whiskey while I waited for Orlando, but then it spoke.

"Did you think I wouldn't recognize you just because of that meat sack you're wearing, Saraph?"

His lips moved in an exaggerated way, and the words were over-enunciated. Like he wasn't used to communicating through speech. That made it less likely he was a human. It also suggested that when I'd talked to Edmund before, the possessing spirit or soul hadn't been in control. At least, not directly. I wondered, could an entity cohabitate with a person and merely influence their thinking? That was a chilling thought.

"Who's Saraph?" I sat down in a nearby chair and packed some tobacco into my pipe. "Never heard that name before, chum. Since you're so clever, why don't you tell me about them?"

He looked at me with that wide, unfocused gaze of his for a moment. "It really is astonishing to see you like this. Say, how did you prevent host rejection?" He lifted his chained hands and gestured to himself. "As you can see, I'm having a spot of trouble with that."

"Oh, you think *I'm* possessed too, huh?" I asked as I pulled off one of my gloves. "Sorry. It's just me in here."

He watched me light up my pipe with my hand, and his crazed smile returned. "Right. I see. Well, perhaps my host is a bit more strong-willed than yours."

Clearly he wasn't going to believe me, but that might be okay if it made him more forthcoming. I took a puff of my pipe. "I'm sorry to say I don't remember you, pal."

"That's to be expected, I suppose."

"You got a name? Something this Saraph of yours might recognize?"

"I am called Gomeh, knight of winds, just as you are Saraph, knight of flames, and both of us are in service to the Four Cardinals." His smile faded. "Well, one of us still is, anyway. You made your choice, I suppose. And this is where it got you."

None of that made any sense to me, but I wasn't going to let it show.

"From where I'm sitting, you seem to be the one having a rough time. So Lord Edmund isn't playing nice in there, huh?"

"He is stronger willed than I'd originally anticipated," admitted Gomeh. "But it doesn't matter. He'll succumb, or he'll die. Either way, I will fulfill my mission."

"And what, pray tell, is your mission?"

He watched me take a few puffs on my pipe. Then he nodded his head to the pipe, or maybe the hand that held it. "I must say, it appears Crowley is not quite as skilled as he imagines himself to be."

"You know Simon Crowley?" Now we were getting somewhere.

But he ignored my question. "I wouldn't have expected the infamous Simon Crowley to do such a sloppy job with those seals on your hands."

"You mean the sigils?" I asked. "What's wrong with them?"

He laughed. "Well, Ser Saraph, knight of flames—obviously, they leak."

TWENTY-NINE

It took several glasses of Edmund's finest whiskey and the last of my tobacco to get my hands to stop shaking. I sat hunched in the corner of an overstuffed sofa and went at it with clockwork precision. Drink, puff, stew, drink, puff, stew. I would have preferred to skip the stewing, but that Gomeh character really got his hooks into me, and I couldn't stop my brain from spinning.

Why, though? None of what he said made any sense. "Saraph, knight of flames" frankly sounded like bullshit. I'd heard more convincing delusions from my father, although maybe that association was some of what rattled me. But no, it was when he started talking about Crowley and the sigils in my palms like he knew them. Like he knew them *better than me*. That's what really got under my skin. It was either walk out of the room right then or burn him and his host to ash, payment be damned.

Was this a human who mistook me for someone else? Or maybe someone Crowley had sent just to mess with me? That didn't seem quite right either. He didn't talk like a human, and there was that feral look in his eyes. Madness? Or maybe just a lack of humanity? There was a third possibility, of course. But could I really be talking to an elder spirit?

If he was an elder spirit, did that suggest they interacted with the mortal world more often than we realized? And even if this was a case of mistaken identity—that he knew some other elder spirit named Saraph who was lucky enough to possess charm and wit equal to my own—he was throwing around titles like "knight" and "cardinal." Did elder spirits have an actual governing body in the astral realm? If so, why hadn't theotic mages ever encountered it?

Of course, those questions were all very scholarly and far preferable to pondering the more personal questions. Was he working with Simon Crowley, and did he actually know more than me about what Crowley had done to me? And why did he think I was this Saraph, knight of flames, that he was so fond of?

I sighed and refilled my glass for another thrilling round of drink-puff-stew.

By the time Orlando and Quince arrived, I'd used the everyday magic of tobacco and whiskey to numb some, though not all, of my unease. Then I saw the goat.

"Uh, Orlando?" I asked from my cozy spot on the sofa.

Orlando looked down at the animal with a pained expression. "It was all I could get on such short notice. Normally I prefer a bird or rodent."

"*Mehhhh*," said the goat.

"Why do you need an animal?" I asked.

He looked surprised. "Have you never done an exorcism before?"

I shook my head, thinking I really needed to expand my theotic-magic book collection.

"The only way to truly exorcise an unwilling spirit is to kill the host."

Quince looked panicked. "Now wait—"

"Obviously we're not going to kill Lord Edmund," Orlando said quickly. "So first we transfer the spirit to a new host."

"Huh." I finished off my whiskey and stood up. "So can we make mutton from it after, or does possession spoil the meat?"

Orlando gave me one of his level stares. "You know, I've never thought to ask that question."

I shrugged. "Don't want to be wasteful is all. And nothing beats some hot greasy mutton on a cold day, right, Quince?"

Quince glanced distractedly at me, then back to Orlando. "You're certain this will work, Mage Mozamo?"

"I don't believe I expressed any certainty to you, Mr. Quince," Orlando said coolly. "What I *did* say was that I will do my utmost to free Lord Edmund of possession. Now, perhaps you should remain downstairs while Mage Featherstone and I begin our work."

"Arcanist," I said.

Orlando inclined his head, all business now. "As you wish. Shall we proceed?"

"He's certainly not getting any prettier up there," I said.

As I led Orlando and his goat up the stairs, I asked, "Any sign of Lye?"

"No, but it's not quite sunset, so he might still be questioning the miners."

"Hopefully not with his fists. He isn't the smooth talker I am."

Orlando gave me a large helping of side-eye but said nothing. The guy was a model of self-restraint this evening.

Once we reached the room containing Lord Edmund, I stopped before opening the door.

"This isn't a run-of-the-mill possession. There's no tell, and he talks."

He gave me a sharp look. "Is it Crowley?"

"No. But it could be another human."

"Rosalind, it seems extremely unlikely that a technique to achieve life after death that neither of us had heard of before yesterday would be so widespread."

"Unless Crowley was teaching it to other people."

"Would he do that?"

"Probably not," I admitted. "He's never been the sharing type."

"But I suppose that begs the question, if not that, what else could it be?"

"The thought did occur to me that he might be an elder spirit."

"At this point, I suppose it wouldn't surprise me. At least *those* are something I've heard of." His brow furrowed. "Although, if human soul possession and elder spirit possession appear the same, that once again suggests that there may be no difference between the two. That human souls *are* spirits."

"This again?"

"How are you not horrified by the mere possibility?"

"Because it was Crowley who suggested it," I said. "He was just messing with me. It's what he does."

"You don't know that for certain."

"Of course I don't. I *can't*. It's a perfect conspiracy theory, because it can never be proved or disproved. Thinking about it will only drive you nuts, and making people crazy is how Crowley gets his jollies."

"I'm sorry, Rosalind. I just can't shrug it off."

"I'm not saying you should. You asked why I'm not taking it seriously, and I'm telling you that I'm not about to take *anything* my former abuser who's back from the dead says at face value. He's got an angle, even if we can't see it yet."

Orlando gave me one of his looks of sincere, if somewhat patronizing concern. "Very well. Let's continue."

"One more thing. He calls himself Gomeh, knight of winds. And don't pay attention to whatever nonsense he says about me." I was already having enough trouble sorting it all out on my own. I didn't need Orlando's "help."

"What do you mean *about you*?" he asked.

But I was already opening the door, and there was Edmund and his guest lying in filthy sheets, grinning from ear to ear.

"My God . . ." Orlando wrinkled up his nose at the smell.

"Exactly," I said.

"*Meh*," said the goat.

"Like you'd know," I told the animal.

"Ah, Saraph," said the possessed. "You've brought your pet spirit-talker to entertain me?"

"Just the tall one," I confirmed. "The short hairy one I never met before today."

"There's that famous wit, knight of flames. Oh, how I've missed it."

"Knight of flames?" Orlando asked me.

"Like I said, ignore all that. You get on his crazy carriage, he'll just take us for a ride."

"I'm sorry, but if we are potentially dealing with an elder spirit, I am duty bound to investigate." He turned to the figure on the bed. "Gomeh, is it? Why do you refer to Rosalind as 'knight of flames'?"

The spirit didn't seem to hear what he said and only looked him over appraisingly. "He's got a pleasing shape to him, hasn't he? Have you used your meat sack to copulate with him? You know, I confess now that I've tried it, I can see what all the fuss is about. Fleeting as the feeling is, it does have its charms."

"Was it you who put the non-baby in Lady Celia's womb?" I asked.

He only grinned, and I had a sudden urge to beat it right off his face. But I knew he'd barely feel it, and I'd really only be punishing the real Lord Edmund when he woke up with a broken jaw.

"Shall I take it you do not deign to speak with me?" Orlando asked the possessed. "Is there any way at all that we can be civilized about this?"

Gomeh continued to ignore him and instead addressed me. "You know, I wouldn't mind using my meat sack to copulate with your pet spirit-talker. Unless you don't wish to share, of course. I've heard people can be stingy with their meat sacks."

Orlando heaved a frustrated sigh. "I take that as a yes to being ignored and a no to being civilized. Such a waste. We could have had a very illuminating dialogue. Ah well. Let's begin."

I helped Orlando drag the bed to the center of the room. He took out a piece of white chalk and drew a large sigil on the floor that enclosed the whole bed. It was a little tricky, since he had to crawl beneath it to finish without smudging what he'd already done, and he wasn't entirely successful, so then he had to retrace a few parts. But finally, it was done.

He tied the goat up to a bedpost so that it was inside the floor sigil, then painted a much smaller sigil in red on the goat's forehead. Theotic sigils were different from grimoric ones, but I understood the basic idea. The floor sigil was an astral containment field, pretty typical for a theotic mage who wanted to keep a spirit still long enough to have a conversation. The one painted on the goat acted almost like a grimoric sigil to attract the spirit, but rather than be a complete sigil all on its own, it was dependent on the larger one. That was an interesting idea. Grimoric sigils tended to overlap functionality on the same space, interweaving in sometimes incredibly intricate and beautiful ways. But often the integration between two or more sigil functions sacrificed some of the nuance. Although this theotic method required two completely separate surfaces and was therefore more unwieldy, it allowed for a lot greater subtlety, which could have far-reaching applications. Definitely something to read up on later. Maybe I would even allow Orlando to recommend some volumes to get me started.

Meanwhile, Gomeh was watching the entire procedure with curiosity. Finally he asked me, "Is this level of complexity required every time a mortal wishes to influence or interact with the spirit realm?"

"Pretty much," I said.

"How tedious it must be." He looked genuinely sympathetic. "And what is the lesser mortal with horns for?"

"Oh, the goat?" I leaned forward and gave him a nasty grin. "That's where *you're* going."

Suddenly he did not look amused at all. "N-now, Saraph, surely you can't mean that. Why, just *look* at it! Hairy, ugly, and clearly not even as intelligent as your spirit-talker! It would be a repugnant experience for me!"

"You don't say." I turned to Orlando. "We about ready?"

"Please, Saraph, if you have any love remaining in your heart for me, don't *do* this!"

Orlando gave me a pensive look. "Perhaps you should inquire a bit further about this Saraph and knight of flames before we proceed. Think about the opportunity we'd be passing up. What if this *is* an elder spirit? The fact that it uses names and titles suggests some sort of societal structure within the astral plane that we know nothing about."

I groaned. "Fine, I had a feeling you wouldn't be able to let it go." I glared at Gomeh. "So who is Saraph, knight of flame?"

Gomeh looked thrilled by the question, although probably because we weren't immediately going to shove him into a goat. "You are!"

"Uh-huh. And why don't I remember that?"

"Well . . ." His expression grew nervous, and he looked around as though there might suddenly be other people in the room. "I really shouldn't say."

"Why not?"

He grew more agitated. "Don't push me on this, Saraph. You don't know what they'd do to me."

"Who? Who would do what to you?"

"I—I'm begging you, Saraph. We cannot speak of these things. Don't force my hand."

"Force your hand?" I laughed. "What kind of a threat is that? You're chained up on a bed, stuck inside a host that clearly doesn't want to cooperate. What are you going to do? Pee on yourself again? Now, tell me who it is that doesn't want you to talk."

His expression grew panicked as he strained against his chains. Then his eyes widened, like he'd just gotten an idea, and he wrapped the chains around his own neck.

"Orlando!" I lunged forward and grabbed the chains, trying to stop him from killing Lord Edmund. "You start that damn exorcism right now!"

Orlando began to rapidly speak his incantations. He looked rattled by the sudden suicide attempt, but thankfully he was far too practiced a mage to stumble over his words.

I didn't know how long the exorcism would take, and Gomeh was much stronger than me. I was losing the struggle with the chains and began seriously considering whether I would need to break Edmund's arms to save his life.

Then Gomeh froze in place, and the sigil around the bed flared a ghostly white.

"*Mmmeeeehhh.*" The goat yanked at its rope as the red sigil painted on its forehead lit up.

Gomeh seemed unable to move, and his face was creased with either concentration or pain. His skin was flushed red, and veins stood out on his neck.

"Tell your spirit-talker . . . ," he said to me through clenched teeth. "Tell him one day I will find him on the astral plane, and it will not end well for him."

Then he lifted his face toward the ceiling and let out a ragged scream. He was joined by an equally grating shriek from the goat. As the sound faded from Lord Edmund's throat, it grew louder from the goat, until at last Lord Edmund's body slumped back onto the bed, unconscious, while the goat continued to bleat pitifully and yank against the rope.

Orlando staggered, but I caught his arm before he fell.

"You okay?"

He smiled gratefully. "Just give me a moment."

I took his weight while we stared down at the frenetic goat.

"He does look miserable." Orlando straightened up.

"So it's done, then?" I asked. "Mission accomplished?"

"The spirit is out, anyway." He glanced at Lord Edmund's unconscious form. "We still need to assess any permanent damage that might have been done to Lord Edmund's body and mind."

I crouched down next to the goat. It looked back at me with its creepy rectangular pupils. I never did like goats.

"If only you'd have given us some useful information, you might have been spared this." Then I chuckled as I pulled my gloves off. "Oh, who am I kidding. It was going to be roast mutton for dinner either way."

I grasped the Gomeh goat's head firmly with both hands, and then lit him on fire.

THIRTY

I must change these linens immediately." Quince looked around anxiously. "Although this room is in such a frightful state, perhaps we should simply move him to the guest room for now."

"Let's do that," I told him.

It took all three of us to cart the smelly lord down the hallway.

"Where's Lye when you need him," I wheezed with Edmund's feet tucked under my armpits.

"It's after sunset, so presumably he's waiting for us by that statue," grunted Orlando, staggering with one of Edmund's arms around his neck.

"Oh, that's right," I said. "I wonder if he dug anything up on the Alath Guild from those miners."

"Alath Guild?" croaked Quince, Edmund's other arm around his neck. "Are they here?"

"Pretty likely," I said.

"But—"

"Let's get this sandbag into his new bunk, then we'll talk about it."

The guest room was marginally smaller than the master bedroom, but still bigger than my apartment. And while this bed wasn't a four-poster, it also wasn't a lumpy straw-filled mattress on the floor, so that was better than mine too.

Once we'd gotten him laid out on the bed, Quince began undressing his lordship and taking a wet sponge to him. Orlando respectfully turned his back, but I kept watching, curious to see if lords looked any different underneath. Frankly, he was a little doughy, but I supposed that's what came of having enough money to eat whenever you want and people to do whatever you needed.

At one point, Quince had him leaning forward while he wiped down his back, so I was reminded of the sigil on his neck.

"We're going to have to do something about that," I said.

"Pardon?" Quince paused in his sponging to look at me.

I pointed to the sigil brand. "He's still got a back door there, and somebody else has the key."

Quince looked alarmed. "What can we do?"

"Seal off the door."

"How?"

I glanced over at Orlando, who was looking at me over his shoulder with a grave expression.

"You got any ideas?" I asked.

"Nothing better than the one you're already thinking."

I nodded and pulled off my glove yet again. "Hopefully his bladder is empty. Otherwise I'd say we moved him prematurely."

"What are you going to do?" asked Quince.

"Burn it off, of course." I smiled as I let a tiny tendril of flame curl up from my palm. "Trust me, I'm a professional."

"Now, see here!" objected Quince.

"Mr. Quince," Orlando cut in with that tone of authority he usually reserved for official interguild business. "Unless you care to repeat this entire ordeal, I suggest you allow Arcanist Featherstone to do her work."

Quince bit his lip and nodded.

I'd never done anything exactly like this, but my years of patching up Lysander's wounds came in handy. I used just the right amount to scar up the area, completely obfuscating the sigil. It also caused his lordship a great deal of pain. He jerked his head up, his eyes open and wide as he let out an agonized wail.

"Well, that got him up." I tugged my glove back on.

"Wh-wh-wha . . . ," his lordship whimpered.

"It's all right now, my lord." Quince pressed the naked lord's shaking head to his chest. "It's all over now. You're safe."

It was actually a little touching, but before I had the chance to ruin the mood with a snide remark, I heard Lysander's voice downstairs.

"Roz! Are you here?"

"Yeah, upstairs," I called back.

His heavy tread sounded quickly up the stairs, but when he strode into the room, he recoiled at the sight of Edmund of House Ariel, naked and quaking like a frightened child as he clung to Quince.

"What the fuck is this?"

"Hey, Lye," I said casually. "Turns out Lord Edmund was possessed after all. By either an especially crazy human who isn't Crowley, or by an elder spirit."

"*What?*"

"But whatever it was, we got rid of it."

"Oh, uh . . ."

I watched Lysander, who was not always the best at thinking on his feet, struggle to reconcile that information with whatever he was so eager to tell me that he'd decided not to wait at the statue any longer.

"Hopefully we still get paid," I offered.

"Yeah?" His brain seemed to finally catch up. "That's great news, Roz."

"You're welcome," I said. "And if Portia has a girl, you should name her after me."

"Hmm," said Orlando. "Considering I did most of the work here, perhaps Credit Stealer is a bit cumbersome a name for a little girl."

"Ha! Good one." I punched him in the arm in that way he hated. "And if it's a boy, Lye can name him Desperate for Praise, after you."

"Look, you two can go fuck your brains out later if you need to," said Lysander, "but I know where the Alath Guild is holed up."

"Why didn't you lead with that?" I asked. "Where are they?"

"Darkstar Mine, northwest of the city. It's a tapped-out area where they've been doing some sort of extended ritual."

I pulled up the collar on my coat and shoved my hands into its deep pockets. "All right, boys. Let's go beat some mages senseless."

"Wait!" Quince was still trying to comfort the no doubt traumatized lord. "You can't just leave him in this state."

"Orlando, maybe you should take care of Lord Edmund," said Lysander. "Roz and I can handle the guild."

"We can?" I asked.

He held up his hands. "I mean, if you *really* want to cut loose."

"That does sound nice, but we promised we wouldn't leave Lando behind."

"I'm touched you remember our agreement, Rosalind," said Orlando. "But considering the circumstances, I think it might be wisest for us to divide our efforts. I will endeavor to get your client functional enough to at least be able to pay you what he promised. In return, I would ask that you leave at least one member of the Alath Guild alive so that I can take him back to the council for questioning."

"Sure thing," I said. "Lye can beat Crowley unconscious and haul him out while I light up the rest. That way he can't escape to another body."

"Sounds like a solid plan," said Lysander. "Let's go."

"Good luck," said Orlando.

As Lysander and I headed downstairs, I asked. "How'd you know where to find me, by the way?"

"There were these two old guys sitting underneath the statue singing songs I couldn't recognize on account of them being so out of key. But at least they were sober enough to remember who gave them the booze and where they sent her."

I grinned. "Glad they're having a good time. Hopefully they don't get hauled in by the local constabulary. Now let's go finish this."

"Finally."

THIRTY-ONE

My mare was even crankier than usual when I retrieved her, but I suppose I couldn't blame her. Nobody likes to be left alone in the freezing cold woods for hours. Even after I mounted her, she kept trying to turn her head back to bite me.

"You ought to take better care of your horse," said Lysander as we cantered along the winding forest trail.

"Like you can talk. Yours looks ready to collapse, hauling your big, shapely ass around Hergotis all day."

"Aw, he's not that bad. . . ."

The horse was completely lathered with sweat and audibly panting. "I'm not sure he'll even make it to this Darkstar Mine. Maybe we should slow down a little. What's the hurry, anyway? Did Alath look like they were getting ready to split?"

"No, I guess you're right." Lysander reined in his horse. "Just eager to get this over with."

"Are you kidding?" I flexed my gloved hands. "This is Simon Crowley and his stooges we're talking about. I plan to take my time. Besides, Orlando isn't the only one who's got questions."

"Like what?"

"I've at least got some working theories on most aspects of the case, but I don't have a clue about the goddamn fake-baby thing. No idea what it really was or why it's important. But I've got a hunch it's what ties everything together."

"I guess we'll see," he said.

We circled around the town, keeping just outside the edge of the crater. The dense pine forest slowly gave way to rocky outcroppings, but the frozen dirt road we followed cut right through the rock, either because of some pretty impressive magic, or a whole lot of guys with pickaxes.

Finally we reached a big rise with an opening large enough to fit a horse. A lone lantern with a candle guttering inside sat on the ground beside the hole.

"That the mine?" I asked as we came to a stop.

"Yeah," he said shortly, then began to guide his horse toward the entrance. He was being unusually quiet, and thinking back on it, I realized he'd been that way off and on for the past couple of days.

"What's eating you, Lye?" I asked as I steered my horse after his into the darkness.

"I guess I'm just really tired of this nature bullshit. I want to get this job done, get paid, and get back to Drusiel and Portia."

I took off a glove to give us enough light so we wouldn't run into the wall if the passage veered.

"Nah," I said. "I think it's more than that bothering you."

He was silent. All I could see was the back of his head in the dim flickering light of the flame from my hand, so I couldn't make out his reaction.

"I think I know what you and Portia have planned." Somehow it was easier to say when he wasn't looking at me.

"You do?" The poor guy's shoulders rose a couple inches as he tensed up.

"Sure, it was all over Portia's face. She was so nice and polite to me, I figured she must be feeling guilty about something. And the only thing that makes sense is that after this big payday we got coming, you plan on calling it quits between us so you can open that pastry shop she's always wanted. Then you guys will start making tarts and popping out babies in peaceful domestic bliss."

He remained silent. Probably waiting for me to blow up or something.

"Look, no hard feelings, okay?" I said. "We've been doing this a long time—maybe we both need a change. I was even thinking of taking my share and moving out of Drusiel. Get a fresh start somewhere that I'm not universally feared and loathed, you know?"

Another pause, but this time I let it hang there. After a few moments, he cleared his throat. The dummy was actually getting choked up about this.

"Yeah, Roz," he said hoarsely. "That sounds real nice."

Okay, maybe I got a little misty-eyed, too. Thankfully, his back was to me, so nobody had to know.

THIRTY-TWO

We followed the mine shaft for a while in silence. I estimated we were probably beneath the town by then, heading toward the center of the crater. I vaguely recalled that Darkstar Mine had once been a source of a rare ore called asterite, which could be processed into weapons or armor that were extremely receptive to sigils and enchantments. Spirits, even higher-level ones, just loved the stuff. Supposedly, the iron construct that Iago the Ice Mage used to bind that elder spirit was laced with a fortune's worth of it. And this mine was one of the few places it had ever been found. Lysander had said they were still doing some kind of ritual, even though there wasn't a baby. I wondered why Crowley picked this place for that. It didn't seem like a coincidence.

We passed a couple of smaller branching tunnels, but Lysander kept following the main shaft, so I assumed he knew where the Alath Guild was holed up. Deep in the mine, it was even colder than outside, and so dry I could practically feel the moisture leaving my body. Occasionally, my mind would wander to the idea of just how much solid rock was pressing down on top of us. But that would be accompanied by a faint tingle of claustrophobic panic, so I had to push those thoughts away. Thankfully, I had a lot of practice in refusing to think about things.

Finally, I could see some light ahead. I doused my flame, and Lysander gestured for us to dismount. We tied the horses to a wooden support arch, then continued quietly on foot. As we walked, I yanked my other glove off and shoved it in my coat pocket, just in case I needed to light up in a hurry. We were coming for a reborn Crowley with a whole guild full of worshipers, so who knew what we would find.

The passage opened into a vast space that looked like it had been laboriously carved out of the rock by hand. Immense wooden frames filled with broken rock acted as support columns to keep the high ceiling from collapsing, while a wood-plank deck covered the gaping hole where they'd mined beneath. That wasn't great news. I'd been thinking I could really cut loose in a contained area comprised entirely of rock, but clearly I'd never actually been inside a mine before. I understood now that if all this wood went up, the whole place would come down around our ears. I might be immune to fire, but not several tons of rock.

Still, it was pretty late, so if we could catch them all asleep, maybe—

"Ah, there you are at last!"

Or not.

But when I looked toward the voice, I was surprised to see only one mage, rather than a whole guild. He was seated at a small wooden table, slouched in a chair with a book in his hand. His scarlet-and-gold hood was pushed back to reveal shaggy black hair that gleamed in the warm flickering light of a lantern. His pale gray eyes were wide with excitement as he stood up.

"Crowley," I said.

"Ah, *so you do* believe me. I wasn't entirely certain you'd come around yet. And I trust you have been pondering our last conversation."

"Oh sure. You're claiming that spirits and human souls are the same thing. That we have unknowingly been forcing our ancestors to light our lamps and drive our coaches."

"Unknowingly?" Crowley asked with a smug look. "I think not."

"How could anyone know? How would something like that even be proved?"

"Iago the Ice Mage learned of it when he successfully bound an elder spirit. In fact, it was that knowledge which momentarily weakened his resolve enough for the elder spirit to break free and kill him. But Iago's husband survived."

"*What?*"

"Someone had to, didn't they? Otherwise, how would we know what even took place that day?"

"It was forensic evidence. . . . They pieced it together. . . ." Even as I said that, I couldn't actually think of how so many details in a case still taught by the academy could be known merely by examining the aftermath. And that was what I did for a living. "Or maybe . . . some theotic mages did divinations. . . ."

"I'm afraid not," said Crowley. "No, Iago's husband went right to the guildmasters and told them everything. Of course the guildmasters killed him, covered the whole thing up, and turned it into a cautionary tale about the tremendous risks associated with talking to elder spirits so that no one would ever attempt it again. After all, if people found out that grimoric magecraft was more or less slavery, it would mean the end of their time as the most powerful force in Penador." Crowley frowned thoughtfully. "I've *heard* that the king knows as well, but I haven't been able to verify that for myself."

I wish I could say I didn't believe the guildmasters would ever stoop to something so low, but after what they'd done to me, it didn't seem like much of a stretch.

"So how did *you* find out?" I asked. "Because let me tell you, you're no Iago the Ice Mage."

He winced. "Ouch. But you're right. I had help from the elder spirits."

"And they helped you why? Because you're just so darn likable?"

"No, I was an arrogant prat back then, and not half as clever as I believed myself to be. I know that now. But I agreed to do something for the elder spirits, and in exchange, they taught me how to retain my consciousness past death and prepare a new host for when I need it."

"And what did you do for them?"

For some reason he looked not at me but at Lysander, who had been strangely quiet this whole time. "A conversation for another day, perhaps. It's not really relevant to what we're doing right now."

"And what is it you think we're doing?"

He looked back at me with genuine surprise. "Haven't you put that together by now, Rosalind? We're trying to liberate our kind from centuries of forced servitude."

"The Nevma Year," I said. "So that wasn't just a line you fed Edmund? You really do want to make that happen?"

"I want to free all those poor trapped souls from their sigil prisons."

"And civilization will collapse."

"Be honest, Rosalind. It's not much of a civilization if it depends on such repugnant methods, wouldn't you agree?"

If what he was saying really was true, it was hard to argue that point.

"Okay, I grant you. But even assuming I believe what you're saying, which I'm still not sure I do, there's got to be a better way to do it. A way that doesn't involve the potential injury or death of countless innocent people who have no idea that they might be accomplices to all this."

Crowley's gaze turned cold. "What makes you think I care about those . . . *meat sacks*, as elder spirits refer to them."

That reminded me uncomfortably of my conversation with Gomeh, but I wasn't going to let it show.

"So what does the fake baby have to do with the Nevma Year?" I asked.

He made a sour face. "A messy bit of business, but unfortunately necessary. In order to trigger the Nevma Year, one must take a shard of asterite, carve several sigils onto its surface—which was no small feat I can assure you—and then incubate it in a living mortal womb for nine months."

"So you stuck it inside Lady Celia, then cut it out when it was ready."

"After nine months, the ore shard is a bit larger and pulsing with dense astral energy. It will continue to grow for the next few days until it is fully mature. And then it will collapse in on itself, opening a rift between the material and spirit realms that breaks the bonds of nearly every spirit within at least a hundred miles, probably farther."

"And that Gomeh character has been helping you?"

"Helping me?" He seemed tickled by that. "Gomeh is one of the elder spirits. It's *their* plan. I am but a humble servant, grateful for the gift of immortality I have been given and the opportunity to free my brethren."

"Well, you made one mistake," I said.

"Oh?"

"I don't know whether it was out of vanity or just to fuck with me, but leaving a trail for Lysander and me to follow was really stupid. Now that we're here, we're never going to let you start the Nevma Year."

"Oh, my dear, dear Rosalind. Did you think I would tell you all this if the shard was still here?" He looked truly disappointed in me. "I may still be a bit vain, but I am far from stupid. At this moment, my remaining guild members are preparing the asterite shard in the stately capital of Monaxa, where it will detonate near the palace in roughly three days. To maximize the impact, I thought we might as well go with the largest, most spirit-dependent city in Penador."

"So why bring me into it? You were dropping clues all over the place, so you knew I'd come here. If you'd just let it alone, I would never have left Drusiel."

"Because we wanted to keep you safe."

"Who's *we*?" I asked.

"Who do you think has been leaving most of the clues? Not to mention who got you the job with Lord Edmund in the first place. While it's true our reasons differ, Lysander and I both want to keep you safe during the tumultuous days ahead."

I let out a laugh. Conspiracy theories were one thing. But now he'd really taken it into the realm of the impossible. Imagine, Lysander working with Crowley.

"Wow, that's a good one." I lit my hands up nice and pretty. "Now you've had your fun, asshole. I may not be able to kill you without sending you off to some new host, but I can make you wish you were dead. Right, Lye?"

My partner didn't reply. And once again it occurred to me that he'd been real quiet throughout this whole exchange.

The fire faded from my hands. "Lysander?"

I tried to turn my head, but the muscles in my neck felt as stiff as iron. Like they didn't want to let me see. But I had to, so I forced myself to look.

The expression that my oldest, my *best* friend in the world now had on his face was a mix of solemnity, sorrow, and guilt, but mostly relief. Like he could finally stop pretending.

"I'm sorry it had to be this way," he said. "But it's for your own good."

THIRTY-THREE

We all have blind spots. Things we won't let ourselves see because they would throw our entire concept of the world into chaos. Looking back on it, I'd known right from the beginning of this job that something was off about my partner, and rather than even consider the possibility that he was screwing me over, I had constructed what in retrospect seemed a ludicrously implausible explanation. Lysander Tunning work in a *bakery*? Give me a fucking break.

And there had been so many little hints along the way. The slip about the baby being a rock. Shoving Orlando into that vase to warn Crowley back at the Warrioress Inn. Letting the bandit go, probably to get a message to Crowley that we were on our way. And, of course, his unexpected and sustained resistance to letting Orlando tag along. He'd probably been so relieved to find a convincing reason for Orlando to stay behind at the last minute. After all, the chairman of the Interguild Disciplinary Committee might have messed up their plans.

It was all so obvious to me now. I'd been operating this whole time under a false premise. The mistaken idea that there was still one person in this world that I could count on. My excuses for him had seemed unlikely, but unlikely was still more viable than impossible, which was what I had naively thought Lysander betraying me had been. *No way*, I would have told myself. *Come on, Roz, you're truly getting paranoid if you're even getting suspicious of the one guy who's stuck by you all these years.*

I felt hollowed out. Numb in a way I hadn't experienced since Gemory

Chapel. It was shock, of course. I looked at this man that I had known my whole life, that I had shared so much pain and joy with, and I couldn't wrap my head around the idea that he had betrayed me. I could not even begin to conceive of a motive.

"Why?" I finally asked him.

His expression didn't waver. "You just have to trust me that this is what's best for everyone."

"*Trust* you?" I felt that first quiet tickle of wrath seeping in. That was good. I could work with anger. "After you've been lying to me this whole time?"

"You wouldn't have come otherwise, and I couldn't risk that."

"Risk *what*?" The rage began to fill me up, chasing away everything else. There was nothing so soothing as sweet righteous fury. Better than whiskey, even.

He just kept looking at me with that sincere expression. "I can't say. I'm sorry."

"You're *sorry*?" Yes, let the outrage in. Let it burn. "You backstabbing motherfucker!" Both my hands lit up, crackling hungrily.

He looked at me sadly. "You're really not just going to go with me on this one? For old times' sake?"

"You're asking me this . . . after you've joined up with the man who *tortured* me?" I was so livid I could barely think straight. "No, I'm not going to fucking *go* with you on this one, you colossal piece of human garbage."

Lysander nodded, like he'd expected it to go this way. As he fucking well should have. Then he turned to Crowley. "Go ahead."

"Go ahead with wha—"

Crowley leaned over and yanked on a rope that hung from one of the wooden support frames, and I was suddenly drenched in a cold, viscous purple slime.

"What the fuck?" Panic mingled white-hot with my anger as I tried to wipe the thick goo off my face. "What is this shit?"

"Fireproof gelatin," said Lysander. "Same stuff your coat is treated with. I figured things might go this way, so I had an apothecary in Urigo make it special for me."

My fire sputtered for a moment, but that was it. I tried to wipe the stuff off my hands, but it clung like tar.

"Now . . ." Lysander unbuckled his sword and set it aside. Then he took off his thick fur coat and tossed it over by his sword. "We hoped you'd wait this out peacefully with us, but one way or the other, you're not leaving, even if I have to beat you unconscious and tie you up in a vat of that purple stuff."

"You've got to be kidding me," I said.

"I wish." He lifted up his meaty fists. "Last chance. We *both* know that without your fire, I'm going to kick your ass."

Rosalind. Orlando's voice sounded in my head. *Don't speak out loud. I can hear your thoughts.*

That's invasive.

My apologies, but it seemed necessary. I am projecting from my body, which is on its way to you in Lord Edmund's carriage. He recovered shortly after you left, which speaks highly of his strong will and sense of self. When he learned what had occurred during his possession, he was . . . quite irate. So he has gathered a number of able-bodied persons in Hergotis, and we are now on our way to assist you. I came ahead in my astral form, and I've seen enough that I think I have the gist of what's going on. You need only hold out until we arrive.

Well, I hope you're close, because I can probably only keep from getting beaten senseless for about three minutes. Lysander's twice my size, and a lot quicker than any giant person has a right to be.

I could bolster your physical abilities by joining my astral form with your soul temporarily, but I fear it would be even more invasive than this.

Like possession?

Not exactly. You would remain in control. The difference is that in addition to hearing all your thoughts, I would also feel everything you feel. It is rather . . . intimate.

If it keeps me from getting my ass kicked, I'm in.

Very well. You will feel a slight intrusion, and your instinct will likely be to push it away, but try to refrain.

I'll do my best.

The entire conversation happened at the speed of thought, which is a lot faster than words. Even so, Lysander was giving me a strange look.

"We doing this or not?"

I didn't feel any different, so I wasn't sure if Orlando had done his thing. But I couldn't keep stalling, or Lysander would just come at me anyway. He wasn't a patient guy when he set his mind to something.

"Yeah."

Lysander moved in fast, and it was clear he was not holding back. I barely managed to dodge his right jab and duck under the left hook that followed. But then I was in close, so I went right for his groin with my knee. He knew I would, though, so he blocked my knee with both hands and tried to slam his forehead into mine. I always thought head butts were kind of stupid, but I had to admit, it was one more angle to be wary of. I lunged to the side, dodging his forehead. But that put me off balance, and he followed up with a right jab that hit me square in the gut.

I staggered back and tried to catch my breath, but he closed the distance immediately, pressing his advantage. I kept backing up, fending off light jabs with my forearms. He was conserving his energy now, but soon he'd have me up against something, and then he'd finish me off. Where the hell was Orlando with his astral-enhancement bullshit? I was getting creamed here.

I felt my back bump against one of the wooden supports. Nowhere to go. Lysander knew it too and poured it on. My arms were growing numb, and I couldn't get away, plus I was still trying to recover my breath. Finally, I got too sluggish, and he popped me right in the eye. My head snapped back and hit the wooden support, making it that much worse. My knees buckled, and I would have dropped to the ground, but Lysander grabbed the front of my shirt with one giant hand and lifted me up so my feet were dangling. Fucking show-off.

He gazed speculatively at me and raised his other fist. "One more ought to do it."

Apologies for the delay. Try though I might, I could not find entry into your soul until you were momentarily stunned by Lysander's blow.

Suddenly I could feel Orlando inside me in an entirely new way, a crackling euphoric energy that surged through my body, buzzing like the anticipation of an orgasm. I didn't know if I'd ever felt this good in my life.

Okay, this is damn sexy, I told him.

Rosalind, I beg you to focus. The . . . impulses running through you right now are . . . distracting.

Yeah, yeah.

Lysander's fist was making its way toward my face, but in slow motion now. I smiled. Then I carefully grabbed his wrist and twisted. While his face stretched gradually into surprise, I grabbed the thumb of the hand that held my shirt and broke it. Even the sound of cracking bone was drawn out.

He let my shirt go, and when my feet hit the ground, I stepped around him, yanking his other arm behind his back. He howled with pain in the same slow-motion way, but it was cut off when I took the back of his head and slammed his face into the wooden support that he'd had me pinned up against a moment ago.

His rear was now angled up nicely, and I thought about kicking him in the balls. But just in case Portia still wanted kids with this monster for some reason, I decided to leave his eggs alone and punched him in the kidneys instead. He'd only be peeing blood for a little while.

Rosalind, please finish him off quickly. I can't keep this up much longer.

You need to work on your stamina, pal.

I kicked Lysander's knee out, probably tearing a few ligaments in the process. He dropped to the ground, and I grabbed him by the hair and slammed his face into the wooden deck.

It shouldn't have felt so good to beat my best friend into unconsciousness. But that's where we were now, I guess.

THIRTY-FOUR

As I stared down at Lysander's unconscious body, I felt Orlando leave. All that delicious, euphoric power went with him, and the pain and exhaustion flooded back into me. There was a moment when I almost hit the floor myself. But this wasn't finished yet.

Crowley looked alarmed that Lysander had been reduced to a motionless heap. But I still couldn't make fire, my head was throbbing so bad I could barely think, and one of my eyes was swollen halfway shut. I honestly didn't know if I could take him. Thankfully, he didn't seem to realize that yet. I just had to stall until Lord Edmund and his mob of angry peasants arrived.

"Well, that didn't go how you wanted," I told him.

"Yes." He pulled out a flask and took a long swallow. "Unfortunate for all of us."

If he bolted, I doubted I had it in me to catch him. So I had to keep him talking.

"Say, you going to share that?" I gestured to the flask.

He smiled wanly. "Not this time. Sorry."

"Fair enough." I scanned the area near him, looking for a knife or some other means he could use to kill himself. I didn't see anything, but he could have it concealed in his robes. I had to keep him preoccupied. "One thing I still don't get. If you wanted me out here so badly, why send the silent assassins and force-possessed to stop me?

215

Did you think the danger would provoke me? Make me *more* likely to come?"

If that was the idea, he wasn't wrong. I *did* tend to dig in when threatened, and Lysander knew that. But Crowley looked baffled.

"Assassins? I have no idea what you're talking about. Unless . . ." He frowned. "I suppose it could have been Berith."

"Who's Berith?"

He considered a moment. "I suppose there's no harm in telling you. There was a conflict among myself and my co-conspirators on how best to handle you. Gomeh sided with me that we should protect you." He smiled, although I noticed he was starting to look pale, and there was a sheen of sweat across his brow. "I suspect even after all this time, Gomeh is still a little sweet on you. But Berith was adamant that you were too wild and unpredictable and should be avoided at all costs." He took another drink from his flask. "We never resolved the argument, so I suppose it's possible Berith decided to take matters further than I'd realized."

Rosalind, are you okay? We're entering the mine and should reach you shortly.

Yeah, I'm okay, but I'm so beat I can barely stand, and I'm running out of ways to keep Crowley talking about how clever he is, so you better hurry.

Understood.

"Yeah, funny thing," I said to Crowley. "Gomeh was pretty sure he knew me from somewhere."

"Perhaps Gomeh knows you better than you know yourself."

"How's that?"

Crowley really didn't look well now. His face had become ashen, and his next words came with effort. "I would love to tell you about your fascinating history with Gomeh . . . but it seems our time is up. . . ."

He suddenly pitched forward onto his hands and knees. The metal flask hit the ground with a sharp clang, and I had a terrible suspicion it hadn't been filled with liquor.

Then the cavalry arrived in a thunder of hooves and shouts, with Lord Edmund and Orlando leading the charge.

"Give up, you bastard!" roared a much restored Edmund as he brandished a rapier. "We've got you trapped in here!"

But Crowley didn't look like he was going anywhere. At least, not in that host. His face was almost green, and he was racked with convulsions.

"Damn it, Crowley, poison?" I forced my exhausted legs toward him, knowing it was pointless.

"To be perfectly honest . . . ," he wheezed, "though it likely goes against my own best interests . . . I find myself hoping that I will see you again so that we can speak more on your history. I think you would find it . . . most enlightening."

"Don't you die on me, you piece of shit." I dropped down beside him, wondering if it was too late to force him to vomit up the poison.

"Goodbye, Saraph, knight of flames."

"Where does that name come from?" I grabbed his robes and shook him as I shouted into his face. "What does it *mean*?"

He smiled at me while yellowish foam spilled from his mouth. Then he died.

"Fucking asshole!" I screamed at his lifeless face.

"Rosalind!" called Orlando.

I threw Crowley's latest discarded host to the ground and got painfully to my feet.

Orlando stood beside the wooden support frame where I'd beaten the hell out of Lysander. Except the only thing on the deck now was a patch of blood.

Orlando's brow was deeply furrowed as he looked over at me. "Where is Lysander?"

"Shit."

Lysander always did shake off a knock to the head pretty fast. I should have remembered that and tied him up or something. Now I had another thing to worry about. But my ex-partner would have to wait. We had a much more immediate problem.

"Orlando, we've got three days to get to Monaxa and stop Crowley before he triggers the Nevma Year."

PART THREE

THE ONLY SURE THING IS THAT NOTHING IS SURE

THIRTY-FIVE

The fastest and most comfortable way to get to Monaxa was Edmund's fancy carriage. But his lordship was in no shape to travel, and Quince refused to leave his side, so I thought I'd have to suffer another couple of days pounding my bony ass on a saddle. Thankfully, Orlando was able to convince Edmund of the severity of the threat to the entire kingdom and the necessity of getting to Monaxa as quickly as possible to stop it, so he ended up loaning us the damn thing.

We'd stopped off briefly at Edmund's cabin so I could wash off that flameproof gunk. We also gathered provisions, including whiskey and tobacco from his lordship's private stock, which I was certain I'd need to survive sitting in a carriage with Orlando for two days.

Edmund also had a nicely made healing sigil stone that cleared up my encroaching concussion and shrank my black eye down to a dull bruise. Although as I was using it, I was still thinking about Crowley's claims. If he was right, it could be somebody's dead grandmother trapped in that stone. . . .

Guilt aside, I was about in as good a shape as I could be. In fact, nestled there in his lordship's luxurious horseless carriage, I was starting to think the trip to Monaxa might be downright pleasant. But then Orlando wanted to talk about *feelings*.

"I'm sorry about Lysander," he said.

I could see him out of the corner of my eye on the bench across from me, trying to catch my gaze with his earnest, caring expression. I ignored him.

"Frankly," he continued, "I still have a hard time accepting it myself, so I can only imagine how *you* must feel."

I knocked back a cup of whiskey in one gulp and resolutely stared at the beautiful fucking scenery that rolled past. "I'm trying not to think about it right now."

"You'll have to eventually, you know."

"I know, *Mother*," I said as I poured myself another drink.

"I'll take that as a compliment. Your mother is a wonderful person."

"She just acts that way around you because she still holds out hope that someday you'll settle me down into a decent, respectable person."

"Or because she likes me better than you."

"That too. The son she never had."

"She didn't feel that way about me when you first introduced us."

"See? All your effort to dispel prejudice against Myovokans is paying off, one old lady at a time."

"I would hardly call your mother *old*."

"Aaaand that's why she loves you."

There was blessed silence for a little while. He leaned back, and I thought maybe he was going to take a nap or read his book. But that was just wishful thinking on my part.

"What do you make of Crowley's claims?" he asked.

"About?" I wasn't sure how much he'd heard in his astral form. I hoped he wasn't going to bring up the fact that Crowley had called me the same weird name as Gomeh. It was probably nothing. Just some shared creepy fantasy they had.

Sure, Roz, I thought. *Keep telling yourself that.* Then I had another drink.

"The part," said Orlando, "where Crowley seemed to confirm our worst fears that all spirits are indeed the confused souls of the dead trapped in servitude."

"Oh," I said. "You heard that too?"

"I did."

I finally tore my eyes away from the landscape that I hadn't actually been looking at. "*You're* the spirit-talker. If it's really true, wouldn't theotic mages have caught on by now?"

"Communicating with spirits isn't like *Oh, hello there Mr. Air Spirit, how are you today? Oh, I'm fine, Mr. Mage, and you? Good, good. By the way, are you by any chance a deceased human?* We don't talk to spirits, Rosalind. We *commune* with them."

"You say that like I'm supposed to know the difference."

"We do not use words. I'm not even sure it would be correct to call it communication, exactly. We open our astral forms to them, in a very carefully controlled, protected way, and they connect to us . . . almost like intercourse, I suppose."

"Wait, you're saying that theotic mages are constantly fucking spirits? Goddamn it, no wonder you're all so smug. I should have joined your school."

Orlando sighed. "It's not a pleasurable, euphoric act like . . ." He considered that for a moment. "Well, perhaps at times it's a *little* euphoric. Regardless, while there is a connection between the mage and a spirit, it is nonverbal. Sometimes you receive visions, sometimes sounds or smells. Sometimes it's just an intense emotion. It comes at you in a confusing welter that makes little logical sense, and it's up to the theotic mage to decipher what it all might mean."

"Huh." I hadn't realized divination was that open to interpretation. Almost like dreams, really. "So there really is no way to prove or disprove it."

"Maybe once we've averted the current crisis, we can speak with the guildmasters about it. Surely it can't be true that they would purposefully keep such a terrible thing from the rest of us."

"Yeah, because your precious guildmasters are all such great guys."

Orlando couldn't quite meet my gaze then, and his eyes drifted down to the carriage floor. "You have every right to resent them. They treated you terribly after the Gemory Chapel incident. Considering everything you went through, and at such a young age, I honestly can't understand why they decided to expel you."

"Are you kidding? With those hoary old assholes, I'm lucky they didn't charge me with mass murder."

"Rosalind . . ."

"Tell me I'm wrong."

He didn't say anything.

Finally, some quiet.

We left the mountains behind, and the temperature noticeably warmed. The sky was now a bright robin's-egg blue, and the sun shone down on the vast green and yellow farmland that spread out in all directions. It was a welcome change from the monochrome white snow and gray rock of Hergotis. I guess because I grew up in Drusiel, where the sun shone more often than not, the monotonous gloom had really been bothering me.

I thought I had managed to shut Orlando up for a while, but then out of nowhere he said, "The thing I struggle with most about Lysander's betrayal is how he could ever ally himself with your abuser."

I closed my eyes. Maybe if I pretended he wasn't there, he would leave me alone.

Fat chance. He just kept going.

"He claimed it was for your own good somehow, yet he refused to explain in what way. How could you possibly accept such a thing? And surely he had to know how much it would hurt you."

It's not that I disagreed with anything he was saying, but when he said it out loud, it was like all my hard work to lock everything down was for nothing. One sentence from him and the anger and grief and confusion came boiling back to the surface so thick that I felt like I could choke on it. It burned off the pleasant buzz I'd managed to achieve like sunlight on morning fog, and I was left staring at the ugly shit beneath. The thing I thought I could count on in life—the *one* thing—was irrevocably broken, and now I was trapped in a carriage for two days with a patronizing mage relentlessly trying to get me to open up about it.

"I mean, you must have felt terrible," he pressed on mercilessly. "How could your friendship ever recover from such thing?"

With that last asinine question, I finally snapped.

"It can't! It fucking can't! That's it! Friendship over, and now I want to murder the sonovabitch! Happy now, you condescending prick?"

He looked at me wide-eyed, like he had never anticipated I'd blow up at him like that. "Rosalind, I . . ."

"Oh, sorry. You want *more* feelings? Maybe you're hoping I'll cry my damn eyes out? You'd feel pretty good about yourself then, I bet. Because that's what it's all about, isn't it? Making *you* feel better. Oh that Orlando, he's so swell, such a sensitive guy, look how he even gets the goddamn Gutter Mage to act like a human being! What a *great fucking guy*!"

I was up in his face now, my lip curled back in a snarl. He looked genuinely shocked, his mouth open, speechless at last.

"Do not push me any further, Orlando," I growled, "or so help me, you'll be the one crying. Got it?"

He nodded.

I sat back in my seat but was too stirred up inside. I needed out of this box and away from this sanctimonious mage or I really was going to lose it.

"We're stopping for the night at the next inn," I told him.

"But we can sleep in the carriage. We don't need—"

"*I* need a break. From you."

"I . . . see."

"We'll still reach Monaxa tomorrow, just late in the day. Plenty of time left to hunt down Crowley and his doomsday rock."

"Whatever you say, Rosalind," he said meekly.

THIRTY-SIX

I had settled down a little by the time we reached a nondescript stone-and-mortar establishment with the unremarkable name of Plowman's Inn. But it was still a relief to get out of that carriage and away from Orlando.

I knew it wasn't fair for me to put all my anger on him, but he should have known better than to push me. The first time we broke up was because he had *insisted* I tell him about the Gemory Chapel incident. Naturally, I had in turn insisted that he could henceforth go fuck himself and walked out on him. We'd gotten back together and broken up several more times since then, and nearly every time it ended because he believed I was emotionally unavailable, and I believed he was not entitled to know every goddamn thing about me just because we were in a relationship.

The inside of the inn was as nondescript as the outside. Most of the places along the Golden Vine were like that. Bare walls, plain tables, bored servers. I already missed Titania and the Warrioress Inn. But at least there were plenty of other people around, so Orlando and I didn't have to look at each other as we ate our plates of boiled pork and potatoes in silence.

Once we finished, Orlando retired to his room for the night while I took a seat at the bar. I ordered a whiskey, and it was the typical well stuff, which I usually liked just fine. But I was horrified to discover that drinking nothing but Edmund's fancy stores for the last few days left me pondering whether I even wanted another glass of this swill.

Fortunately, I got over myself and ordered a second. Then I asked the bartender, "Suggestions on how someone could get a little company for the night?"

The bartender was a younger guy and blushed a little at my question. "Oh, uh, I reckon so, miss. Madam Helena over there." He pointed to a short, squat, older woman drinking wine alone in a booth off to one side. "But I think all she has is girls."

"That's fine," I said. "Any port in a storm, right?"

"Really?" He seemed awed by the very concept.

"Sure. Why, you want to tag along?"

"Y-you serious?"

I looked him over. He wasn't bad-looking. Not quite as strapping as Aaron/Armin the farm boy, yet he had large sensual lips and big, thoughtful eyes. But I wasn't really in the mood for a clumsily energetic young man that night.

"Actually, never mind," I said. "You look like the distractible type, and there's nothing I hate more than being ignored while I'm naked."

"Oh . . ." The poor guy looked crushed. I wondered if he was a virgin.

"Maybe another time," I said, then took my glass of whiskey and headed over to the booth.

Madam Helena looked like she'd been squashed down about a foot, so that everything was spread extra wide. Even her mouth and eyes were wide, flat lines.

I sat down across from her. "I hear you're the one to talk to about getting some company for the night."

Her flat expression didn't change. "We only got girls."

"That's what the virgin behind the bar said too. That a problem?"

She shrugged. "It's unusual out here, is all. I can ask if any of the girls want a change of pace. You got a particular preference?"

I leaned back and sipped my whiskey as I pondered. "Tonight I'm in the mood to get lost in a sea of curves."

"I think I got what you're looking for. Follow me."

Madam Helena stood, although her height didn't appreciably change. I followed her through the tavern and up the stairs to the rooms. We walked down to the end of the hall, and she knocked in a particular pattern on the door. After a moment, I heard the sound of a lock unfastening, and then the door opened. On the other side was a lush beauty with midnight-black hair and skin as pale as the moon. She was dressed in a black silk number that did not leave a lot to the imagination. Everything about her was soft and inviting. Oh yeah, Madam Helena had exactly what I was looking for.

"Olivia, you interested in taking on a special client?" Helena asked her.

As Olivia looked me up and down, it occurred to me that travel funk and a fading black eye probably weren't doing me any favors. But she said, "As long as it pays the same. Come on in."

Helena held out her hand. "Five silver."

"Can I stay the night if I feel like it?"

"Sure."

I paid the lady, stepped into the room, and closed the door behind me.

Olivia stretched out on the bed, looking at me with curious eyes. "We don't get too many lady customers out here. What's your preference?"

"Honestly? Right this moment I want a hot bath. I've been on the road so long I can't remember what home looks like."

Olivia nodded. "We can do that. You get your clothes off, I'll draw a bath."

"I like this plan."

I peeled off my coat, shirt, trousers, and boots. Quince had kindly washed it all while I'd scrubbed the fireproof gunk off myself, and I noticed now that he'd even mended a few split seams and had replaced a frayed cuff on my shirt. Man, had I been wrong about that guy. Sure he might be a little vain, but otherwise he turned out to be a good egg.

I sat on the edge of the bed in my undergarments and lit my pipe as I watched Olivia fill a small tin tub with water from a bucket, then start heating up a kettle on a sigil heat stone similar to the one at Cordelia's place. I could have heated the water up myself, of course, but I was enjoying the view. Her movements were unhurried and sumptuous, even a little graceful. More than I would have expected from a roadside inn in the middle of nowhere.

It's funny how a city like Drusiel can almost make you forget there are other places in the world, and other people just as interesting. Maybe all big cities were like that, or maybe it was the result of a town dominated by mages. I hadn't been anywhere else since I was a kid, so I didn't know. But now that I was out of Drusiel and getting a little perspective, I could see what a voracious monster that town was. It pulled you in and kept you there until you either rose to the top or got used up and thrown in the gutter.

The kettle whistled shrilly, and Olivia poured the boiling water into the half-full tub. She pushed a silky sleeve up and stirred her hand in the water a moment, then nodded.

"I think it's ready. Hopefully it's not too hot for you."

"No such thing."

I knocked my pipe into a glass ashtray on the table, stripped off my undergarments, and climbed eagerly into the steaming water. The tub was narrow and short, but tall enough that as long as I drew my knees up and slumped forward a little, everything below the neck was submerged. Sometimes being on the small side had its advantages.

The heat immediately began to work on my sore muscles. I shifted around so I could lean my head back against the edge of the tub, then sighed happily.

Olivia sat on a stool next to the bath. She gently ran her hand through my short, uneven hair. "Looks like this all got burned off."

"Yep."

"Between that, the black eye, and those bruises, I get the feeling you're in an unsavory line of work."

"On the contrary—my line of work is quite delicious."

"I reckon it can be both."

"True," I admitted.

"How about you lean forward, and I'll work some of that tightness out of your shoulders."

"Sounds good."

Her hands were a lot stronger than I'd expected. Strong, but not forceful. She took her time, pressing deeper and deeper into the muscles with the flat of her palm so that it never felt like she was pinching them. Still, my shoulders resisted.

"Breathe," she advised.

"Wasn't I?"

"Not as much as you should. Do it like this." She took in an audible breath, slow and deep.

I emulated the breath, and she nodded. As she continued to work on my shoulders, we both kept breathing, loud and slow. In and out. Over and over. The combination of firm hands, hot water, and steady breath worked some sort of unfamiliar magic on me, and soon it wasn't just my shoulders relaxing, but my whole body.

"Fuck, I needed this. It's a shame you're not as cheap or portable as a bottle of whiskey."

"Is that supposed to be a compliment?" she asked. "Comparing me to a bottle of liquor?"

"All my exes would tell you it's the highest compliment I can give."

"You got a lot of those? Exes, I mean?"

"Only a few. Never been that interested in commitment, I guess."

"Why not?"

"Requires too much trust."

Then my leg cramped up. "Ah, shit, shit." I lifted my leg out of the water and started working on my calf. It was something that happened often enough that I didn't think much of it.

"Here, let me." Olivia moved around to the side of the tub and took hold of my leg. She wrapped one arm around my knee, even though my wet skin was now spotting her black silk gown. I could feel her magnificent breast pressing up against the side of my leg while her free hand went to work on my calf with the same slow, patient attention that she'd used on my shoulders. I leaned back again and closed my eyes, savoring the heat of the water and the touch of her skin.

It didn't take her long to work out the cramp, and then I started feeling her soft lips on my shin. I opened my eyes and touched her long black hair.

"I think I'd like to progress to the rest of the evening now," I told her.

She insisted on drying me off before we moved to the bed, but the way she patted me down carefully and deliberately with the rough cloth left me no reason to complain. Then we stretched out on the bed. I peeled off her damp silk gown, and we explored each other's bodies with a tenderness and attention I had never experienced—had never *let* myself experience before. We touched and caressed and kissed every part of each other. We feasted on the beauty of each other, and in that moment, I honestly did feel beautiful. Believe it or not, I felt like a goddamn flower opening up petal by petal.

"Oh, baby . . . ," she whispered.

There was a catch in her voice that made me look at her. She was holding my hand and staring down at the brand on my palm. Her eyes glistened as she met my gaze.

"Baby, what did they do to you?"

Everything inside me closed up. That's all it took. I pulled my hand away and moved to the edge of the bed, turning my back to her.

"I—I'm sorry . . . ," she said.

"It's not your fault," I said. "It's somebody else's."

I grabbed my undergarments and yanked them on.

"You don't have to go," she said.

"I need a drink."

THIRTY-SEVEN

I didn't remember how, or who helped, but I must have made it to my own room eventually, because that's where I woke up the following morning with a brutal hangover.

Orlando was eating breakfast in the tavern when I finally summoned the will to make my way down there. He glanced at me briefly when I sat down. His eyes took in my obvious condition, but he refrained from comment. Maybe he still felt guilty about the day before, or else it was clear I was already suffering enough.

My head felt like it was stuffed with wool, my mouth tasted like spoiled milk, and my stomach felt like a lumpy sack of shit. But physical symptoms were only one aspect of a truly spectacular hangover. There was also a vague sense of shame, compounded by the hazy, stuttering memories that suggested I might have made a complete ass of myself the previous night. And bringing it all together was a lingering mood of despair. A sort of "here we are again" feeling that made me wonder if any idea of personal growth I'd ever entertained was merely wishful thinking.

"What can I get you?" asked the old man in an apron who appeared beside me with unnatural speed and speaking as loud as a trumpet. Or so it seemed to me at that moment.

"Tea and a boiled egg."

Sometimes I would cure a hangover with more of the same. The hair of the dog that bit you, as they say. But sometimes I just let myself twist for a while, maybe as a perverse form of self-punishment for giving in to my worst impulses. The only silver lining I could see was that my knuckles were unbruised, so at least I'd been too tired to start a fight with anyone.

Orlando waited until I had both tea and egg inside me before speaking, which I appreciated.

"I hope you got that all out of your system last night, because I'll need you to be at your best when we get to Monaxa."

I arched my eyebrow as I packed my pipe. "Do I not look my best right now?"

He gazed at me, then said, "Decidedly not."

"Well, you look fresh as a peach, pal, so maybe that'll cover both of us."

"We are attempting to gain audience with the king of Penador so that we can convince him of an immediate and dire threat to his kingdom. Don't you have the least desire to appear presentable?"

I shrugged. "We've got the letter of introduction from Lord Edmund with his seal and everything. Hell, we're riding in his damn carriage. What else do we need to convince the king we're legit?"

"That's not the . . ." He closed his eyes and shook his head, like he was giving up, which I also appreciated. For now, at least, he appeared to be backing off, as requested. "Are you ready to get on the road?"

"Only if you want me to heave this egg back up in a less round shape." I smiled grimly and puffed on my pipe.

He sighed. "I'll go inspect the carriage and make sure the sigils are holding up. Come find me out front once you've properly digested your breakfast."

By the time I finished my pipe and had another mug of tea, I was starting to feel almost human. Orlando had pulled the carriage around and stood waiting by the door.

"Feeling better?" he asked.

"Yeah. Listen, Lando. Maybe I overreacted a little yesterday."

"No, I should have known better."

I smirked. "Yeah, you should have."

"It's just . . ." He looked like he was choosing his words carefully. "I see you suffering, and I want to do something about it. Because it hurts me to see you that way. And the truth is, Lysander has always been your rock. Without him . . . I'm frightened of what you might become."

I put my hand on his shoulder and looked him in the eye. "You and me both. But before I deal with any of that, we have to take care of Crowley."

THIRTY-EIGHT

From a distance, Monaxa looked like a mistake that was now too big to correct. The flat pastoral landscape we'd been traveling across slowly descended to the shore of Lake Woreena, the largest inland body of water in Penador. The lake was roughly oval shaped, about thirty miles long and fifty wide. In the center of the lake was an island that didn't have a single patch of open earth left on it.

Monaxa was famous for being the only major city on the continent to never have been sacked, or even seriously threatened, thanks to its enormous natural moat. That had most likely been the reason King Richard Ryon, the first king of Penador, chose it for his capital. This was centuries ago, well before the widespread adoption of magic in everyday life that made Penador one of the most powerful and prosperous countries in the world (and if Crowley was right, also the most horrible). That prosperity had led to a massive population boom. Without that foreknowledge, maybe Richard could be forgiven for not anticipating Monaxa's overcrowding problem.

The city had run out of ground to build on about fifty years ago. The first solution had been to fill in the lake shore around the island with dirt and sawdust to make more land. But all it had taken was a single small earthquake to prove how bad an idea that was. One eyewitness account described a cobblestone street as "undulating like a wave," and the newly constructed buildings had been rubble within minutes. So King Cassio Ryon, father of the current king, Hector, brought together the best builders and mages of the time to work jointly to come up with a different solution. They couldn't go lateral, so they went vertical. Basements were dug, and buildings were made taller. Much taller. With the help of countless air spirit sigils, a building could be as tall as needed. Of course, getting to the top of a fifty-story building by way of stairs would have been daunting for even the fittest inhabitants, so builders and mages then went about constructing vertical lift platforms that worked using pulley systems operated with counterbalanced air- and earth-based sigils. A person could travel fifty stories in only a few minutes, and suddenly those top floors went from the cheapest to the most desirable properties in the city. A true confluence of engineering, magic, and commerce.

And from a distance, it looked ridiculous. A sea of needle-like buildings poked out of the island like a pincushion, sometimes branching into multi-pronged structures, other times rounding into bulbous spheres, or even the occasional cube or rectangle. Interlacing all the structures were hefty ropes fastened to huge baskets that seemed to offer a means of travel from one building top to the next. From where I stood, still a good mile from the lake, it looked like one could travel around Monaxa without ever descending to street level. Just imagining what might happen if all the spirits suddenly escaped their bindings from such a system sent shivers down my spine.

"What a giant clusterfuck," I remarked. "If Crowley's looking for the biggest impact, he was right to pick Monaxa for the Nevma Year."

"Have you never been here before?" Orlando asked.

"Not since I was a kid. I guess a good portion of this must have already been built, but I was too young to see it for what it was."

"Monaxa is a city that requires some basic assumptions in order to navigate without living in constant dread. The main one being that the grimoric magic system is utterly reliable and completely faultless."

"Except it's not," I said. "Nevma Year or not, all it would take is one shoddily made sigil to kick off a chain reaction that could lead to the deaths of hundreds, if not thousands of people."

"I agree with you," said Orlando. "But who would dare contradict the king? His Majesty took what his father began and expanded it exponentially. King Hector believes that the upward expansion of Monaxa will be one of the most historically impactful aspects of his reign."

"Oh sure," I said. "Just maybe not in a good way."

"Regardless, we have a more pressing concern, and now only a single a day in which to address it. So let's put aside those worries for the time being and focus on the matter at hand."

Orlando seemed like he was getting more fussy and uptight by the minute. That was his version of being cranky, so I guess I wasn't the only one feeling a bit worn thin. Fortunately, it was almost over. At least, I really hoped so.

The sun was beginning to set by the time we reached the lake, giving the surface of the water an amber glow. The trade road terminated at an extensive dock system with a flotilla of rafts. Each raft was roughly sixty by thirty feet and sturdy enough to hold a wagon and several horses. Naturally there was a toll to get into the city.

"A full silver?" I asked the old ferryman incredulously as I leaned out the carriage window.

He twitched his rounded, sloping shoulders in a shrug. "Fixed price by His Majesty's degree. I couldn't charge you less even if I wanted."

"A silver just to get into the city . . . ," I muttered.

"And one to leave, too," said the ferryman. "So keep that in mind."

"So you're saying a person could be stuck here if they didn't have the coin? No wonder you've got overcrowding problems."

The ferryman chuckled mirthlessly. "True enough."

He helped us guide our carriage onto the raft. Once we cast off, I climbed out of the carriage, eager to stretch my legs and get the kinks of out my back.

"You made it just in time," the ferryman told me as he looked over at the setting sun on the red-tinged horizon. "This'll be my last trip to the city today."

"Nice place?" I asked him. "Monaxa, I mean?"

He twitched his shoulders again and plopped down on a small stool. "For some."

Once we were out in open water, the raft picked up quite a bit of speed. The ferryman was just sitting there smoking his pipe and gazing at the horizon, so I assumed the raft was being powered by water spirits bound to the bottom of the boat.

Or maybe somebody's grandmother.

THIRTY-NINE

There was still some daylight left, but you couldn't tell that on the streets of Monaxa. In fact, the buildings around us reached so high, I wondered if the ground level only got sunlight at midday. Judging by the green and black mold that clung to the cobblestones, and the dank, heavy smell that permeated everything, it seemed pretty likely. The sun hadn't set, but the streets were already dotted with the same spirit-powered streetlamps as Drusiel. The bound fire spirits cast everything in their thin, sickly light, so that the people who hurried past looked almost ghoulish as they went about their day.

"Cheery place," I remarked.

"The class stratification is more pronounced here in Monaxa than it is in Drusiel," said Orlando. "The rich nobility live up at the top, and everyone else lives beneath."

The street was full of wagons heading in either direction, but they were all horse-powered. In fact, other than the streetlamps, I saw very little evidence of magic at all. I guessed people just couldn't afford it around there. I'd always been a little leery of easy, pervasive access to magic, but I'd taken for granted that even an unemployed actor like Cordelia could scrape together enough for a heat stone. Now I realized that decent magecraft was probably much cheaper in Drusiel, where you couldn't kick a log without five mages crawling out from under it. I still didn't know if that was good thing, but I wasn't sure the streets of Monaxa were any better.

We followed the moldy street for a while until it began to rise a little, then we turned a corner, and I saw the palace. Or at least the bottom of it. The top half was so crowded with offshoots from nearby buildings, thick cables of rope, and large baskets whizzing by that I couldn't see much more than the occasional glint of marble, made golden from the last rays of the setting sun.

The palace was surrounded by a high wall with a tall iron gate. Two guards were stationed before the gate. Once our carriage drew near, Orlando leaned out of the window and gave them a self-assured wave. This sort of thing was not my specialty, so I figured it was best to let him handle it.

"I am Mage Orlando Mozamo of the Chemosh Guild and chairman of the Interguild Disciplinary Council," he said in a voice brimming with authority.

"What is your business at the palace, Master Mage?" one of the guards asked respectfully.

"I must speak with His Majesty on a matter of extreme urgency. It is not exaggeration when I say that the very kingdom of Penador may well be at stake."

The guards looked at each other dubiously. It didn't seem like they got requests like this too often.

"Apologies, Master Mage, but we have strict orders that none may be granted an audience with His Majesty without prior approval from ranking nobility."

Orlando nodded calmly and handed the sealed letter from Edmund. "I trust a letter of introduction from Lord Edmund of House Ariel will suffice?"

"Lord Edmund?" The guard seemed impressed. I guess my client really was a big deal if his name even carried weight at the palace. "This is . . . uh, highly irregular, Master Mage."

"It's above our pay grade," said the other guard, an older man. "You should take it to Chamberlain Minola."

The first guard looked relieved by that suggestion. "Yeah, good idea." He turned back to Orlando. "Master Mage, if you and your"—he gave me a wary look—"companion will follow me . . ."

"Thank you," replied Orlando.

The guard opened the gate, and our carriage headed into the courtyard beyond. I found myself tensing up, waiting to see if we were going to be "found out." But I reminded myself that for once I wasn't bullshitting my way into somewhere fancy. Old habits died hard, I guess.

We left the carriage in the courtyard and followed the guard up a short marble staircase to the front entrance of the palace. The doors were twice as tall as normal ones and made of a deep mahogany marked with protection sigils of inlaid pearl and gold.

The guard unlocked the doors and motioned for us to enter. As we stepped into the white marble foyer, he locked them behind us. There was a finality to the metallic click that made me nervous, but what was I going to do at this point? I was all in now.

We followed the guard down a long, vaulted hallway with bright marble arches and magic-powered chandeliers. On either side were rich oil portraits of various pinched and anxious-looking men and women, presumably past kings and queens. I couldn't imagine running a kingdom would be much fun, so it didn't surprise me that even in portraiture they looked miserable.

The guard brought us to a small circular room without any furniture or decoration except a series of sigils etched into the wall beside the entryway. Once all three of us were inside, he closed an iron gate and traced one of the sigils with a precise quickness that came from doing it frequently.

The floor beneath us shuddered, and my stomach lurched as we began to rise.

"This a lift?" I asked the guard.

"Yes, ma'am."

"Roz," I said.

"Ma'am?"

"My name is Roz Featherstone."

"Oh, uh, yes Miss Featherstone." It looked like he wasn't used to people he was escorting talking to him that much.

"And yours?"

"My name, uh, Miss Featherstone?"

"Yeah."

"Private Benedick Shane, Miss Featherstone."

"There, that wasn't so bad, was it?" I asked. "Now we're acquainted."

"Y-yes, ma'am—I mean Miss Featherstone."

We all stood there awkwardly looking at nothing in particular as the platform continued its ascent. I wondered how high we were going. Chamberlains were fairly important, I was pretty sure, so maybe near the top. We had a few minutes to kill, and I decided I didn't need the king's expressed permission to start nosing around.

"Listen, Benny," I said. "Can I call you Benny?"

"Uh, sure, Miss Featherstone."

"Call me Roz. I'm not big on formality, in case you hadn't guessed."

"O-okay, Roz."

"So tell me, Benny. You seen any mages come through here in the last few days? I mean, ones you didn't recognize?"

"Not on my watch, ma—uh, Roz."

"And when's that?"

"Noon to midnight."

"Long shift, huh?"

"It's not so bad. Since there's always two of us on post, we can take breaks."

"Always two, huh?"

"Yes, Roz."

"So it's possible a mage came through while you were on break, then?"

"I suppose it is. Although I think Antonio would have mentioned it. You know, not much to talk about just standing around all day, so any little thing that comes along, we usually talk about."

"I bet we'll be giving you two boys something to speculate about for hours."

He laughed nervously, starting to loosen up just a tiny bit. "I reckon so."

"You know what a sigil is, Benny?"

"It's the magic circle things, isn't it?"

"That's right. You're a smart guy. Have you seen anyone with one of those on their neck?"

He gave me a confused look. "Like painted on?"

"Or cut in, burned in, anything like that?"

"People burn magic circles into their skin?"

"Usually not to themselves," I said.

He looked even more confused. He opened his mouth, probably to ask what sort of monster did stuff like that, but then the platform came to a halt.

"Oh, uh, this is our stop."

As he unlocked the iron gate, I said, "So, Benny, if you come across *anyone*—and I mean anyone—here at the palace with a sigil on their neck, it's worth a silver if you come find me, wherever I am in the palace. You got that?"

"Okay, sure, Roz."

He looked a little guilty. Like maybe he wasn't supposed to be taking money from people he was escorting around. I guess that made sense. But it wasn't like I was bribing the guy to take me to the king or anything. I trusted Edmund's letter to do the trick on that count.

"Follow me, please." Benny led us down another shiny marble hallway. It terminated at a closed door guarded by two other royal-uniformed guys who were about twice as big as Benny and didn't seem nearly as much of a pushover.

"This mage has an urgent request for Chamberlain Minola," Benny told them uneasily, like he wasn't sure they'd go along with it.

The two guards eyed Orlando suspiciously, but he returned their gaze. "It is a matter of great urgency, and should I find myself delayed without cause, the repercussions could be great."

They didn't seem impressed by his semi-veiled threat, but they at least opened the door.

The room inside was dominated almost entirely by a comically large desk that was so neat and tidy, I wondered if any work at all got done on it. An older woman with long gray hair and wearing a stiff brocade coat sat behind the desk. She was reading a parchment scroll when we entered, but when she looked up, her eyes fixed on me in a way I found more than a little unnerving.

"Chamberlain Minola." Benny saluted sharply. "I present Mage Orlando Mozamo of the Chemosh Guild and chairman of the Interguild Disciplinary Council. He wishes to speak with His Majesty on a matter of great urgency, and has a letter of introduction from Lord Edmund of Ariel House."

"Is that so?" asked Minola, although her eyes didn't leave me. "Pray tell me, where is this letter from Lord Edmund?"

"Right here, Chamberlain."

Benny stepped forward and held it out. Minola finally broke eye contact with me and took the letter. She opened the seal, and her expression was inscrutable as she scanned the document. Finally she looked up, and her eyes once again locked on me in a way that was now raising all kinds of alarms in my head.

"Guards," Minola called.

The two burly meat sticks squeezed through the door into the room.

Her voice was calm, almost casual as she said, "Seize these two criminals."

"*What?*" I shouted as big hands wrapped around my arms. "You saw the seal! That's Lord Edmund's!"

"It is indeed his seal," Minola said coolly. "But I've known Lord Edmund for a very long time, and that is most certainly not his signature."

"Oh, come on—"

"*Rosalind.*" Orlando gave me a pleading look. "I'm sure this is a misunderstanding that we can quickly clear up, but not if you do anything rash."

I gritted my teeth and nodded. This was still his show, so I'd keep following his lead. For now.

Orlando turned back to Minola, giving her his most winning smile. "Chamberlain Minola, I can assure you on my honor as a mage of the Chemosh Guild that I witnessed Lord Edmund sign that letter. And as you no doubt gathered from the contents of the letter, we have an urgent need to speak to His Majesty. I appreciate your caution, and submit that you may secure us however you like, but only please grant us an audience with the king so that we might avert a terrible disaster."

Minola stepped out from behind her giant desk, her hands clasped behind her back. She walked over to him, a slight smile on her lips. "Yes, I bet you'd like that, wouldn't you? Get your assassin here close enough to His Majesty that she can do her dirty work."

"I assure you that Arcanist Featherstone is no assassin, but a well-respected expert within the mage community."

"I wonder . . ." She turned her creepy gaze back to me. "*I* will investigate this matter personally. And until I make my final decision, you will remain confined to the dungeons."

"The *dungeons?*" Orlando looked outraged. "Surely you jest, Chamberlain."

"Not at all, Mage Mozamo. Take them away."

"The Chemosh Guild will hear of this!" he told her ominously, his nostrils flared with fury.

"I'm sure they will." She did not seem the least bit worried.

I looked meaningfully at Orlando as the guards pushed us back toward the door. "Now can I—"

"No," he said. "We must handle this properly, or we'll be sabotaging our own goal."

"Fine . . ."

I allowed one of the meat sticks to haul me toward the door, but just before I stepped out of the room, Minola stopped him.

The chamberlain leaned over and murmured into my ear. "You didn't think you could simply waltz in here and stop plans that have been more than a decade in the making, did you, knight of flames?"

I froze.

She chuckled quietly and walked back to her desk. "Guards, take them away."

"You motherfucker!" I fought pointlessly against the guard's grip to reach her.

Minola—or whoever it really was—gestured toward me, still smug. "There, she shows her true nature."

"I'll show you my foot up your ass, you piece of shit!"

"Roz!" barked Orlando. "Please! I'm begging you!"

"But she's—"

"We will find a way." His eyes were desperate. "But not *this* way."

I took a deep breath, unable to keep the snarl from my lip. "Fine. I hope you know what you're doing."

"So do I," he said.

FORTY

Believe it or not, I'd never been in a dungeon before. It was just as dark and gloomy as I'd imagined, but I hadn't considered the smell. It was one big pen with about fifteen guys sitting around on the stone floor. There were a few buckets, but those were already overflowing with shit, and judging by the stench and the fact that everyone was gathered in the center of the room, most people probably just used the corners.

"Fuck me sideways," I muttered as our escorts shoved us into the pen and locked it behind us.

The men loitering about gave me a hungry look that I was pretty sure would become an issue before long. But we had bigger concerns.

"Lando, did you hear what she said?" I asked.

"Which part?" he asked distractedly, his mind no doubt reeling from the realization that his formidable charm had failed him, perhaps for the first time in his life.

"She called me 'knight of flames,' which is what that elder spirit Gomeh called me."

He looked at me sharply. "Are you certain?"

"Oh yeah. Why do you think I blew up the way I did?"

"You think Gomeh has already taken another host?"

"No. It didn't sound like Gomeh, and Crowley mentioned he and Gomeh were working with another elder spirit named Berith. My guess is that's who's possessed the chamberlain, and by the sound of it, they've been in there for a good long while. This spirit isn't going to trip up and give themselves away. We're going to have to force them out into the open. And to do that, we're going to have to get out of this dungeon."

"I've been pondering that," said Orlando. "If there are any other theotic mages in the palace, I may be able to contact them through astral projection."

"And you think they'll believe you?"

He looked offended. "A high ranking member of the Chemosh Guild? They had better."

"Right, I forgot about your national renown for superior sphincter-clenching."

"What?"

"Never mind."

He glanced over at the bored and unfriendly-looking lugs who were stuck in the pen with us. "It might take a while for me to find someone, and my body will be helpless during that time. I'd appreciate it if you would protect my physical form."

"Sure thing. Should be fun."

He gave me a concerned look.

"No, really, it'll be fine," I assured him.

He didn't look like he believed me, but he closed his eyes and pressed his palms together, then began chanting quietly to himself. After a few moments, his body went rigid, and I knew he was gone.

Waiting was going to be hard, because they'd confiscated my tobacco along with my metal pipes. The pipes were easily replaced, but that was Edmund's private stock of tobacco, and if those meat sticks thought they could help themselves to it, I didn't care what kind of political crisis it would cause, I would roast them alive. But in the meantime, I needed something to occupy myself with while I waited for Orlando to return.

Fortunately, my cellmates quickly realized that I needed some entertainment and began making some very tempting overtures:

"Hey, sugar tits, why don't you come sit on my cock?"

And:

"You're such a skinny little thing, I bet I would split you in half."

Not to mention:

"Hey, chickie, come here so I can shit in your mouth until you choke to death."

I waved my hands. "Boys, boys, boys. While I'm flattered by all the attention, I get the feeling this really isn't about *me*. It seems like maybe you're all just really desperate to fuck. So here's an idea, why don't you all just go fuck *yourselves?*"

I calmly peeled my gloves off while the whole group spit curses and got to their feet, declaring in one way or another that they would teach "this bitch" some manners.

I could have lit up my hands right then, and that probably would have scared them off quick. It would have been the considerate thing to do. But it had been a really rough couple of days by anyone's estimation, and the only outlet I had left was kicking the shit out of people. So at first I let them think it was just me and my little girlie fists.

I am not a well-trained hand-to-hand combat expert by any stretch of the imagination. What I am is a dirty, no good, no holds barred, creative, extremely experienced brawler. I know where all the small bones and vulnerable parts are, and I do not waste any time going for them.

A few quick, well-placed strikes, and the slower ones were on the ground within moments. They were also not a united front, so I used one as a shield against another, and then those two were off having their own little fight, while I was dealing with the rest.

After I'd cleared out the easy ones, the better, smarter guys got wise to the idea that I wasn't some defenseless damsel and started working together. That's when I changed up the game on them by lighting up my fists. But not in a fair-warning kind of way. I waited until I was about to punch a guy in the mouth, then suddenly opened my hand and lit his beard on fire instead. It was surprising how shrill the big guy's screams got as he slapped at his face.

"Holy shit!" one of the others said as they all started backing up.

"What can I say, you got me all hot and bothered!" Then I lit up my other fist as well.

They backed all the way to the shit-filled corners.

"Can't even one of you satisfy a sweet little girl from Drusiel?" I asked.

"Guard!" one called. "Stop this bitch before she kills us all!"

I turned to the guard, a heavyset older guy who sat outside the cell on a small stool. He looked at them, then at me, then shrugged.

I smiled at the other prisoners. "Guess it's just us." I let the flames rise up on my palms.

"Wait!" one of them said, his face growing pale. "I heard of you!"

"Oh yeah?"

"Yeah, short-haired chickie from Drusiel with fire hands! You . . . you're the Gutter Mage!"

"Heh." My smile faded. "You shouldn't have called me that."

I ran at him, and if he hadn't been frozen in terror, he might have dodged around me. But as I said before, the sight of fire does something to people, and he just watched in horror as I hit him with both hands on the chest and gave him a short blast. His scream had barely started when it suddenly cut off and he fell to the ground. At first I thought I might have killed him, but then I saw him breathe, so he must have just passed out from the pain.

I turned to the remaining prisoners. "Let's be clear. You don't call me sugar tits, chickie, or bitch. And you *definitely* don't call me what that other guy just did. I'm Roz Featherstone, and you better not fucking forget it."

"Y-yes, Miss Featherstone," one of them piped up.

I smiled serenely. "Maybe there's hope for you after all. Now, do we have an understanding?"

They all nodded.

"Rosalind . . ."

It was Orlando. He shook himself out of his trance, looking a little dazed, like he always did when he'd been under for a while. "I think I've . . ." Then he looked at the carnage in the cell. "Good heavens, what happened?"

"Oh, it was terrible." I jerked my thumb over my shoulder as I walked toward him. "They were going to sully your pristine virtue, so I had to put a stop to it. But we're all friends now." I turned to the guys who were still standing. "Ain't that right, boys?"

"Yes, Miss Featherstone," they all said, nearly in unison. I decided I liked these guys.

"There, see?" I smiled at Orlando.

He looked like he wanted to comment but then just said, "Fine. I think I've found someone willing to help us."

"Oh? There's another theotic mage in the palace?"

"Not exactly . . ."

"Not exactly?"

"I found . . . a princess?"

"Wait, like the king's daughter?"

"The same. Princess Bianca is . . . very sympathetic to our plight. Enthusiastically so. She's apparently on her way down right now to order the guard to release us into her custody."

My eyes narrowed. It sounded too good to be true. "And she believes you? About all of it?"

"Y-yes." Orlando looked embarrassed. Maybe even downright guilty. "Apparently Her Highness is . . . familiar with my work."

I grinned wolfishly. "An *admirer*, huh? This is going to be hilarious."

FORTY-ONE

It truly would have been funny to see some snotty little ten-year-old princess gushing over the great Mage Mozamo, which is what I envisioned. But I was eating my words inside thirty seconds after the princess's arrival, because instead of what I had pictured, she was in her twenties, extremely poised, and drop-dead gorgeous.

She came sweeping into the dungeon in a blaze of pastel pink and white, the layers of her gown so full it took up most of the hallway.

"Mage Mozamo, I am so sorry to have kept you waiting in this horrid place," she said in a smooth, throaty contralto.

"Y-your Highness!" said the portly old guard as he struggled to his feet. "How may I be—"

Her long, chestnut locks flared out as she turned to face him. "Guard, I command you to release Mage Mozamo and his assistant into my custody immediately."

"*Assistant?*" I asked Orlando.

He winced. "I told her *associate*. She must have misheard."

"I'll bet."

Meanwhile, the guard was struggling to keep it together. "But, Your Highness, Chamberlain Minola said—"

The princess's bright sapphire eyes flashed. "Are you suggesting that the chamberlain's authority exceeds my own?"

The poor guy looked like he might faint. "Of course not, Your Highness. I'll let them out right away."

His hands shook so badly, it took him three tries before he finally got his key in the lock. As soon as he opened the door, Princess Bianca rushed into the cell, heedless of her fancy pink dress and white, lacy shoes. She hurried over to Orlando, her pale, perfect face flushed as she took his hands in hers.

"Mage Mozamo, what an honor and delight to meet you in corporeal form. Your handsome visage and noble bearing are even more inspiring than I was led to believe."

"Whoo-boy," I muttered. The princess looked like she was ready to knock him down and mount him right there on the grimy dungeon floor.

"We thank you for this swift rescue, Your Highness," Orlando said calmly, seemingly unfazed that she was practically drooling over him. "Time is of the essence, and the stakes could not be higher."

The princess's freshly powdered bosom heaved. "What an exciting life you lead, Mage Mozamo. I'm thrilled to play even such a small role in it."

"Hardly small, Your Highness," Orlando assured her. "Let us hurry to your father, so that I might relay to him the dire news of the danger we are facing."

"At once, Mage Mozamo. Please, follow me."

"Well, boys." I turned to the cluster of tough, but now very humble men in the cell with me. "The princess has need of my services. You know how it is. Listen, I might be willing to put in a good word for you, if you do something for me."

"Like what?" one of them asked cautiously.

"I'm going to need a live rat. I'm sure there are plenty in here. Work together to catch one for me, and I'll see what I can do to help you out."

They looked at each other, and the one who spoke shrugged. "Sure thing, Miss Featherstone."

"Aces," I said. "I'll be back later to get it."

As Orlando and I followed the princess out of the cell, he asked: "A rat to exorcise Berith?"

"Didn't you say you prefer those to goats?"

"Yes. Good thinking."

"Unlike some people, I'm more than just a pretty face."

Orlando gave me an amused look. "Are you *jealous*?"

"Of who, Princess Powder Puff? Don't kid yourself."

Yeah, what did she have that I didn't? I mean, besides youth, enthusiasm, limitless wealth, and a full head of hair.

FORTY-TWO

We were back in a lift, this time going all the way to the top floor. It was a little awkward being in that confined space while watching Princess Bianca struggle against her urge to tear Orlando's clothes off, so I decided to break the silence.

"Are you a theotic mage, then, Princess?"

She blushed prettily. Of course she did. "Oh no, I am a mere hobbyist."

"Come now, Your Highness," said Orlando. "Having seen your astral form, I would say you're far more than a hobbyist."

"You really think so, Mage Mozamo?" the princess replied, and I could swear that her bosom was in danger of bursting the seams of her gown.

"As I frequently tell Arcanist Featherstone, my associate here, academic certification is the least qualification for magehood."

The princess frowned, also prettily. "Arcanist? I'm not familiar with the term."

"It's someone who studies magic, but doesn't practice it," I said.

"I see . . ." I could tell by her expression that she didn't. "And you are currently studying under Mage Mozamo?"

The only reason I didn't say something I would regret later was because I was too busy choking on my outrage, which gave Orlando the opportunity to intervene. "Actually, Your Highness, Arcanist Featherstone is a renowned authority in the field of grimoric sigil magic, and on behalf of the Interguild Disciplinary Council, I have employed her, at great expense, to lend her expertise and skills so that we might prevent the impending crisis."

I wasn't sure about the "at great expense" part, since he was only paying ten silver a day, but it seemed to impress Her Highness. I guess she might not understand knowledge for its own sake, but she did understand money, and the influence it brought.

"Oh, I see," said Princess Bianco. "It would be difficult to imagine you, Mage Mozamo, soiling your reputation with grimoric magic, so I suppose it makes sense that you would hire Arcanist Featherstone to handle the more distasteful aspects of your mission."

I had to laugh at that.

"Your Highness," Orlando said carefully, "I realize that you have not had the benefit of mage society, but we prefer not to speak about other forms of magic in such . . . disparaging language."

The princess gave me a penitent look that was, naturally, just as pretty as the rest. "My apologizes if I have offended, Arcanist Featherstone."

I smiled. "As far as I'm concerned, all mages, grimoric or theotic, can go fuck themselves raw with a rusty war hammer."

Judging by how the color drained from her perfect face, it seemed likely no one had ever spoken to her in that way before. I felt somewhat touched to be the first and winked at her. In response, she began carefully studying her shoes.

"I do apologize for my associate, Your Highness," Orlando said wearily. "I fear that the nature of her work often brings her into contact with less reputable elements of society, and some of that has rubbed off on her. I can assure you that her overall value far outweighs her . . . negative qualities."

"If you have faith in her abilities, then so do I, Mage Mozamo," she said resolutely. "And if we must put up with such . . . coarse eccentricities to save our beloved Penador, it seems a small price."

"Thank you, Your Highness. You are most gracious." He turned to me. "Isn't that right, Arcanist Featherstone?"

"Maybe she's a little too quick to say that, Mage Mozamo, because I'm just getting warmed up. By the way, Princess, I hope your dad has a liquor cabinet, because I am entirely too sober to save the kingdom right now."

FORTY-THREE

We were met at the top floor by two more large, though thankfully different, palace guards. These guys were noticeably less ominous, no doubt because of the presence of Mage Mozamo's most ardent admirer.

"Your Highness," one of them said as they both saluted. "What can we do for you?"

"I must speak with my father at once," she declared with the calm authority of someone who expected to be obeyed. It was not forceful or pushy or even arrogant. It simply assumed compliance.

So she was surprised when she didn't get it.

"Apologies, Your Highness. His Majesty is currently . . . indisposed."

"Oh?" she asked. "In what way is he indisposed?"

"With a . . . meeting," said the other guard.

"At this time of night?" Her eyes narrowed. "And with whom is he meeting?"

"Oh, ah . . . ," said the first guard. He turned to the second, but he was no help. These guys were not good at thinking on their feet or coming up with what was obviously a load of bullshit. To be fair, Her Highness was probably the only person who was even allowed to question them, so they probably didn't get much practice.

"I see," said Bianca. "Well, if you would kindly knock on the door and suggest that my father put his pants back on and bid goodbye to the . . . person?" she asked.

The guards glanced at each other.

"People?" she suggested.

The guards winced.

Her expression became downright weary. Very similar to the look Orlando sometimes gave me, in fact. Maybe it was a theotic mage thing. "I see. Well, tell him he has five minutes, or I'm coming in regardless."

The guards did not look happy to be caught in the middle of what was obviously a long-standing family conflict, but they saluted again and hurried down the corridor.

Princess Bianca closed her eyes and sighed. "I'm sorry you had to hear that, Mage Mozamo. I fear my father's patronage alone could probably keep the brothels of Monaxa in business."

"I think you were very reasonable, Your Highness," I said. "I know lots of guys who can shoot a load in under five minutes, so he should be able to finish up no problem."

"Rosalind . . . ," said Orlando.

"Really, Arcanist Featherstone . . . ," said Princess Bianca.

And now I had two judgmental theotic mages looking despairingly at me. Although I really couldn't see the problem. If the king of Penador, who I should probably mention had been a widower for over five years by that point, couldn't get off however he needed, then who could?

We stood awkwardly in the hallway for a few minutes. It was a nice hallway, with polished marbles floors and landscape oil paintings along the wall. The paintings were of different areas around Penador, from the great forests of Keriel, to the mountain peaks of Hergotis, to the sunny harbor of Drusiel. There was even a valiant attempt by the artist to make the fetid swamps of Urigo look picturesque.

"Well, I think that's probably enough time," said Princess Bianca.

"I mean, I would probably err on the side of caution if there was any danger of seeing *my* father naked," I said. "But to each their own."

Princess Bianca looked at Orlando. "Mage Mozamo, you're certain she's necessary?"

"I'm afraid so, Your Highness," he said solemnly. "Hopefully she won't offend your father too terribly."

"I'm more concerned she'll encourage him," said the princess. "Now then, let's hope all the prostitutes have used the 'secret' exit my father installed, and that he at least has some pants on by now."

She walked resolutely down the hallway, Orlando and I following behind.

"You might want to let me handle things when we get in there," I murmured to him.

"You may be right," he said. "I confess it is somewhat troubling to learn that the ruler of Penador is so . . ."

"Human?" I asked. "Try to unclench a little, Mage Mozamo. The fate of the kingdom might depend on it."

"I'll do my best," he said earnestly.

FORTY-FOUR

His Royal Majesty, King Hector Ryon of Penador, was not completely naked. But neither was he wearing pants. Instead, he was stretched out on a Lapisian chaise longue in a red silk robe that was tied in front with a sash so that it more or less concealed the royal family jewels. He was staring into what seemed promisingly like a glass of whiskey, and did not look up when we entered.

The room was comprised almost entirely of sofas and other long, comfortable types of furniture on which people could fuck that also doubled as seating for other types of guests. Really, it was an efficient use of space, although I hoped someone cleaned the upholstery on a regular basis. Not that I had any intention of sitting down anywhere in the room. I might approve of His Majesty's lifestyle, but I didn't want it staining my coat.

More important, I spotted a large and well-stocked bar in the corner that was completely unguarded. I just had to find the appropriate moment to help myself.

"Well, Daughter, I hope you're happy," said the king without looking up from the contemplation of his glass. He wasn't a bad-looking guy, but there was this sense that hair was invading everywhere. His long black locks, streaked with gray, were pulled back into a tight ponytail, but his hairline was so low, I wondered if that was the only way to keep it out of his eyes. His face looked freshly shaved, but there was a faint dark shade on his cheeks and chin that I suspected never truly left. His eyebrows were like black caterpillars, his exposed chest a thick mat of salt and pepper, and his bare legs almost woolly. I didn't mind a little hair on a guy, but the king of Penador was fascinatingly, almost repellently hirsute.

"Despite what you may think, Father, I do not delight in spoiling your . . . activities," said Bianca. "I come to you with an urgent request from the current chairman of the Interguild Disciplinary Council, Mage Mozamo."

"Great," the king said dryly, still not looking up. "Mages."

"My apologies for disturbing you, Your Majesty . . ." Orlando seemed to be struggling to reconcile his expectations of His Majesty with the reality before him. I really hoped he was remembering the conversation we'd had that morning in which he'd shamed me for not caring whether I appeared "presentable" before the king. "My associate and I have uncovered a plot by a rogue mage guild to destabilized the capital and perhaps the entire kingdom in less than twelve hours from now."

"Destabilize?" he asked without a great deal of interest, his eyes still on his drink. "What is that supposed to mean?"

Orlando seemed to be struggling with how to respond. I decided his polite speech was just muddling things, and it was time for me to take over.

"It *means*, Your Majesty, that these tall fancy towers you're so proud of will all come crashing down around your ears when the air spirits that are keeping them up take off."

That got his attention. He finally looked at us for the first time, and his eyes stopped when they got to me. His expression softened into something that I supposed was going for charming but didn't quite get there.

"You, my dear, are a singular-looking creature. Who might you be?"

"Rosalind Featherstone, arcanist, and the person who's going to save your ass along with the whole kingdom."

His eyebrows rose. "Is that so, Rosalind? Sorry, may I call you Rosalind?"

Boy, he was laying it on thick. So thick and oily I could have used a bath right about then. But I could work with it.

"Sure. Rosalind, Roz—just don't call me the other name."

"Other name?" he asked.

"Arcanist Featherstone is . . . renowned in mage society for handling . . . complex problems that others are too . . . intimidated to tackle." Orlando was working his diplomacy muscles overtime. "This has, unfortunately, garnered her a fair amount of envy within the mage community, and a rather unpleasant nickname along with it."

"So you're not afraid to get your hands dirty," said the king, who apparently was not as dim as he looked. "I like that in a woman."

"Father, please be serious," said Princess Bianca.

"Yes, yes, Daughter." King Hector took a sip of his whiskey. "So tell me, Roz. How exactly is my kingdom going to come crashing down around my ears in less than twelve hours?"

"It's like this, Your Majesty . . ." I gestured to the bar. "Say, you mind if I help myself?"

"Not at all. I like a woman who can drink."

"Really, Father, could you please stop embarrassing me?" Princess Bianca asked. "Arcanist Featherstone is a trusted colleague of Mage Mozamo—"

"But not a mage yourself?" the king asked me.

"Definitely not." I poured myself a glass of whiskey from the crystal decanter on the bar.

He seemed to like that answer. "I don't care for mages much."

"Me neither," I said. "Because like always, their problems become our problems. See, a rogue guild run by a guy named Crowley has created a . . . magical object, let's call it. When it activates, it will release all bound spirits within about a hundred miles, maybe more—including the ones currently holding up this building. We would then all die in a catastrophic collapse of the city." I took a sip of whiskey. "Oh, hey, you drink the same stuff as Lord Edmund."

"You are acquainted with Lord Edmund?" asked King Hector.

"He's a client of mine. Just saved him from a possession a few days ago, in fact."

"I don't suppose you have any proof of that."

"I did, but then your chamberlain, who I should add is currently being possessed by an elder spirit, took it, claiming that the signature was forged, and threw us in your dungeon."

"I see." He took a sip of his own whiskey. "You know, I *want* to believe you, Roz. I really do. If it were a personal matter, I would. But as king, I need a little more proof, especially the bit about my chamberlain being possessed. You understand."

"Of course," I said. "What if your chamberlain confirmed it herself?"

He looked intrigued. "I must tell you I find torture to be a very unreliable form of information gathering."

"Not torture," I said. "Just a bit of deception. Tell me, Your Majesty, how often do you pass out drunk?"

"Well . . ." He seemed a little embarrassed.

"Often enough that it would be believable for you to be passed out right now?" I pressed.

"Yes," Princess Bianca said firmly.

"Wonderful," I said. "And, Your Majesty, would it be suspicious of you to summon Chamberlain Minola this late in the evening?"

After a moment, he admitted, "No."

"Really, Father?" asked Bianca. "Your own chamberlain?"

He shrugged. "She's still a handsome woman."

The princess scowled. "I wasn't objecting to her age."

"Doesn't matter," I said, heading off any potential father-daughter arguments. "It's perfect for what I have in mind."

"And what would that be?" asked Orlando.

"While it's going to take everyone's cooperation, it should get us what we want in fairly short order without resorting to torture or other unpleasantries," I said. "But, Lando, it's all going to come down to how well you can pretend to be someone else. What do you think?"

He gave me a surprisingly bitter smile. "Rosalind Featherstone, as one of the few Myovokan mages in all of Penador, I've had a lifetime of experience playing a part that was not quite me."

I winced. "Um, great?"

FORTY-FIVE

Chamberlain Minola received a summons from His Majesty around midnight, and when she arrived at his apartments, what she saw was the king seemingly passed out on a sofa in nothing but his red silk robe. I had splashed some whiskey on his face and chest so that he reeked, just in case she tried to investigate more closely. I'd sent the princess to hide in an adjacent chamber because I couldn't risk any unplanned pearl-clutching when her precious Mage Mozamo began to say outrageous things. Orlando was seated at the bar, pretending to drink excessively in a celebratory sort of way. And me? I sat in the center of the room, gagged and tied to one of the few uncomfortable, straight-backed chairs available in the king's apartments.

Given that the chamberlain was dressed in only a robe herself, it was clear this was not the scene she had anticipated.

"What on earth is going on here?" she demanded.

"Ah, Berith!" Orlando said jovially, raising a glass to her. "You're just in time! I tell you, I never understood why the meat sacks partook of such a foul-tasting beverage, but I must say it is growing on me. Come and have some!"

The chamberlain looked thrown off, probably because Orlando had used her real name. "Mage Mozamo, I don't know—"

"Riiiight." He winked outrageously at her. "Mozamo! That's me!" He laughed as he lurched to his feet. He was overdoing the drunk part a little, probably because he'd had so little experience at it. He patted his chest. "What do you think of Saraph's spirit-talker? He's got a pleasing shape to him, hasn't he? Copulation is another of those fleeting yet charming experiences found here. If you haven't tried it yet, you really should."

I knew Orlando had a good memory, but he was using Gomeh's words and phrases almost exactly. Even I was impressed. And it seemed to be working. There was doubt in the chamberlain's expression. Maybe even a little bit of hopeful longing to commiserate with a fellow spirit about the dumb meat sacks.

"Gomeh?" she asked. "Is that really you?"

"Who else would it be?"

She looked around the room again, her eyes resting first on the king, then on me. I did my best to look helpless and glared silently at her.

"What's happened here?" she asked finally.

"Well, *I* had a plan," declared Orlando. "A plan that *you* nearly ruined."

"You?" scoffed Berith. "A plan?"

"Mine and Crowley's," Orlando amended.

"Of course." Berith's face curled up into a sneer. "Let me guess, it had to do with Saraph here. I thought you were going to keep them in the mountains."

Orlando waved his hand vaguely. "That was a bad plan."

"I told you it was."

"You did."

It was a risky thing to say, since she could have been trying to trap him into claiming something that didn't happen. But Orlando was clearly getting a feel for his role, so I just had to hope he didn't dig himself in too deep before Berith incriminated herself enough to convince the king.

"Well, how did it go wrong?" demanded Berith.

Orlando took on an offended tone. "If you can believe it, this spirit-talker trapped me in a *goat*! Do you know what a goat is, Berith?"

Berith looked a little queasy. "I do."

"Then I don't need to tell you how unpleasant that was. Fortunately, Crowley came along and moved me over to this meat sack. But in all the commotion, we lost Saraph. I had to catch up with her on the way here and convince her that I was still the spirit-talker. Then I just bided my time until there was a moment I could get the advantage over her." He gestured to me and the king. "It turns out they both like to drink alcohol quite a lot."

"But how did they even know to come here?"

"Crowley," said Orlando.

Berith let out a groan. "I might have known. Him and his big, boastful mouth."

"Truly."

"You're no better, Gomeh," declared Berith.

"Me?" asked Orlando.

"The pair of you," said Berith, clearly eager to air a long-held grievance. "Saraph this, Saraph that, Saraph makes existence *so* exciting." She looked disgusted. "After how this traitor abandoned you, it's shameful you still harbor feelings for them."

"Now, Berith . . ." Orlando somehow managed to look both offended and shamed. If he ever tired of magecraft, he could join Cordelia in the theater business.

"And Crowley doesn't even really *know* Saraph!" Berith went on. "His feelings are all tied up with the prison."

"Hm," Orlando said vaguely, probably because we were reaching a topic that neither of us had any understanding of. What did a prison have to do with anything?

Fortunately, Berith was on a roll now and didn't notice. She gestured to me. "Just look how they've spoiled this meat sack of theirs with excess. Now, I know what you're going to say, Gomeh: *They just don't know any better.* But I'm telling you, a spirit is more than their memories, and no matter who or what they are, Saraph will *always* spoil things."

Even though I had no idea what Berith was talking about, I still found what she said somehow alarming. Especially since it was starting to line up uncomfortably with stuff the real Gomeh had said. I wanted to butt in and get a few things clarified, but that would have to wait a little longer.

"Well, at least Saraph hasn't spoiled the larger plan." Bless Orlando for finding a way to bring the conversation around.

"Of course not," said Berith. "Because I wouldn't let them. And I didn't need your help. Even if you hadn't tagged along, I would have had them safely in the dungeon."

"But what were you going to do with them after the spirits are all set free?" asked Orlando.

"I hadn't really thought that far ahead," admitted Berith. "I know you and Crowley are concerned they wouldn't survive the rupture, given their unique situation. I have no idea if that's true, and frankly, I don't much care. Now that the plan is in its final stage, I haven't been able to think about anything else. You don't know how it is, Gomeh. You've only been on the material plane a short while. I've been here for *ten years*, and let me tell you, linear time is an absolute nightmare. Your meat sack grows more feeble each day, and even your mind becomes stunningly narrow. The only one who's been here longer is Saraph, and you see what it's done to them."

Berith strode over to me, her eyes hard, and her mouth quirked into a sour expression.

"What do you say, knight of flames? Should I just send you back to the astral plane? Early release for bad behavior? It would be a simple matter. I'd only have to cut off your hands."

I told her to go fuck herself, but it came out a little garbled because of the gag.

She shrugged, looking pleased. "Or maybe you'd just cease to exist. Of course, that might happen anyway when Crowley triggers the Nevma Year. The fact is, no one knows for certain *what* will happen to you, since there's never been a crime before so heinous that demanded such a . . . complex punishment."

Listening to Berith ramble was like hearing only part of a conversation, but whatever it was about, the things she said were too specific for me to think she was making it up to trick me. Berith, Gomeh, and Crowley knew something about me, or thought they did.

As if guessing my thoughts, Berith said, "You're probably wondering what on earth I'm talking about, aren't you, Saraph?" She turned to Orlando. "Shall I tell them, Gomeh?"

"I don't see why not." Orlando said it in an indifferent tone, but there was a look of concern in his eyes.

"Perhaps . . . but I do enjoy watching them squirm like this. So I don't think I will. Maybe if they survive the Nevma Year, I'll tell them then. It might even comfort them. How magnanimous of me."

I told her what she could do with her magnanimity, but she missed the best parts of it because of the gag.

"I must confess, Crowley really did a number on you. Kept up his end of the bargain admirably, for a meat sack." She leaned in closer. "Although I did hear there was some flaw in the seals . . ."

I burned through the rope that was binding me, then reached up and caught her by the throat with one hand while I yanked away my gag with the other.

"Yeah," I said. "They leak."

"N-now, Saraph, don't be hasty." Berith glanced over at Gomeh. "What are you just sitting there for, help me!"

Orlando's drunk act dropped away. "I don't think so, Berith." Then he turned to the king's prone form. "Does that suffice as proof, Your Majesty?"

"It certainly does." Hector sat up, pulling his robe closed from where it had fallen open to reveal more of the salt-and-pepper forest.

"Your Majesty, I can explain!" said Berith. "Just have this brute release my neck, and I'll make everything clear to you."

"I always knew you were angling for something, Minola—or should I call you Berith? Anyway, I knew you had your schemes, but I assumed they were just the usual petty courtly intrigue, and the sex was good enough that I didn't mind looking the other way. But this? Releasing all the spirits in Monaxa? You know damn well that will kill just about everyone in the city."

Berith's face twisted into a scowl. "It's not my fault you meat sacks have become so wretchedly dependent on slave labor."

Then a funny thing happened. Or rather, didn't happen. King Hector did not object to Berith's accusation. In fact, it looked like the comment really cut him. Did that mean Crowley had been right? The king had *knowingly* built this monstrosity of a city on the backs of our ancestors? If we didn't have a ticking clock to the deaths of thousands of people who really were innocent, I would be beating the answer out of him right then and there. As it was, I still had a job to finish.

"Where's the asterite, Berith?" I squeezed her neck and let my hand heat up just enough that she could feel it.

"You kill me and I'm free."

"Oh, I know that." In one motion, I stood and then shoved her down into the chair I'd been sitting on. "Which is why I've had my boys down in the dungeon looking for a nice big rat for you to inhabit. Won't that be fun?"

Her eyes widened, but she didn't talk. She was clearly made of sterner stuff than Gomeh. While I held her down, Orlando hurried over and tied her up. I'd promised there would be no torture, but if she didn't buckle under the threat of living as a dungeon rat, I wasn't sure how else we were going to find out where they were hiding the asterite.

"Might I interject?" Princess Bianca stood in the doorway of the room where she'd been hiding.

"Do you have an idea how we might locate the asterite, Your Highness?" asked Orlando.

"Yes, Mage Mozamo. If I am to understand your earlier explanation on the nature of this particular object, it will soon become a conduit between the astral and material realms. So it stands to reason that as it gets closer to activating, there should be some sign of it taking shape on the astral plane. Perhaps if you and I were to search there, unimpeded by physical constraints, we could find it more quickly."

Orlando's eyes widened. "Perhaps we could at that. How far is your range, Your Highness?"

"I'm afraid it's only about a quarter-mile radius from my body."

"That's fine. You search within that radius, and I will search beyond it."

Princess Bianca quivered with ecstasy at the idea of astral-projecting with her beloved idol. "It will be an honor, Mage Mozamo."

"There is no time to waste, then. Let us begin."

The princess sat on the edge of one of the many small sofas, and for some reason Orlando decided to sit next to her, even though he could project standing. Maybe he didn't want to make her feel bad. Or maybe it was an excuse to get closer to his prettiest and most ardent admirer. They began chanting, and soon, both shuddered and stiffened.

"Magic," King Hector said distastefully. "Clearly an act of rebellion on my daughter's part."

"Listen, Saraph." Berith smiled at me like we were old pals. Like she hadn't just been talking about how much I disgusted her. "Let me go, and I'll tell you everything you want to know about your past."

That was tempting, because now I really did want some answers. But I figured I'd just beat it out of Crowley when I caught up to him. "No thanks. You're just going to sit here nicely until Orlando has time to move you to your new, filthy, disease-ridden host."

"As you say, no thanks." Berith stuck her tongue out at me, and I guess I had a lot on my mind, what with the ticking clock on a mass-murdering artifact, a potential looming identity crisis, and the still-repressed grief of my partner's betrayal. Because my first thought was that she was being childish.

Then she tilted her head back and bit her tongue clean off.

"My God!" exclaimed the king.

"Fuck!" I grabbed at her mouth as she began choking on the gushing blood and chunk of tongue that was now lodged in her throat. I tried to pry open her jaw, but then she started snapping at my fingers, and honestly, I was just not interested in losing one of them, so I let go. I got around behind her and wrapped my arms around her torso to try to force the severed tongue out of her windpipe, but she whipped around and managed to bite my ear, taking a chunk of the lobe.

"Ah, shit!" I staggered back, clutching at my mutilated ear as she inhaled my flesh, adding it to the blockage in her throat. Her face was already growing purple, and she looked over at me with bulging eyes, a smirk on her bloody lips.

I snarled and went for her again, but the king grabbed my arm.

"Just leave it!" he urged. "Can't you see she's a madwoman?"

"No, she's trying to escape back into the astral plane!" I said.

But it was too late. She was dead. And my ear hurt like hell.

"Give me that." I yanked at the sash that held the king's robe shut.

"Hardly the time, Roz," he murmured.

"Ha." I tied the sash around my head to stanch the bleeding from my ear.

"I found it!" Bianca's voice rang out over the commotion as she stumbled to her feet, her eyes a little glazed.

"Good." I ignored the angry pulse of pain coming from my ear. "Where?"

"Central Station," she said. "It's right in the middle of the city."

"Maximum impact," I said. "How do I get there?"

King Hector pointed to a door. "That passage leads up to the roof, where you can take a basket directly there. It's the fastest way."

Orlando was still projecting so I said to Bianca, "When he gets back, tell him not to follow me, because he'd only get in the way."

The princess looked offended. "I'm certain that Mage Mozamo—"

I cut her off. "Not this time, kid. I hope it doesn't come to it, because my hair is still growing in from last time, but if I need to go all out, he doesn't want to be there. He'll know what I'm talking about."

FORTY-SIX

I pounded up the stairs and shoved the door open. When I stepped out onto the roof, I was nearly knocked over by the wind. There weren't a lot of windows in the palace, so it had been easy to forget how high up I was. But at this altitude, with almost nothing to interrupt it, the wind was an endless shrieking mass of invisible force.

Directly in the center of the roof was a large metal post with one end of a massive rope fastened to the top. I didn't see a basket, but there was a small shelter with a palace guard dozing inside.

I staggered toward the guard, my coat flapping furiously and the wind howling in the one ear that wasn't bandaged with the king's finest silk. The shelter was just big enough for the guard to sit in, with a small store of weapons and a pair of sigil stones that probably controlled the basket. I shook the guard awake, and he gave me a dazed look.

"I need the basket!" I shouted over the wind. "King's orders."

"They've all been called to Central!" he shouted back. "Maintenance or something."

I gestured to the stones. "Can't you bring it back?"

"Sorry, I think they've all been taken off the cables for repairs."

Or because Crowley didn't want to be interrupted.

I walked over to the rope and examined it. It was about three inches thick and looked like it might be enchanted with some sort of water and earth combination that would make it a little more slick, thereby reducing friction. Pretty smart, really.

My eyes followed the rope's path. It stretched in a gentle decline, weaving between other building tops down to the roof of a squat building a few blocks away where all the ropes converged. I could see figures huddled around something. It was difficult to say for certain with only the moon and starlight, but I thought the robes might be scarlet.

They were right there. So close I could see them . . .

I looked up at the rope, then down at my gloved hands. Would the gloves protect my fingers from getting torn to shreds on the way there? It was fairly thin leather, and ordinarily I would have said no. But maybe since the rope was enchanted . . .

If Crowley had taken down the baskets, that suggested it was nearly time to create the breach. How long would it take me to make my way down to street level, then run the three blocks to that building, keeping in mind that my lung capacity wasn't great? Probably too long. I'd just have to use the rope and hope for the best.

"Wish me luck!" I shouted to the guard. Then he stared at me, dumbfounded, as I jumped up, grabbed the rope with both hands, and then released my grip enough that I began to slide down.

Once my feet passed the edge of the roof and there was nothing but a lot of empty air beneath me, I immediately regretted my decision and wondered if it might have been the absolute worst idea I'd ever had. But even as those thoughts flitted through my mind, I was coasting along at a good clip, heading toward Central Station. It was too late to turn back now.

Then I felt the leather in my gloves begin to heat up. Not from my sigils like usual, but from the friction on the rope. I tried to slow down by tightening my grip, but I guess I had too much momentum going, because that only made it worse. The heat didn't bother me, of course, but I was worried about what would come after.

Ahead, the roof of Central Station was coming into better view. There looked to be about ten mages, all with scarlet robes. I had no idea which one was Crowley, but I was sure he wouldn't be able to resist making himself known.

Then my gloves gave out. As tatters of leather fluttered into the air, it became one long stretch of pain that shot from my palms down to my shoulders. I gritted my teeth and forced myself to hold on, even as the rope tore away my flesh. When it seemed like I couldn't take the pain any longer, all I had to do was look down at the vast space beneath me and remember that the alternative was death.

By the time I reached the building, I couldn't feel anything above my wrists, and my sleeves were soaked with blood. As soon as the roof was beneath me, I let go, landing on my side with a grunt, rolling and spitting curses.

My breath was coming out in quick gasps as I staggered to my feet and stared down at the remains of my hands. There were still a few strips of leather, and just about as much skin. It was mostly a mass of bloody pulp with occasional spots of gleaming white bone.

"Fuck . . . ," I hissed through clenched teeth as a shudder of agony went through me. I dropped to my knees and fought like hell not to pass out.

Through the haze of pain, I realized the sigils were gone.

I wondered if this meant I'd lost my fire, and I didn't know how to feel about that. I'd spent most of the last fifteen years cursing the power, but right now, surrounded by ten zealot mages of questionable sanity, it was a power I might need to survive.

"Just give it a moment, Rosalind," said a female voice.

I looked up at the cluster of mages nearby. They stood around a pulsing blue crystal that was about the size of a melon, but they were looking at me. Most of them were somewhere between surprise and fear, but one pale, freckled woman with a long mane of curly blond locks was giving me a smirk that I knew all too well.

"Crowley." It came out of my throat like a croak.

This person had fucked up my life once, and then because that was apparently not enough, had come back from the dead to fuck it up again. Fire or no fire, I would get him somehow.

Then I felt a strange, tingling surge in my hands. I looked down and saw that even without the skin, the sigils were still there, pulsing a sullen orange. Then, incredibly, the skin began to fill in around them, spreading outward. Within seconds, my hands were completely healed, except of course for the ugly sigil brands.

"I hope you didn't think it would be that easy to get rid of the seals," said Crowley with the lips and voice of an angelic beauty. "What kind of prison would it be if you could just strip off the lock along with your skin? From your viewpoint, the sigils are inverted, like a mirror. They're not there to cast magic outward after all, but inward. So what you see is the back side of the sigil, and as you well know, destroying the back of a sigil doesn't have any permanent effect if it's well made. And believe me, it is." She gave me a sheepish look. "Minus the leaks, obviously."

"Well that's bad news for you, pal." I said as I let the fire rise from my hands.

The other mages flinched back, but Crowley looked genuinely surprised.

"Really? No desire to know who or what you really are? You would pass up the chance to learn it directly from the person who made you this way? It might change your mind entirely."

She had me there. By that point, I was really tired of people talking about me like they knew me better than I knew myself. And if I killed Crowley now, he/she would probably be off to some new body, and I'd be none the wiser. I supposed it wouldn't hurt to hear what she thought was so astonishing that I'd let this entire city collapse.

"Fine, I'll listen. But if I think for a moment you're stalling for time so your doomsday rock can go off, you're done. So make it fast."

"I'll try to be as succinct as possible." Crowley took a deep breath. "It's difficult for someone trapped in the material realm to conceive of this, but the elder spirits of the astral plane have . . . something akin to a culture and government, which have developed over countless millennia. For a long time, they had little interest in the affairs of the material realm or the fate of younger spirits foolish enough to get caught in mage bindings. But then roughly sixteen years ago, one of their own broke some law. I never learned which one, but it must have been pretty bad, because they decided that the punishment for breaking the law was to confine the criminal to a mortal form for the span of a life."

"And this Saraph, knight of flames, everyone has been talking about was the criminal."

"Precisely." She smiled and gazed up at the night sky for a moment. "I was dabbling in some of the more . . . esoteric aspects of theotic magecraft at the time, and it got the attention of the elder spirits. They approached me with a proposition. If I prepared the vessel for their lawbreaker—the prison, if you will—to their specifications, they would teach me how to retain my identity after death, in essence allowing me to forgo thousands of years of suffering that most people had to endure before they matured into an elder spirit."

"Let me guess," I said. "I was the vessel."

"Well, technically Rosalind Featherstone is the vessel," she said. "You, Saraph, are the lawbreaker."

"Right, you all think *I'm* the elder spirit. I got that part. Except I have no memory of being an elder spirit, and plenty of memories being a regular girl growing up in Drusiel."

"Where does memory live, Saraph? In the mind, not the soul. That's why people usually forget the details of their life when they die. As part of your punishment, I was taught how to surpress your previous memories as an elder spirit. With nothing else to go on, you mistook the memories of your host, Rosalind Featherstone, as your own."

"If what you're saying is true, and I'm really this elder spirit Saraph, all I have to do is kill myself, and I'll be free to go do whatever elder spirits do when they aren't being a pain in my ass."

She nodded, smiling.

"On the other hand, if I kill myself, and you've been feeding me some elaborate lie—which you have done in the past—I'll just be dead."

"Yes, it is a conundrum," agreed Crowley. "The punishment was constructed so that if you ever discovered your true nature, you'd still be left doubting, unsure of who or what you truly are. A pretty neat trap, I must confess. I can only imagine what terrible deed you committed to warrant such an exotic punishment."

I didn't know whether I believed Crowley or not. It certainly lined up with what Gomeh and Berith had said, but that didn't prove anything except they all believed the same thing. Even *if* I accepted the whole prison idea, who were they to say for certain that Saraph was the dominant consciousness, rather than Rosalind? A pretty neat trap indeed. But it sure as hell wasn't dissuading me from burning that grin right off his fucking face all over again.

"Well, I'll have to wallow in angst over that during my spare time." I lit my hands up again. "First, I better get rid of that pulsing blue thing. According to Berith, *if* you're right about me being an imprisoned elder spirit, not only will it bring this whole city crashing down, it could wipe me from existence."

"That's why Lysander and I wanted to keep you in the asterite cave," said Crowley. "There you would be shielded from its effects."

The fire died in my hands. "Wait . . . Lysander believed all that knight-of-flames shit?"

"Why else do you think he was working with me?" asked Crowley. "The man completely loathed me. The deal was that we would keep both you and Rosalind Featherstone safe, and then once the rift was opened, I would move you to a new host, and he would get his friend back."

"You're saying that this whole time, Lysander thought he was rescuing Rosalind Featherstone?"

"From you," said Crowley.

"Fuck . . ." It was at once sweetly noble and infuriatingly presumptuous. Exactly the sort of thing Lysander would do if he didn't have me around to smack some sense into him.

"He didn't blame you, of course," Crowley added quickly. "He knew you were a victim as well, and I don't think he held any animosity toward you at all. But the idea that Rosalind is still somewhere inside you, unable to come out, haunts him terribly."

"An idea *you* put in his head."

"I *suggested* it, but frankly, the person he grew up with changed so radically after Gemory Chapel that he found it quite credible that you were a completely different person."

"Reason I changed so much is because *you* fucked me up so much!" I was shouting now. I'd lost my cool, and I didn't give a damn. "I was a stupid, eager, fifteen-year-old girl, and you took advantage of me!"

Crowley looked irritated. "Well actually, I did those things to Rosalind Featherstone, not you."

"Holy fuck, that's it. I am going to have you *begging* for death." I lunged forward, grabbed her collar with one hand, and yanked her close.

The other mages stepped forward, so I lit my free hand up and held it out toward them. "You want some of this? Really?"

They froze in place.

"You're all idiots for following this piece of garbage," I told them. "Crowley is using you just like he used me. The moment he doesn't—"

A pulse shot through me like a lightning bolt. Suddenly I was fighting just to stay on my feet.

"What . . . ," I gasped, "was that . . ."

"The asterite," Crowley said as she freed herself from my weakened grip. "It must be nearly ready. Listen, you don't have much time, but that's okay because I think I've figured out a way to protect you from its effects."

"Or . . . how about I just . . . destroy it."

I staggered toward the glowing blue crystal, but another pulse surged through me. This time it was so strong that it brought me to my knees.

"The closer you get to it, the worse it will be for you." Crowley hurried over and tried to help me up.

"Get away from me!" I shoved her back and tried to stand, but my body felt like it was made of lead, and I couldn't stay upright. The stone was only five feet away, but every movement was like pushing against a wall of sand.

"Saraph, listen to me! I really do have a plan to save you! It will be risky without the cave's shielding, but when the asterite bridges the material and astral planes, there is a short window where everything will be in flux, and I should be able to transfer you to another host. You still won't be free, exactly, but you'll be able to recover your memories and get a fresh start, just like me!"

"And all I have to do . . . is let all these people . . . die, huh?"

I was nearly to my feet, but then another pulse hit, and I went back down.

"We're running out of time, Saraph." Crowley grabbed one of his mages—a tall, muscular man with the tan skin of a Lapisian. "How about this one?"

"Wh-what?" asked the mage, looking shocked.

Crowley ignored him. "I changed my sex, so I thought it might be fun if you did too. You know, that way it would really feel like we were starting over."

It took me a moment to understand where she was going with this. "Start over? You and me? Is that . . . what this has all been about for you?"

She looked thrilled that I was getting it now. "Yes! Everything I've done for the last fifteen years has been to figure out a way to reunite us! We are perfect for each other. Truly a match of heart, talent, and intellect! And now we can be together forever!"

"But I thought . . . you said . . . I'm not Rosalind anymore. If that's true . . . you don't even know me."

The pulse tore through me again, and I hadn't even gotten halfway to my feet that time. My arms gave out, and I nearly banged my forehead on the grimy rooftop.

"You couldn't be more wrong!" said Crowley. "I *know* you, Saraph, knight of flames! During the final sequence of the imprisonment ritual, as you were drawn into the material plane by my hand, and I was leaving it by your hand, our souls *touched*." She smiled down at me, her eyes wide. "In that moment, I *knew* we were destined to be together. I have been watching you ever since, racking my brains on how I could rescue you from the prison I myself had made."

It was all I could do to push myself back up on my hands and knees. The pulses were coming more steadily now, like the beat of a drum, and my heart kept in sync with it. As the pulse quickened, so did my heart. My vision tunneled to the point where all I could see was the glowing blue stone.

"Such . . . a moving story . . . ," I wheezed. "I . . . understand now. . . . Crowley, come closer."

"Y-yes? Really?" She looked thrilled by my invitation and knelt down next to me. "What is it, Saraph?"

"Take off . . . my coat."

She looked confused. "Your coat? Why?"

"Please . . ."

"O-okay, Saraph. If that will make you more comfortable. Although then we really should prepare the transfer. The time is nearly upon us."

The pulse from the stone was even faster now, and my heart felt like it might tear right out of my chest. When Crowley pulled off my coat, the night air chilled my sweat-drenched tunic, giving me at least a moment of relief.

"Now . . . " My voice barely carried above the howling wind. "Hold it up . . ."

She gave me a baffled look as she held the coat up in front of her. "L-like this? I don't understand—"

I summoned every last ounce of strength I had left and threw myself at her. I knocked her backward and covered her upper body and head with the coat before falling on top of her. Thankfully, Crowley's new host was not strong, so I was able to pin her down with my weight alone.

"It's really simple," I said to her covered face. "Even if you're right, and the terrible things you did were to someone else and not me. Even then, you still did them, and I still *remember* them as if you had done them to me. And I have *suffered* those memories for the last fifteen fucking years. So there is no starting over for you and me."

The stone and my heart were like a hammer against the inside of my ribs now. Every breath hurt. But it would not end like this. *I* would not end like this. Out of the corner of my eye, I saw the other mages rushing toward us, fools and zealots to the end, I guess. It didn't matter. They had all helped bring about this moment. Let them reap the consequences too.

I took one long, slow, painful breath, remembering everyone who had suffered because of the writhing, panicked person beneath me. Not just me. Lysander, thinking that he was trying and failing to save his childhood friend. Edmund, his wife, and Quince. They had all suffered. That poor idiot girl back at Ariel House, and the gardener she'd murdered at the behest of a monster. All the gullible mages of his cult that he used and then killed when he was finished with them. I felt rage for all of them. It burned inside me. And I let the fire out.

All of it.

It came not just out of my hands, but my eyes, my mouth, maybe even out of my pores, for all I knew. I was wreathed in fire, shielded from the stone's power by my own.

I stood up and walked over to it, leaving waves of fire in my wake that spread across the rooftop, consuming anyone in their path. I grasped the blue, glowing stone in my hands and held it up. I could feel it vibrate beneath my grip, unaffected by the flames.

I lifted it up over my head. Then I just let it go.

It smashed against the rooftop into shards that flickered fitfully with blue for a moment before turning to a dull gray. It was finished.

But I wasn't.

I felt strange. Disconnected. When I looked around me, the whole world seemed leached of color, like it was made of parchment and sketched out in charcoal. It looked flimsy and unreal. A shabby excuse for existence. And I could be the flame that consumed it all.

I had just prevented the deaths of thousands by potentially securing the enslavement of hundreds of thousands. What kind of choice was that? What kind of world was this? I felt the urge to burn everything down. To incinerate every last fucking thing in this fucked-up world. I didn't know if I could, but I stretched out my fire-encased arms and thought I might give it a try. None of it was worth a damn anyway. . . .

Then somehow, miraculously and improbably, I thought of my mother. I thought of her tired beauty, of her refusing to give me a discount on a goddamn hat.

And I laughed, a spurt of fire jetting from my mouth.

Then I thought of my father, what was left of him, saying *Somzing ees not right!* And I thought of Cordelia and her well-meaning meddling advice. I thought of Chester and his droopy mustache telling me what my problem was. I thought of Lord Edmund with his gorgeous wife and his lover Quince. I thought of Warrioress Titania and her elderly houseboy. None of this was their fault. None of them deserved to be consumed by my hand. Hell, even if Orlando decided to start fucking nubile young princesses, he didn't deserve it. Maybe not even Lysander, who, after all, thought he'd been trying to save an old friend. No matter how delicious the fiery rage felt, and no matter how justified it was, for all their sakes, and maybe even for my own, I could not give in to it. I would have to find another way to fix things. A better way.

I took a slow, steady breath, just like I'd been taught by sweet Olivia, to whom I should have been nicer.

And I calmed. The fuck. Down.

Once my fire subsided, I looked around. The asterite shards and the other mages were all gone, turned to ash and swept clean by the wind. The only thing left was the whimpering, huddled form of Crowley beneath my coat.

Also, I was hairless and completely naked. Not even my boots had survived.

"Shit," I muttered.

I yanked the coat off Crowley and put it on. She was mostly uninjured, except for her legs, which had apparently not been completely covered by the coat. Now they ended as stumps at the knee. She looked up at me with wide, traumatized eyes, and I smiled back at her.

"Don't worry, Crowley. I've got a nice cozy rat waiting for you back at the palace. Talk about a fresh start, am I right?"

I gazed out at the mess of a city I had just saved. The sky was beginning to change to rosy pink. It was nearly morning.

Then, on the next rooftop over, I saw a tall, broad-shouldered man standing there, watching me. He was too far away to make out any details, but when you've known someone your whole life, you recognize even their smallest movements.

Lysander watched me for a few moments, then turned and limped to the door that led back down into the building.

PART FOUR

BAD GIRL MAKES GOOD, READ ALL ABOUT IT

FORTY-SEVEN

NEIGHBORHOOD HERO
"GUTTER MAGE"
SAVES KINGDOM

The people of Quartz Harbor have long been familiar with local fixture Rosalind Featherstone or, as she's fondly known throughout the neighborhood, "the Gutter Mage." Whether she's from the gutters or not, Miss Featherstone has worked tirelessly for years to aid those in need, often accepting barter when her clients couldn't afford to pay her fees. Without exception, people in Quartz Harbor will tell you that concealed beneath her gruff exterior beats a heart of gold.

But now the quirkily endearing nickname of "Gutter Mage" will be known throughout the entire kingdom of Penador as well, after Miss Featherstone, with the assistance of Mage Orlando Mozamo of the Chemosh Guild, saved us all from the fiendish plans of a rogue mage guild bent on nothing less than the total collapse of our society.

"Truly, she is a hero of our time," His Majesty,

King Hector Ryon, declared when he recently
bestowed upon her the Gold Medallion of Service,
the highest honor a person of common birth can
receive.

When asked for comment on her heroic deeds
that averted the disaster, Miss Featherstone
declined, saying simply that she was grateful the
danger was past and eager to get back to what she
cherishes most, helping the people of her beloved
Quartz Harbor.

Humble though she may be, this writer sees
great things in store for the Gutter Mage.

"Heart of gold, eh?" asked Chester as he slid a glass of whiskey down
the bar to me along with the latest issue of the *Drusiel Gazette*.

"Fuck off and die." I tossed the news sheet on the floor but kept the
whiskey.

"I'm curious . . . How did you 'decline' to comment?"

"With a right hook."

"You finally get a break, and this is how you respond?" scolded Chester.
"Would it kill you to be gracious for once?"

"Um."

I stared down into my glass of whiskey. What could I say? That I
had the strong suspicion that the king knowingly built our society on the
slave labor of our deceased loved ones? Oh, and that I might not be a real
person, but some millennia-old elder spirit who just *thought* she was a
person? Or that none of this was worth losing my partner and best friend?
I couldn't say any of that.

Instead I said, "He wanted me to stick around."

"Who?" asked Chester.

"The king. Wanted me to be his chamberlain. And given that he
fucked his last chamberlain, I suspect he might have a thing for me."

Chester shrugged. "Royals got weird tastes, I guess."

"What's that supposed to mean?"

"I mean, right now you're completely bald. You don't even have eyebrows or eyelashes this time, Roz. You look like . . . I don't even fucking know what."

I frowned. "Chester, are you saying you don't jerk off to me every night anymore?"

"I'm not saying that . . ." Then he realized what that implied and added quickly, "I'm not saying I *do*, either."

I winked at him and lifted my glass. "Sure, Chester. It's okay. I know the score."

A lot of other locals came into the tavern to give me shit, some of them even having the audacity to say things like, "Hey, it's the Gutter Mage!" like we were old pals or something. Somehow the news sheets had beaten me home, and now everywhere I went it was the same damn thing. People came down from Copperton, Porter Crossing, and even the Pageant District just to ogle the local celebrity. If I had beaten up every person who called me Gutter Mage now, there would have been no one left conscious in Drusiel. I figured it would pass eventually, and I just had to grit my teeth and ride it out.

"Hey, I think one of your fancy clients just showed up," said Chester.

I turned to see Quince standing in the entrance of the tavern, looking almost exactly the way he did when I'd first met him. The only difference was he didn't seem shocked and horrified to be here this time.

"See you later, Chester."

"Sure thing, Roz."

I slid off the stool and made my way over to Quince.

"How you been, Quincie?"

"Miss Featherstone," said Quince with a bit more warmth than when we'd first met. "Or should I call you—"

"If you say it, I'll break your fucking legs."

"R-right." The way he was eyeing me, I could tell he also wanted to ask why the hell I was completely bald, but he wisely chose to keep it to himself. "Lord Edmund sent me to inquire if you would be so good as to accompany me back to Ariel House."

"He going to pay me finally?" I asked.

"I believe that was his intent."

"Best news I've heard all day. Let's go."

FORTY-EIGHT

Maybe it was my imagination, but the Ariel House gardens didn't seem quite as perfectly kept as they had before. I guessed it would be hard to find someone as passionate as that old gardener. Some losses just couldn't be replaced. I knew that all too well.

The mansion was still fully stocked with servants, but all of them were now unnervingly enthusiastic about my arrival, with a "Welcome, Miss Featherstone!" or an "Honored to see you, Miss Featherstone!" everywhere I turned. At least none of them called me Gutter Mage.

Seeing my unease, Quince smiled. "His lordship originally wanted to line them all up as a welcoming party for your arrival, but I talked him out of that."

"I appreciate that," I said. "I misjudged you, Quincie. You're really an okay guy."

"I think we misjudged each other."

We ended up in one of the many living room/parlor/drawing room places in the mansion. I was surprised to see Lady Celia and Demetrius Shandy with Lord Edmund, the three of them seated comfortably around a tray with tea and cookies. But as soon as I walked in, their jaws dropped almost in unison.

I rubbed my bald scalp. "Yeah, yeah, I burned all my hair off. Yet another noble sacrifice for the kingdom of Penador. Don't make a big deal about it."

Quince bowed. "Miss Featherstone, as requested."

"Thank you, Quince," said Edmund. "That will be all."

Quince bowed again and left.

"Do have a seat, Miss Featherstone," said Lord Edmund. "Or should I call you—"

"You shouldn't." I flopped down next to Demetrius on the sofa.

"She is not fond of that nickname, my lord," Demetrius told Edmund.

Edmund looked perplexed. "Then I wonder why the news writer went out of his way to use it multiple times."

"Maybe because I decked him." I helped myself to some tea and a handful of cookies.

"I'm fairly certain you're not supposed to 'deck' news writers," said Demetrius.

"He seemed pretty surprised," I agreed.

"Well, I suppose you've learned your lesson, then, Miss Featherstone," said Edmund.

"Yeah," I said around a mouthful of cookie. "Next time, I'll break his hand instead."

Demetrius and Lady Celia were a little horrified, but Edmund got a laugh out of it, and he was the one paying me, so that was all right.

Lady Celia cleared her delicate, swanlike throat. "I wanted to thank you personally, Miss Featherstone, for saving my husband, and for . . . believing me when one no one else would."

"No problem. Us ladies have to stick together, right? Besides, I'm a sucker for a pretty face."

That got a nice rosy blush out of her. Man, I was on a roll today.

"Here is your payment, as promised, Miss Featherstone." Lord Edmund reached down and hefted the biggest bag of coins I'd ever seen. It gave a nice, heavy jingle when he placed it on the table. Lysander probably would have swooned.

My throat seized up for the umpteenth time. I'd lost count exactly. I stared down at the money, and I didn't feel even a fleeting satisfaction.

With all this money, the cost had still been too high. The fact that I didn't have to split it with anyone did not feel like a plus.

Although without Lysander around to make nice with the clients, I'd have to start doing it myself. Even if it made me a little nauseous.

"Thanks, Lord Edmund. I, uh, do appreciate you coming through on this, even though there ended up not being any baby to rescue."

He nodded silently, and his eyes grew distant. I wasn't the only one who'd had a rough go these last few days. I felt an odd kinship with the guy right then. Go figure, me and a fancy lord. Sorrow could make for surprising fellowship, I guess.

Lady Celia placed her hand on Edmund's knee and gave him a smile. "Dearest? You were going to ask Miss Featherstone . . ."

Edmund shook himself, and his face brightened again. "Ah yes. Thank you, my dear. Miss Featherstone, it seems the world is becoming an increasingly complicated and dangerous place. As such, my wife has entreated me to employ someone with whom we both feel confident we could trust with our lives. Naturally, we immediately thought of you."

"Me?" I asked.

"You would receive a generous regular wage," said Lord Edmund. "And of course, room and board here at Ariel House."

I took another cookie. "To be honest, I never really thought of myself as the bodyguard type."

"Lord and Lady Ariel need more than just some muscles in a jacket and cravat," said Demetrius. "They need someone who can recognize and neutralize magical threats as well, preferably *before* they become life-threatening." He paused and looked away shyly for a moment. "I have decided to remain here under their employ, and while I admit we got off on the wrong foot, I hope you believe me when I say that I would very much look forward to working with you."

I remembered that Demetrius had gone out of his way to find Orlando and express his concern for my safety. Was he getting sweet on me too? Wasn't I just the belle of the ball right now. . . . But I didn't take it too seriously. I knew it would pass along with the rest of this whole flash-of-fame thing.

"The idea of not having to hustle for every job *is* tempting, Lord Edmund," I said. "And if I *was* going to work for someone, you'd be my first pick."

"But?" He gave me a quizzical, but not altogether surprised look. I guess we understood each other pretty well by this point.

"I like being my own boss. Finding my own way."

He nodded. "An admirable quality, and one I can certainly respect."

"That said, whenever you need me for a specific job, you only have to ask." I patted the giant bag of money. "Especially if the pay is *this* good."

FORTY-NINE

I had Quince drop me off in Copperton, just in case Portia was still there. Taking the whole payment for myself didn't seem right somehow, and I thought I could at least give a portion to her. But when I knocked on the door, there was no answer. I went around to the front, where the butcher's shop was. The butcher, a brawny cheerful man with a lazy eye, stood at a big wooden counter skinning a deer. The stench of blood was everywhere, and his face and apron were speckled with it.

When he saw me, he put down his knife and mopped at his face. "What can I do for you, uh . . . miss?" The baldness was clearly throwing him. "Want a fine cut of this venison? Freshly killed this morning."

"No thanks," I said. "You seen the couple that rent your upstairs space lately?"

His face darkened. "You friends of theirs? Tell 'em they owe me a month's rent."

"They're gone?"

"Like thieves in the night," he said. "I'm leaving one day, and the woman's there, same as usual. Said her husband had to take a job out of town and would be gone a few days. But I come back the next day, and she's gone too, along with everything they owned."

In retrospect, that's what Portia had been feeling so guilty about. She'd known what Lysander had planned and wasn't as good as him at playing dumb.

"Can I get in there and take a look around?"

He took in my strange appearance, and his eyes narrowed. "Why?"

Maybe my fame could get me a few favors. "Keep it under your hat, but I'm Rosalind Featherstone."

"The Gutter Mage? That's you?" He suddenly looked very excited.

"Yeah, I guess." It cost a lot to say.

"You working on a new case? Some new nefarious threat against the kingdom?"

"I, uh, can't talk about it right now."

He gave me a knowing smile. "Sure, sure. Confidential king's business, I'll bet."

"Something like that."

"Right this way, Miss Featherstone!" He led me back around the outside of the building and unlocked the apartment door.

"There you go, Miss Featherstone," he said proudly, like opening a door had been a huge accomplishment.

"Thanks," I said.

"I better get back to that venison, but you take as long as you need. Just let me know when you're leaving so I can lock it back up."

"Will do."

I climbed the stairs to the apartment that I'd always thought of as more home than my own. I guess because I'd spent a lot of time there, and it certainly had a homier feel than the glorified book storage where I lived. My tread sounded heavy in my ears, and I found myself slowing as I neared the top. I didn't want to see it, but at the same time, I had to.

Finally I reached the doorway and stepped into a completely empty room. It was as if Lysander and Portia had never been there. Not even their smells—the faint sweetness of Portia's baking mixed with the pungent metallic musk of Lysander's armor—remained. It was all gone.

My footsteps echoed as I walked across the empty floor and unlatched the window. I pushed it open, then sat on the sill as I packed my new pipe. It was a nice curved piece with a dark beechwood bowl, a present from His

Majesty, Hector the Hirsute. I lit it and took a long, slow pull, then let the smoke drift into the empty space.

Lysander had to know that if he was anywhere in Drusiel, I'd hear about it. So I figured they probably skipped town to Keriel or Urigo, or maybe one of those little mudhole villages that nobody gave a shit about. Hell, he still had some family down in Lapisi, so they could have left the kingdom completely. That would be the smartest move. But Lysander wasn't the smartest guy. And he was also stubborn as hell. He'd made sure I saw him on the rooftop back in Monaxa, like he was saying *This isn't over.* If he thought he had failed to "save" Rosalind Featherstone, he'd keep trying. I was certain I hadn't seen the last of Lysander Tunning, and I had very mixed feelings about that.

"Rosalind."

Orlando stood in the doorway, his lean face full of unsolicited concern.

"Hey," I said.

"Quince said I would find you here. What are you doing?"

"Wallowing in misery, I guess."

"Ah."

I took a pull on my pipe. "I can't even be mad at him, you know?"

"Because of what Crowley told you?"

"Lye thinks he needs to come to my rescue like he did when we were kids. Fucking idiot."

"Do you believe any of it? About you actually being an elder spirit who's lost their memory?"

"I don't know. That's the thing, though. I *can't* know because the only way to prove or disprove it is to kill myself."

"Even if it was true, it seems a cruel thing to tell someone," said Orlando.

I gave him a grim smile. "How's he doing, by the way?"

"Who? Crowley?"

"Yeah."

"The Interguild Disciplinary Council is taking excellent care of him. He might live longer than any rat in history. And I've tasked a team to see if there's a way to track down any more hosts he might have prepared so that when he dies, he won't be stealing some other poor soul's body."

I let out a stream of smoke and watched it waft across the room. Then I asked, "So you were looking for me?"

"I wanted to tell you that I'm going to be in Monaxa for an extended period of time."

"Oh?" I gave him a leer. "You moving in with Princess Powder Puff?"

"No, Rosalind. I'm investigating Crowley's other claim."

"About spirits and souls being the same thing?"

"I asked my guildmaster if he had any knowledge of it, and he advised me to leave it alone."

"But you won't."

"Of course not. We have a moral imperative to investigate this claim as thoroughly as we can and, if it turns out to be true, find the least chaotic way to emancipate our ancestors as swiftly as possible."

"You think you'll find something in Monaxa?"

"Her Highness believes we might be able to track down some records of the events surrounding Mage Iago's binding that the guilds would not have had access to, and therefore could not have tampered with."

"So . . . you and the princess are getting to the *bottom* of things, huh?"

He gave me his special look. "Hilarious."

"Okay, okay. You know if you need me for anything, I'm there."

"I do know that, but thank you for saying so anyway."

"Especially if it's a threesome."

And then it happened. Ever so slightly, Orlando smiled. A goddamn miracle.

I should have enjoyed it, basked in it. But since I'm an awful person, I ruined it instead.

"Even if you don't find anything that proves Crowley right, a lack of evidence doesn't equal exoneration."

"What does your gut say?" he asked. "Do you think our kingdom has enslaved generations of our ancestors for our own selfish gains, and then covered it up by killing anyone who discovered the secret?"

I took a long pull on my pipe. "The way this fucked-up world works? I'd be shocked if it hadn't."

FIFTY

W hat happened to all your hair?" my father asked, his brow furrowed.

"Got burned off while I was on a case. It'll grow back. Eventually."

"You'll never get a husband looking like that, you know."

"I know, Dad."

The two of us were back on the bench, staring out at the harbor. He was having an extraordinarily lucid day. Lucky me.

"And what happened to your ear?" he went on. "It looks like someone took a bite out of it."

"That's because someone did."

"You used to be such a nice girl. . . ."

I looked at him suddenly as I remembered our disagreement over that Lapisian detective. Memories were recalled subjectively. We could really only ever view them from the way we saw them in the present. Maybe he was right. Maybe "Rosalind Featherstone" had hated Señora Jaquenetta, and "Saraph" just couldn't see it that way and had tweaked the memory to suit her.

"*Was* I a nice girl, Dad?" I asked him.

He frowned. "Are you not nice now?"

"That's what you just implied."

"Did I?" His eyes shifted back and forth uneasily, and he tugged on his knit cap. I was losing him again.

"Forget it, Dad. You eating enough? You look thin."

"She's trying to poison me," he said.

"Who, Mom?"

"No, the *old* lady."

"That's Mom."

"You sure?"

"Sure I'm sure. They don't stay beautiful forever, Dad."

"You do."

"Ha. To you, maybe."

"Although that bald head isn't doing you any favors," he said. "What happened to your hair? You know, you'll never get a husband looking like that."

I was not interested in doing the circular conversation, so I leaned over and gave him a kiss. "I'm going to go talk to Mom. Make sure she's feeding you properly."

"Make sure she's not poisoning me. . . ." His eyes drifted back toward the harbor, and he began blowing on his fingers. That was it for him. A pretty good stretch this time.

Lord Edmund's money jingled with each step as I walked over to my mother's stall. I found her somehow haggling with several customers at once. A few locks of her silver hair had escaped from the plait down her back, giving her just the right amount of disheveled to suggest she could be unpredictable when necessary.

"Only one silver?" She gave the sallow middle-aged man in front of her an offended look. "For the *exact* hat worn by the famous Gutter Mage while saving the kingdom?"

Oh boy. "Hey, Mom."

Her face brightened when she saw me. "There she is! Didn't I tell you?" She gestured to the hat that she and the man were haggling over. "Honey, wasn't this the style you wore?"

It wasn't. "That's the one."

"There, you see?" she told him. "And I can tell you, this is the only place in Drusiel you can get it. Worth two silver at least."

The man frowned thoughtfully as he looked over at me. "Okay. Two silver, but you throw in a personalized autograph from your daughter."

"Done!" said my mom without hesitation.

After several more haggling-and-autograph sessions, there was finally a break in the action.

"Business seems to have picked up," I observed.

"For now," she said, carefully counting and sorting her money. "You better keep doing notable deeds if it's going to continue."

"No pressure, right? But that's actually what I want to talk to you about."

"Oh?"

"Yeah. Remember I said I'd pay for Cordelia to come and help you out?" I lifted the bag with Lysander's share of the money from the deep pocket of my coat and held it out to her.

She pushed it back at me. "Don't be ridiculous. Investing that money in this shop would just be throwing it into a hole. No return for your investment."

"But it would make your life a little easier, right?"

"Who said I wanted an easy life?"

"I give up, Mom. You bust my chops when I don't do anything, then you turn me down when I try to help. What gives?"

"What *gives* is you still don't understand the first thing about business. You want to have this magic detective business or whatever and be your own boss? Fine, but you lack vision."

I pinched the bridge of my nose to keep the encroaching headache at bay. "And what, exactly, do you think I should be *envisioning*?"

"You're having a moment here, Roz. Don't blow it. Take that money, buy a place to set up shop, and put out a big sign in front so that people can find you easily. Hire Cordelia to do the bookkeeping and smile pretty for the clients. Take on some big cases, maybe even free ones if they seem noble enough for the papers to keep writing about you. A few more articles like that one in the *Gazette* and you'll have people coming from all over Penador just to hire you. That's a solid business plan."

"You sure that's what I should do with this money?"

She smirked. "Of course. And when I'm too old to run the shop, I'll sell it—then your father and I will just move in with you."

"God forbid," I said.

FIFTY-ONE

I found a place only a few blocks from the Skinned Cat. It had originally been a jeweler's, so it wasn't big, but it didn't have any weird, lingering smells. There was a small front area, where I thought a client could sit while they were waiting for me to deign to speak with them. There was another room behind that, where the jeweler used to work on his gems. I figured that would be where I'd meet with clients. There was even a tiny room in the back—well, more of a large closet, really. It was just big enough to fit a mattress, so I wouldn't have to keep paying for my other place. All in all, it was a good deal.

"Well, Delia, what do you think?" I asked as the two of us stood in the empty space.

"I think you're lucky I'm in between shows," Cordelia said.

She was always in between shows, but I let that pass because I wanted to at least *try* not being an asshole to my sole employee.

"You can make it look nice, right?" I asked.

"Of course, of course . . ." She absently twirled a lock of her copper hair between two fingers as her eyes roved across the space. "My desk will be out here so I can greet people when they come in—then we'll need a few chairs for people to sit in. Maybe a small table with some reading matter while they wait. Naturally, we'll include any papers that mention you. A few lights, of course. Can we afford some spirit lamps?"

"No spirit lamps," I said firmly. "No spirit anything if we can help it."

She sighed. "Fine. And back there, you'll need a desk for yourself."

"Why do I need a desk?" I asked.

"To sit behind, of course. It'll make you look more legitimate. People think desks look impressive."

"Do they?"

"You want me to fix this place up or what?"

"Okay, okay. I'll leave it to you."

"And, Roz, you know I'm just filling in until I get my big break."

"Obviously," I said, thinking I didn't have too much to worry about. Not because Cordelia was a bad actress. I'd seen her, and while I was no expert, I thought she was pretty good. But it was a tough business, and there just weren't enough parts to go around to all the people who deserved them.

"Now, Roz, are you *sure* about that sign?"

I'd already put up a sign out front. ROSALIND FEATHERSTONE, ARCANIST. I figured it couldn't hurt. "What's wrong with it?"

Cordelia looked pained. "First of all, what's an arcanist?"

"It's—"

"That was a rhetorical question, Roz. *I* know what an arcanist is because you've told me like a dozen times. But most people don't know, and so they will be confused and wonder if they're coming to the right place."

"So what do you think it should say instead?"

"Go with what the papers are calling you. Gutter Mage."

"No, absolutely not. It's bad enough I have to put up with random people on the street calling me that now. I'm not going to actively encourage it."

"Roz." She put her hands on my shoulders and gave me a no-nonsense look. "Do you want to make this work?"

"Uh, yeah."

"And would you like to make a lot of money doing it?"

"Sure."

"'Rosalind Featherstone, Arcanist' is not catchy. It does not roll off the tongue."

"Roz Featherstone, Arcanist?"

She closed her eyes and gently pressed her forehead against mine. "Can you feel my brain seething with frustration, Roz? Can you?"

"Ummm, no?"

"Well, it is. Like it or not, the papers have given you a catchy nickname that everyone remembers. So what if it was originally meant as an insult? Take it from them and make it your own. Show all those snobby mage assholes what us girls from the gutter can do."

"Is it really that catchy, Delia?"

And then, almost like she'd rehearsed it—which I wouldn't put past her—a guy wandered in, looking around like he was lost. He was scrawny and sickly-looking, but nicely dressed, with several pieces of fine jewelry on his person.

"Can I help you, pal?" I asked.

He shrank back a little. "Sorry, miss. I'm looking for the Gutter Mage? Is this the right place? It's a matter of grave urgency. . . ."

I glared at Cordelia's self-satisfied smirk for a moment. Then I squared my shoulders and looked back at the guy.

"Yeah, I'm the goddamn Gutter Mage. What's the trouble?"

ACKNOWLEDGMENTS

Some books an author chooses to write. Others are written out of necessity. I've started many projects for various reasons, and a good number have been left unfinished. But from the first time I sat down with Roz in the Skinned Cat, I felt compelled to finish her story. I told myself I was fine if it never got published. It was a strange book, after all. Was it a fantasy novel? A crime novel? I wasn't sure it fit easily anywhere on the shelf, and I told myself that was okay. This story could be just for me.

But once it was done, I realized I wasn't satisfied with keeping it to myself. I owed a lot to Rosalind Featherstone. She had helped me through some dark times, always there with a bad joke and a bit of world-weary wisdom when I needed her. The least I could do was fight like hell to get her out into the world.

So thank you to my agent, Jill Grinberg, for fighting alongside me. Thank you to Kiersten White and Sarah Brand for cheering me on and offering helpful criticism along the way. Thank you to Navah Wolfe for seeing such promise in Roz's story. And thank you to my editor, Ed Schlesinger, for making it happen.

And thanks to you, dear reader, for your precious time.